A Tine to Live, A Tine to Die

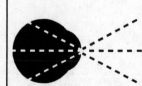

This Large Print Book carries the
Seal of Approval of N.A.V.H.

A LOCAL FOODS MYSTERY

A TINE TO LIVE, A TINE TO DIE

EDITH MAXWELL

THORNDIKE PRESS
A part of Gale, Cengage Learning

Detroit • New York • San Francisco • New Haven, Conn • Waterville, Maine • London

GALE
CENGAGE Learning®

LIBRARY OF CONGRESS CATALOGING-IN-PUBLICATION DATA

Maxwell, Edith.
 A Tine to Live, a Tine to Die : A local foods mystery / by Edith Maxwell. —
Large Print edition.
  pages cm. — (Thorndike Press Large Print Mystery)
 ISBN-13: 978-1-4104-5827-8 (hardcover)
 ISBN-10: 1-4104-5827-X (hardcover)
 1. Organic farming—Massachusetts—Fiction. 2. Family secrets—Fiction.
3. Murder—Investigation—Fiction. 4. New England—Fiction.
5. Massachusetts—Fiction. 6. Large type books. I. Title.
PS3613.A8985T56 2013
813'.6—dc23   2013016231

Published in 2013 by arrangement with Kensington Books, an imprint of Kensington Publishing Corp.

For my sons,
Allan and John Hutchison-Maxwell

ACKNOWLEDGMENTS

I want to thank my agent, John Talbot, for taking me on as a client and nurturing the proposal for this book into a salable work of art. My editor at Kensington Publishing, John Scognamiglio, also took a leap of faith in signing me on without having seen the entire manuscript, and I thank him. None of this would have happened if Sheila Connolly, president at the time of the New England chapter of Sisters in Crime, hadn't sent John Talbot's request for a few names out to the entire chapter and had handpicked several instead. Thanks, Sheila! Thanks, too, to Rosemary Silva, whose keen editorial touch vastly improved the book by nailing inconsistencies and fine-tuning my writing.

My farmer friend Paula Chase of Arrowhead Farm also read the proposal. She helped me fix a few details and has been my consultant all along the way. Software engineer Tina VanRoggen ably served as my geek consultant.

I read most of this book to the fabulous Salem Mystery Writers Group — Margaret Press, Rae Francouer, Doug Hall, Bill Joyner, and Sam Sherman — and am grateful always for their critiques and support. Sherry Harris edited the entire manuscript before I turned it in and made it much bettert. Three talented fellow authors — Jessie Crockett, Liz Mugavero, and Barb Ross — are also represented by John Talbot and had similar deadlines to mine this year. They are the best support group ever.

I wouldn't have arrived at publication without the members of the Guppies (the Great Unpublished) chapter of Sisters in Crime. They provide an infinite supply of information, cheers, and commiseration. May you all be published! My excellent friend and publicist, Jeanne Wallace, has helped me immensely in getting the word out to the world about my stories. I also thank Barbara Bergendorf, Janet Maxwell, and Jennifer Yanco for their love. My fellow Quakers at Amesbury Friends Meeting are endlessly encouraging. I couldn't ask for a better second family.

Many years ago, when I co-owned a small certified-organic farm with John Hutchison, he said, "You like to read mysteries. Why don't you write one?" I started to write this book way back then. Thanks, John. I read drafts at the time to Susan Oleksiw's writing group and learned much about the craft from her, Mary McDonald, Tempa Pagel, and Jan Soupcoff. I'm so happy to have finally finished it. I also learned a great deal about farming from the Massachusetts chapter of the Northeast Organic Farming Association, some of which is reflected in this story.

I am eternally grateful for my sons, Allan and John David, avid readers and awesome writers both, who are tireless cheerleaders for their author mom. And I thank Hugh, who doesn't quite get what I am doing but is happy for me, regardless.

CHAPTER 1

Cam hung the pitchfork on the back wall of her antique barn with a tired hand. The scent of sun on old wood mixed with the aroma of fresh scallions, well-oiled machinery, and a couple of centuries of farmers. Thirty new customers were due at the farm over the next two hours to pick up the first of their weekly farm shares, and she hoped she was ready. She was about to turn back to her errant farmhand when she spied an unfamiliar plastic jug on a shelf behind the organic products. She extracted it and examined the red-and-green label. What the heck? She whirled, then strode toward the middle of the barn.

"What's this doing here?" Cam pushed the jug toward a disheveled Mike Montgomery, who faced her in a wide stance, tattooed arms crossed, breath reeking of alcohol despite the noon hour.

"How would I know?" The young man

glanced at the container and then examined the fingernails on his left hand.

"I did not bring this onto the farm, and I can't have it here." Cam willed her employee to look at her, or at least at the label featuring a skull and crossbones. "You know that. We follow strict organic practices. I explained everything at the start of the season." A hefty gray-and-white cat arched his puffy, long-haired body against Cam's leg. She reached down to stroke him while fixing her eyes on Mike. Great-Uncle Albert had asked her to keep him on as farmhand, and she'd agreed, despite misgivings.

"Maybe it was left over from your uncle's stuff. *Albert* didn't care how I took care of the crops. He was just happy somebody did the heavy lifting for him."

Cam straightened. "Look, Mike." She kept her voice level despite her anger. "I cleaned this barn top to bottom when I moved to the farm last fall. I threw out every product like this. I know it wasn't here."

"Okay. You win." Mike rolled his eyes and shoved his hands into his pockets. "I was tired of handpicking those stupid beetles off the asparagus and the potato leaves. I was going to kill them off with a good spraying instead." As Cam opened her mouth, he put up a hand. "Now, don't get your panties in a twist. I didn't do it yet. Your precious organic crops are all clean and safe."

"They'd better be," a voice said in a shocked tone.

Cam turned to see Alexandra Magnusson, one of the new subscribers to Cam's farm-share program, who wore two blond braids like a Viking princess. If princesses wore cutoff overalls and hiking boots with red socks, that is.

"Hey, Alexandra. Be with you in a minute." Bad timing to have a new customer show up right now, a customer Cam wanted to impress.

The younger woman stuck her hands in her pockets and scowled at Mike. Her pale skin set off intense green eyes.

Cam moved closer to Mike and lowered her voice. "Mike, this is unacceptable. You skip work on my most important harvest day so far. When you do drift in, you've been drinking." She ticked his offenses off on her fingers, her ire rising.

Mike grinned. "It's not a crime to have a morning date, is it?" He leered at Alexandra, who backed away with disgust on her face.

Cam shook her head. "A date? When you're supposed to be at work? But the worst part is that you think it's fine to spray

13

chemicals on my crops. I could lose my organic certification! I won't tolerate it." She took a deep breath. "I'm going to have to let you go. You no longer work here."

Mike stopped grinning. Glaring at Cam and Alexandra, he pivoted and strode toward the wide main doorway. He stopped and looked back. His face darkened into a scowl. He threw a hand in the air as if to dismiss Cam.

"You'll regret this!" Mike stomped away.

The cat surveyed him and then turned and streaked out the open back door of the barn.

Two people stood in the wide doorway, silhouetted in the early June light. The smaller one, carrying a large basket by its handle, nearly fell over as Mike pushed between the two without a word and disappeared.

Cam shoved the toxic container under the table. She hurried toward the newcomers. "Sorry about that. I'm Cam Flaherty. Welcome to the share program. Come on in."

"Who was that poor fellow? He didn't seem too happy." The petite woman with the basket turned toward the barn door, as if sad everyone wasn't as happy as she.

"He used to work here. Don't worry about

14

him." Cam shook her head.

"Well, anyway, I'm Felicity." She beamed up at Cam. She wore a purple tunic over loose turquoise pants. A long gray braid hung down her back. "We met just that once, remember, when we signed up for the CSA? We were so excited to find a community supported agriculture program here in Westbury. And after a New England winter, finally the season is under way. Aren't we excited about our share, Wes?" She gazed at her companion.

Wes nodded without speaking. He was a little taller than Cam's five feet eleven. He also sported gray hair, although not on the top of his shiny head. Friendly wrinkles surrounded blue eyes behind wire-rimmed glasses.

Alexandra still watched the door, her eyes intent. "If that guy tries to put pesticides on your crops, I'll take him down and run a pitchfork through him."

Felicity inhaled sharply, and Wes put a hand on her shoulder.

"Nobody should use those chemicals," Alexandra went on. "They're poisoning our environment."

"I'm sure you won't need to do that, Alexandra. He'll find another job somewhere." Cam then mustered her inner social being, not an easy task for a geek-turned-farmer. "Thank you all for buying a share in the farm. Getting the money up front really helps, because that's when I need it for seeds and other expenses. And I think you'll enjoy your portion of freshly picked local produce every week. Let me show you what we have for today."

Cam turned to the produce table, a rustic plank laid out with the first harvest of the spring. Thirty bundles of asparagus she'd cut over the last couple of days. Thirty bags of spinach she'd harvested earlier in the morning from the bed that she had seeded last fall. Thirty bunches of slim green-and-white scallions. Thirty small heads of Red Sails lettuce, and more. Nine months ago, when she'd taken over her great-uncle's farm, she hadn't been sure she'd ever get to this point. Now she was both proud of these baby crops and a little nervous that her customers wouldn't think it was enough. The beginning of June in Massachusetts was still early in the growing season. They'd just have to be satisfied with the yield.

Several other customers approached from the barn door. Cam said to the group, "We're starting with half portions for the next month. Help yourself to one of every-thing."

Felicity looked over Cam's shoulder. "Lucinda!" Felicity waved. "Hey, when's the next club meeting?"

A wiry woman with curly black hair stood behind the produce table. One of the farm volunteers, Lucinda DaSilva had come early that Saturday morning to help Cam harvest for the shares.

Cam looked at Lucinda and back to Felicity. She hadn't realized they knew each other. She raised her eyebrows.

"Lucinda is the president of our club. The Westbury Locavore Club!" Felicity's voice rose until Cam wondered if she was about to float up to the rafters on sheer enthusiasm. She knew that kind of relentless cheer was not part of her own makeup, and, frankly, was glad.

"She told me. So you're members, too. Now I see how I got so many subscribers in such a short time in February. Well, food doesn't get any more local than this."

Lucinda nodded. "We had just formed when I saw your ad for the CSA on Craigslist. Seemed like a perfect match."

"Some of us are even thinking of joining a CSF." Alexandra spoke behind Cam.

"What's a CSF?"

"Community supported fishery," Alexandra said. "It comes straight from the boat

17

to the consumer. This one's out of Glouces-
ter. Could we have our fish pickup here on
the farm? They can bring the truck during
our farm-share pickup time. Would you
mind?"

"Give me a couple of days to think about
it," Cam said. "Right now I can't see any
problem. Maybe I'll join, too." She wasn't
sure she'd ever embrace these people's
dedication to all things local, but, hey, if it
made her farm profitable, that was enough.

"Great!" Alexandra nodded briskly. "We
do a bulk meat order at Tendercrop Farm
over in Newbury, too, because they raise all
their own animals and treat them hu-
manely." She stuck her hands in her pockets.
"It's part of the sustainability model. We're
building a new world."

Only a recent college graduate filled with
idealism could say such a thing with a
straight face. Cam smiled. She had been
there herself a decade earlier. She didn't
care as long as the model included sustain-
ing her farm.

"Sample the salad on the table." Cam
spoke to the cluster of shareholders. "I'll be
preparing a dish from every week's harvest
and putting recipes out for each share-
holder." Cam gestured at a small table
showcasing a wide wooden bowl brimming

with greens, a stack of small paper plates, a mug full of plastic forks, and a basket holding half sheets printed with recipes.

"What's in the salad?" Wes asked in a deep voice. He walked to the table and peered into the bowl.

Felicity beamed at her husband, then said to the group, "He does all the cooking in our house."

"Well, it's a couple of kinds of lettuce, along with mizuna, which is a mild Asian green, and baby arugula. Then I marinated asparagus in an herb vinaigrette, added chopped scallions, and topped it up with violets."

"I've seen that on cooking shows, but I've never eaten any flowers." Lucinda looked wary.

"They're tasty. Don't worry. I grow several types of edible flowers, although the violets are wild. Wait until later in the season, when you taste a nasturtium. Peppery. Really nice."

Alexandra strode to the salad table and served herself a heaping plateful, making Cam glad she'd put out only tiny plates. The bowl had to last for all thirty subscribers.

Alexandra took a bite. She closed her eyes, tilted her head back, and said, "Ahhh. So perfect." Reopening her eyes, she selected one of the recipe sheets. "Ooh, Herbed Spring-Garlic Quiche, too. I know what I'm having for dinner tonight."

"But paper plates and plastic forks?" Felicity raised her eyebrows. "Next week I'll bring you some bamboo products. Much more green."

Cam thanked her and hoped silently she could deal with all this enthusiasm for sustainability. Just then she caught sight of the pesticide jug she'd shoved under the table after the confrontation with Mike. *Uh-oh.* She glanced around quickly, but nobody seemed to have seen it.

After Felicity filled her basket, she walked up to Cam and leaned in close.

"When's your birthday, Cam?" Felicity asked. "Have you ever had your astrological chart done?"

Cam shook her head.

"Tell me the date and what time of day you were born, and I'll do your chart for you."

"November second, six fifty-eight in the morning. I remember my mother telling me that as if it was significant." She squinted at Felicity. "Is it?"

"Everything is significant. Eastern time zone?"

Cam shook her head. "No, Central. I was born in Indiana." If Felicity wanted to find meaning in the planets, Cam wouldn't stop her, but she didn't think there was much logic in it.

"Hey, everybody." Lucinda held up her hand and waved. "Want to make sure you know we're kicking off the season with a Locavore Festival this Friday evening. Over at St. John's Hall." She turned to Cam. "We reserved a table for you, Cam. You'll be there, right?"

"It's the first I've heard about it, but sure. I'm not doing anything else Friday night."

"I'll just put this up so all the subscribers will know about it." Lucinda drew a flyer out of her bag and tacked it to the wall near the produce table. "It's going to be great."

More shareholders streamed in. The next two hours became a blur of greeting customers, making sure they understood the system of taking one of everything. Cam jotted down the names of new volunteers and showed the fields to several. One asked her about the greenhouse, how she had constructed it from arcs of piping and plastic, how she ventilated it, what the cost had been. A man came with his daughter. The girl, who looked somewhere in her preteen years, seemed excited by the barn and the table full of produce.

The man spoke with a slight accent. "Is Mike Montgomery here?"

"No, he's not." Cam kept it simple.

The man looked relieved and let his daughter lead him out to look at the fields.

All the schmoozing of the event exhausted Cam, but she kept a smile plastered to her face. At two o'clock she stepped out of the barn. Only one share remained for pickup. Lucinda joined her in the fresh air. The cat snuggled up to Lucinda's shin.

"*Tudo bem,* Preston?" Lucinda stroked the back of his neck. "Such a big boy, and very handsome. What kind of cat is he?" She looked up at Cam.

"He's a Norwegian Forest Cat." At Lucinda's expression, Cam said, "Really! You can find pictures of other cats who look exactly like him on the Internet. He has the sweetest nature, too."

"You miss the forest, kitty?" Lucinda murmured to Preston.

"I wonder where the last person is." Cam checked the clipboard in her hand. "It's an S. Wilson. I don't think I met him. Or her. Must have been an e-mail application."

A car pulled into the drive from the road. Gravel spewed as it passed the house and headed for the barn. It didn't slow and even seemed to accelerate.

Lucinda stepped forward. "Hey!" She held up her hand, palm out. "Not so fast," she yelled over the engine noise.

The windows of the car were closed. Cam couldn't see the driver, only the shape of a head wearing a hat.

The car still didn't slow. Who was this maniac? Cam grabbed Lucinda's arm and yanked her into the barn as the car sped straight at them.

Chapter 2

The car screeched to a stop directly in front of the barn door. Cam's heart beat so hard, she could barely breathe.

The car door flew wide open and bounced against its hinges. A slender man with sandy hair sticking out from under a faded Red Sox hat extricated himself and stood. An alarmed look on his ruddy face, he said, "Am I too late?"

Stunned, Cam narrowed her eyes. "What do you think you're doing, speeding like that?" Her heart slowed. This guy had the nerve. . . . Wait a minute. "Stuart?" Her voice rose.

"I wondered if you were the same Cam Flaherty." The man smiled. He extended a hand toward Cam. "Last I heard, you were still head down in your cubicle, creating software, cranking out C++ code for the company."

"I was. Then my position was eliminated

about a year ago. 'Reduction in force,' they called it. A load of you know what, in my opinion. Around the same time, my great-uncle had to give up the farm and asked me if I wanted to run it. My great-aunt died a couple of years ago, and when Great-Uncle Albert had to have his foot amputated, that was it for him."

"That's quite a switch."

"I know. I've wondered if I made the right decision. But I have always loved growing stuff, and with NetSystemics leaving me in the lurch, well, it seemed like a sign." Cam mustered a smile.

"And that boyfriend of yours? What was his name? Tim?"

Cam sighed. "Tom. Yeah, well, he didn't really like me living an hour's drive away. So that's been over since the winter." Cam was surprised Stuart even knew about Tom.

"I never liked the guy."

"Did you know him?"

"We met once, yes."

"But what about you?" Cam asked, leaving the puzzle of how Stuart knew Tom for another time. "What are you doing up here in the country? Last time I saw you, you were Marketing Whiz Boy. Everybody talked about you like you were golden." What she really remembered was a tipsy Stuart getting a little too friendly with her at one of the lavish holiday parties and hoped he wouldn't recall the same. She'd had to push him away repeatedly.

Stuart looked out at the fields for a moment, then back at Cam. "Yeah. I was. New management came in. Must have been after you left. In with the new ideas, out with the old. I wasn't too happy about it. I'm still not. Moving back in with Mother at age forty? Real fun."

"Mother?"

"I grew up here. Wilson is a big name in this town."

"Wilson?" Cam's recording was stuck on the question mark. "You're my last subscriber?" They had never worked directly together, and she'd known Stuart only by his first name.

"Yeah. I just got off my shift at the Food Mart." Stuart looked like he'd tasted a bitter herb. "I go from marketing whiz to slicing meat. Nice, huh? It's the only job I could find. I work there, but I'd rather get my produce here. And my girlfriend, well, my *ex*-girlfriend, is the sister of another one of your customers." He cocked his head. "Am I too late?"

"You're not too late," Lucinda said.

"Good. Who are you?" Stuart addressed

Lucinda.

Cam wondered how someone with such abrupt manners had gotten as far as Stuart had in his former job. No wonder he had an ex-girlfriend. "Stuart, this is Lucinda DaSilva. She's a subscriber and president of the Westbury Locavore Club."

"Loco what?" Stuart frowned at Lucinda.

"Locavore. We believe in eating food grown close to where we live. Starting today, I'm not eating anything from farther than a hundred miles from here." She rolled her eyes as if at the challenge. "For a year."

"Oh, yeah. I think I heard Katie's sister talking about local eating," Stuart said. "But doesn't that mean no coffee? I'd never be able to do that."

Lucinda grimaced as she shook her head. "And I'm Brazilian. That will be the hardest part for me. By the way, what's C++?"

"C++ is a computer language," Cam said. "It's what runs most of the modern world."

"That why you renamed the farm Produce Plus Plus?" Stuart asked. "Wasn't it called Attic Hill Farm before? Being on Attic Hill and all."

"You got it, on both counts. I guess I was trying to bridge my two worlds. Now it sounds a little hokey, but I'm stuck with it.

At least Great-Uncle Albert gave his blessing on my renaming it and going organic."

"That must be a pretty big deal," Stuart said. "Converting to nonchemical growing."

"He wasn't certified organic, but he didn't use much in the way of off-farm inputs." Cam heard herself toss out the jargon like she'd been a farmer all her life and smiled. "Most small farmers can't afford to apply pesticides or chemical fertilizers in a major way. But you're right. Getting certified is a three-year process. I'm just getting started."

"I like the farm's name," Lucinda said. "It sounds like lots of food. Or food plus community plus health. You know?" She put her hands on her hips, ready to gauge Cam's response.

"I hadn't thought of it that way. But sure. As long as it brings in the sales. Stuart, come on in and we'll get you your share."

Stuart had finished stuffing his vegetables into the two plastic bags Cam provided when he grabbed a ringing cell phone from his pocket. He put the bags down and pressed a button on the phone.

"Where are you?" He glanced over at Cam, then quickly away. "I'm on my way." He strode toward the door.

"Wait! Your share." Lucinda held out his bags.

Stuart retrieved them with a sheepish smile.

"And drive carefully, all right?" Cam called after him.

"I'm leaving, too." Lucinda cradled a cardboard box full of produce in her arms. "June first. The start of my locavore year. I have some cooking to do." She beamed.

"Thanks so much for helping out, Lucinda. I couldn't have done it without you."

Lucinda waved as she walked out. "See you next week," she called.

Cam tidied up, including tossing the jug of pesticide into the trash barrel and securing the lid. As she left the barn, she looked back. Motes danced in the sunlight shining in from two high west-facing windows. Her shovels, pitchforks, rakes, and hoes hung neatly on the back wall, next to a Peg-Board with hooks for pruners, hand hoes, and trowels. Large buckets held greensand, lime, and other organic soil amendments. Albert's old red rototiller stood in a corner.

Cam walked toward the house and sank into a lawn chair, grateful for a chance to rest. The big maple in back of the antique saltbox her great-aunt and great-uncle had lived in for sixty years provided blessed shade. The tree had always given Cam a feeling of being protected, even when she was a child playing at being a scientist under its wide limbs during the summers she spent with Marie and Albert. She gazed at the barn, which listed a bit but was still structurally sound after all these years. The greenhouse beyond to its right was technically a hoop house. It looked like a white sports bottle some giant had cut in half lengthwise and placed on the ground. Building it last fall had been her first big project.

To be living here full-time now was a blessing. Cam had thought she was a confirmed city person. She'd had a charming rehabbed third-floor flat in an old house in Cambridge. She had ridden her bicycle to work and had rented a Zipcar or had taken the T when she wanted to go farther than a couple of miles. She'd walked to the farmers' market and availed herself of art films in Harvard Square. But being back in the country gave her room to breathe deeply again.

Preston sidled up to Cam and leapt onto her lap. She rubbed the top of the cat's head with her chin and then leaned back in her chair. She closed her eyes, stroking his lush double layer of fur. She'd chosen him from a shelter three years earlier. Luckily for both of them, he'd made the transition from urban condo pet to farm cat without suffering any apparent angst.

"How's my favorite farmer?" A booming voice made Cam nearly jump out of her chair. Preston executed a quick exit, first gouging Cam's denim-clad thigh in the process, then speeding toward the barn. She turned to look at the voice and groaned. The last thing she needed. One more person she had to interact with.

Jake Ericsson strode up the driveway, carrying a small padded cooler. He approached Cam, gesturing to her to stay seated. "You look bushed."

Cam frowned.

"What?" His tone was teasing, then turned serious. "You're disappointed. Maybe I should leave?"

"No, don't leave. It's just been a long day." Cam tilted her head back and squinted at the chef. "I did tell you I wouldn't be ready to fully supply you for another couple of weeks, didn't I? It's still too early in the season to give you anything in the amounts you need. Plus I have my subscribers to satisfy." Landing a contract to supply summer produce to The Market, the coolest and most gourmet local-foods restaurant in the nearby small city of Newburyport, had been one of the highlights of her spring. "All I'll be able to sell you right now will be strawberries and rhubarb."

"Ya, ya, I know." Jake, his native Swedish accent still in evidence, reached for another chair. He pulled it close to Cam's. He lowered his substantial self gingerly onto the webbing, as if hoping he wouldn't break yet one more aluminum seat. "Thought you might like a little adult refreshment." Jake unzipped the cooler and drew out two brown bottles, the condensation on the cool glass dripping onto his black-checked pants. He extracted an opener from his pocket and pried the lid off of one bottle. "Thirsty?"

She nodded as she reached for the bottle. "Did I say it's been a long day?" She hadn't spent too much time with Jake, but somehow adult refreshment had always been part of the visit, whether on the farm or in the restaurant kitchen. She guessed she could put up with a little socializing for a cold beer.

"That's why you need a cold one."

Cam read the label. "Local Harvest Five Mile Ale?"

"Yup. The Ipswich Ale Brewery started the series recently. We're featuring it at The Market. The beer has to contain least fifty percent Massachusetts ingredients and at least one ingredient from within five miles of Ipswich. You ought to think about growing hops here."

"That's an idea. And maybe we could do a joint event. The farm, your restaurant, the brewery. What do you think?"

"Great idea." Jake opened the other bottle and held it out for a clink before taking a long draught.

"I'll definitely tell my subscribers about this ale," Cam said.

"So how did the first day with them go?"

"It turned out okay. I was a little worried I wouldn't have enough to harvest, it's so early in the season, but my volunteer Lucinda helped me out."

"Lucinda DaSilva?" Jake cocked his head at Cam.

"You know her?"

"I might." He gazed out at the barn, the breeze ruffling his shaggy dark-blond hair.

Cam wondered at the evasive answer, but she was too tired to pursue it.

"So no disasters," Jake said. "That's good."

Cam rolled her eyes. "Almost none. I found a pesticide container in the barn." She suddenly wondered if she should have mentioned it. She didn't really know Jake at all. Too late now. "My great-uncle's employee, Mike Montgomery, thought using poison on the crops would be easier than handpicking pests."

"Montgomery. A name I know. His mother is a farmer, too."

"That's right. Anyway, I had to fire him. And now I have no farmhand."

"That's not good." Jake leaned back in his chair, imperiling the life of the flimsy outdoor furniture, which Cam was pretty sure dated from the 1960s. "Can you manage the work without him?"

"I hope so. I can call on all my eager shareholders for volunteer help, too. Maybe I'll hire Lucinda, come to think of it."

"Maybe." Jake took a long drink of his beer, then eased up out of the chair. He smoothed his black T-shirt over a substantial belly. The man clearly enjoyed his own cooking. Cam realized it was the only shirt she'd ever seen him wear besides chef's whites.

"Give me a tour of the farm before I head back to dinner prep?" Jake held out his hand to her in an oddly courtly gesture, which surprised Cam.

She accepted the hand and stood. His muscular fingers held hers for a moment longer than necessary, and his ice-blue eyes locked onto Cam's. She didn't often stand next to a man a half foot taller than she was. She liked it. A rush buzzed through her all the way to her face. Her pale Scottish-Irish cheeks pinkened. She pulled her hand away, ran it through her short red hair, and cleared her throat.

"To the fields?" She gestured toward the barn, the hoop house, and the fields beyond.

"To the fields."

At just after sunset that evening, Cam puttered in the farmhouse kitchen, which she hadn't yet had a chance to update and wasn't sure she wanted to. It was oddly comforting that the utensil drawer still stuck like it had during her childhood summers with her great-aunt and uncle. Cam found the corkscrew and opened a bottle of Marechal Foch from Alfalfa Farm Winery a few miles down the road. She poured the dark red wine into one of her great-aunt's fragile wineglasses and carried it with her to the barn to get scissors and a basket. The cool twilight air was fragrant with growth and bloom. A fat waxing moon brightened the darkening sky. A bat zigzagged overhead. Cam held the glass by its bowl, swirling the wine. She raised the glass to the moon. "May the season just get better."

Despite having worried about the amount of produce and the shareholders' reactions, she had had a good day, if she didn't count having to fire Mike. The customers had seemed satisfied with their produce and with being part of the farm community. Then there was that moment of spark with Jake, and how comfortable she felt walking the fields with him.

After he left and she cleaned up, Cam rewarded herself with a visit to Mill Pond, a secluded spot on the other side of town. She strolled along the trail that circled the water to her favorite spot, a boulder sitting on a finger of land jutting out into the water. She sat meditating for an hour, relieved to be alone.

All that conversation tired her. She hadn't considered that the farm lifestyle would include interacting with people as much as with the vegetables. In the cubicle, her main interaction had been with her computer, aside from the awkward gatherings in the break room for a coworker's birthday, which were usually accompanied by embarrassing remarks or a horribly inappropriate cake. It was good to get off the farm for a bit, too, although much of her meditation had involved trying to figure out how she was going to get through the busiest part of the season without a farmhand.

Now she planned to clip greens for a salad and a few perennial herbs to top the quiche she had ready to pop in the oven. Spending an evening alone reading a good murder mystery sounded about right, even if it was Saturday night. Cam sipped the wine as she walked.

She rounded the corner of the barn from the yard. The light was on in the hoop house. Had she left it on all day? It looked like a Maxfield Parrish painting, ghostly white walls against a deep blue evening sky. Cam walked along the side.

She slowed, staring. Worn sneakers stuck out of the hoop house doorway. "What?" Cam moved closer, until she could see into the structure.

She inhaled sharply. The shoes were still on their owner. Mike Montgomery lay on his back on the gravel path between raised benches full of green seedlings. A dark stain pooled around his head, tinting the small gray rocks an unpleasant red. A pitchfork rose straight up from the body. Its tines were embedded in Mike's throat.

A mosquito droned its high noise around Cam's head like a tiny chain saw. All the other sounds of a late spring evening were gone. She stared through the doorway. That was her pitchfork.

CHAPTER 3

Her eyes locked in horror on Mike, her difficult ex-employee, this troubled man. She had an urge to tell him everything would be all right. Except nothing would be all right for Mike Montgomery ever again.

A sharp pain pierced Cam's left hand, followed by wetness. She had gripped the bowl of the wineglass so hard, it broke. She looked at her hand. Blood mixing with red wine dripped down her arm to her elbow and onto the ground. She took a couple of deep breaths. She let go of the pieces of glass. They fell to the hard dirt of the path without a sound. She pressed her good right hand to the wound and raised both hands above her head.

A rustling sound came from behind the hoop house. Cam froze, cursing in a whisper. She took a quick glance left, then right. Nobody. She sprinted to the house.

The light she'd left on in the kitchen

pushed out of the window into the dark. No home had ever looked so much like a safe harbor. Cam hurried to let herself in. She gave a quick look over her shoulder, then slammed the door behind her. Just because she didn't see anyone didn't mean the killer wasn't out there. She held her cut hand in the air and locked the door with her right. Her usually reliable legs wobbled with relief. Suddenly her eyes thickened and her head thrummed, with the world at a distance.

She sank to the floor, propping her back against the door. A dead man lay in her hoop house. She had seriously cut her hand. She'd had a few sips of wine with nothing to eat. And now, instead of calling the police, she was about to faint.

Her right ear started ringing. Cam was overtaken by a memory of her great-aunt Marie.

Marie's voice said, "Cammie, you can do anything you put your mind to."

Right. The cool linoleum seemed to fortify her. She gauged the distance to the counter and her cell phone. She couldn't crawl, because of her wound. She started scooting, pushing herself along with her good hand and pulling with her feet. Blood dripped on her forehead from the cut hand, which she still held over her head.

She finally reached the phone. Cam laid it flat on the floor. She punched in 911 with her right index finger and pressed SEND. At the sound of the dispatcher's voice, relief flooded over her. Now she could share the burden.

The dispatcher told her to stay in the house until the police arrived. Within minutes, sirens pulsed in the distance. Cam reached for a dish towel. She pressed it to her cut and waited.

Cam's eyes widened at the police officer at her door. "Ruthie? Ruth Dodge?"

"That's me." Ruth Dodge glanced at Cam's face and at her hand, her smile disappearing. "Hey, are you all right?"

Cam nodded. "I think so. I cut my hand. It hurts."

"We'll get it checked out for you." Ruth adjusted her duty belt. It sat snug on her large frame, accentuating the curves of well-padded hips. "I'd heard you were in town. But responding to a call about murder is a rotten way to get reacquainted with my best childhood buddy."

"I can't believe it's you. How are you? How long have you been a cop?"

Ruth winced. "I've been an *officer* for five years. It's a good gig. And you're a farmer now, it appears. I know Albert's moved over to Moran Manor." A short burst of sound erupted from a device on her belt. She grabbed it and spoke into it. "Sure. Right away," she said, then clicked it off.

"Chief wants to see you. You all right to walk up to the scene?" Ruth, as tall as Cam, fixed deep brown eyes on Cam's light blue ones.

Taking a deep breath, Cam said she was. She wrapped the towel around her hand and followed Ruth out the door. As they made their way toward the barn, Cam wondered why they needed so many emergency vehicles for one poor dead man. The pulsing blue and white lights were nearly blinding, and a fire engine seemed to fill the entire driveway. She guarded her face with her hand and looked at the ground as she walked.

"Here's Cameron Flaherty, Chief, the farmer who found the body. Cam, Chief George Frost." Ruth gestured toward an older man in slacks and a pink polo shirt standing in front of the barn, then stepped back.

"Thanks, Ruthie." Cam extended her hand and shook the chief's. "Nice to meet you, sir."

He shoved a lock of white hair back off

his forehead. "Likewise." He ran a hand down his shirt. "I was out to dinner. We don't get murder calls around here too often. I suppose you might not know that. How long have you been living here?"

"Less than a year, but I spent every summer on the farm when I was young. That's how I know Ruthie." Cam looked at her old friend. Ruth didn't smile, though. Cam wondered why not. *Can't smile on duty?*

He snorted. "Never heard her called Ruthie before. Anyway, what happened here? How'd a pitchfork get into young Montgomery's neck?"

Cam shuddered. "I have no idea. I had been out, and —"

"Where? For how long?"

"A couple of hours. I was at Mill Pond."

"Alone?"

"Yes." Cam frowned. "I got home around six thirty, I think. I came out here just as it was getting dark to cut salad for my dinner."

Frost sniffed. "You've been drinking." He gave Cam a stern look.

"Sure. It's Saturday night. I'm at home. Anything wrong with that?"

"What happened to your hand?"

"I cut it." Cam looked at her hand, then noticed for the first time the spatter of blood on her khaki shorts and her turquoise T-shirt. *Great.* She glanced up to see the chief also focused on her shorts. "That's my blood, by the way."

"What do you think Mike Montgomery was doing here?"

Cam explained how she'd inherited him as an employee along with the farm, and what had happened at midday.

"You had a fight with him."

"Not a fight, really. I merely told him I couldn't have him working for me. Organic certification takes several years, and I'm only in the first year. Pesticides on my farm, in my barn, on my crops could jeopardize the whole process. And he was late, and he'd been drinking before noon. It was too much."

"Was anyone else around?"

"A couple of my customers had recently arrived, plus a volunteer was helping out."

"Had you fought with him before?"

"I didn't fight with him!" Cam's voice rose. She cleared her throat to try to regain control of this ridiculous situation. "I simply let him go." She glanced back, but Ruth was gone. Cam shivered and wrapped her arms around herself, wishing she'd thrown on a sweater. The night was cooling down fast.

"Any idea who might have wanted Mr.

Montgomery dead?"

Cam shook her head. She ran through the events of the day in her mind. Her confrontation with Mike. Alexandra's indignation. *Wait.* What had she said? *Oh, crud.* Cam wrinkled her brow. Alexandra had literally described the actual murder. She should probably tell Chief Frost that, but Cam didn't want to get Alexandra in trouble. She was sure the young woman had not killed Mike. Or hoped she was sure.

A woman in a violet sheath dress with a cap of silver hair strode up the drive toward them. She carried a black attaché case. A heavy gold bracelet encircled one wrist, and a jeweled watch decorated the other. She would have looked like a fashionable businesswoman except for the black sneakers on her feet.

"Ah, Dr. Cobb. You made good time."

Cam was glad to have Frost's focus on someone else.

The woman nodded as she shook his hand. "I was at a fundraiser for the Women's Crisis Center."

"Thanks for getting here so promptly."

The woman looked at Cam. "Glenda Cobb. Medical examiner. You have blood on you."

Cam sighed. "I'm Cam Flaherty. This is

44

my farm. I cut my hand on a glass."

"I see." The ME turned back to Chief Frost. "Where's the body?"

"I'll take you." He faced Cam. "You can go back inside. I'm going to need those clothes, so please change into something else. Officer Dodge will accompany you. She'll take your statement, too." He took the ME's elbow and walked away.

Cam gazed after them. She started as Ruth materialized next to her.

"My clothes? He thinks I did it." Cam rubbed her head as she frowned. "Why? That's crazy. How could I kill someone? He doesn't even know me."

"It's his job. Let's go back to the house, Cam. I want to catch up with you, but tonight's not the time. I need to take what you're wearing and to write down what you told the chief, and then I have to get going."

They walked in silence back to the saltbox. As they reached the antique house — two stories in the front, its back roof slanting down to one story — Cam said, "I can't even imagine who might have killed Mike Montgomery. I mean, he was kind of difficult. But you don't go around sticking pitchforks in people's necks simply because they're a problem to you."

Ruth paused. "We will find who did it."

Cam wasn't so sure.

In the morning, Cam pulled on denim cutoffs, pink socks, and an old purple T-shirt with a head of cabbage on it advertising the NOFA Summer Conference.

Maybe there'd been a murder here last night, but that didn't mean she didn't have a long to-do list. She needed to till in the winter rye in the far field, weed and thin the infant carrots and cornstalks, water the lettuce seedlings, pick strawberries. The digital clock by her bed read 6:35, already a late start. Light streamed in through the antique window glass and burnished the wide pine floorboards. A cool breeze stirred white cotton curtains. The fresh light and air soothed her unsettled feeling, which had endured from the night before. But what was that rumbling sound?

Cam ran a quick brush through her hair and walked into the hall. She peered out the window on the street side.

"Oh, no." Three news trucks had parked at the edge of the road in front of her house, their engines idling. A stylish woman Cam had seen on the news paced briskly back and forth on the driveway, near the street. She wore slacks and a short jacket, and her

46

hair curved perfectly around her face despite the early hour.

Downstairs, Cam brewed coffee and poured a mug. She sat outdoors on the back steps to lace up leather work boots, grateful for the screening effect of an antique lilac next to the entrance. "How am I going to avoid these reporters, Preston?" The cat rubbed his side luxuriously against Cam's leg, arching his back and purring loudly, but not giving a clue as to what she should do.

She judged the distance across the yard to the barn and wondered for how much of it she'd be hidden by the house. She set off at a brisk pace, but as she edged onto the drive to enter the barn, one reporter called out.

"Ms. Flaherty? Cameron? Can you tell me what happened last night?" The chic reporter strode toward Cam. A young woman in black hoisting a camera on her shoulder followed close behind her.

"No, and you need to get off my property." Cam faced them. She put both hands up in the universal halt gesture. The reporter slowed but kept moving toward Cam. "I mean it. I will call the police."

"All right. I just want to be sure the viewing public has the real story, in your own words." The woman flashed a megawatt smile. "We'll be out here when you're ready." She nodded to the cameraperson and headed back to the street.

In your dreams. As Cam rounded the barn, she shook her head. Ruts in the ground described the vehicles that had invaded her land. Seeing them further darkened her mood. A tire tread had flattened the edge of the herb garden, barely missing the tender basil and dill seedlings.

Seeing the hoop house cast an even darker shadow despite the slant of morning light pouring into it. Yellow police tape blocked the entrance where Mike's body had lain only twelve hours earlier. Poor Mike. She would have thought the police would be here investigating, looking for clues to the murderer's identity. She shook her head to clear it. She had a farm to run.

Staring at the hoop house, Cam realized something else. How was she going to water the lettuce starts? She set her fists on her hips. The tender seedlings needed hand watering with a gentle stream. Spraying them with the hose from the doorway would destroy them and probably any evidence the police hadn't collected last night. She wanted to head back to the house to call Ruth or Chief Frost to get permission to cross the tape. She didn't want to destroy evidence, but she had a business to run here. She stopped. It was not even seven o'clock on a Sunday morning. She couldn't be waking people up. Plus, now the pack of newshounds was ready to pounce on her.

Cam sighed. She was about to return to the barn when an object flashed at her in the sunshine from the ground right inside the hoop house door. She knelt and reached beyond the tape and then pulled her hand back. She'd seen enough police shows to know you weren't supposed to touch evidence. She found a tissue in her pocket, then used it to scrabble in the gravel on the ground until her fingers found the object through the thin paper. Cam sat back on her heels and held it up. The slim disk was scratched but had a tiny loop of metal sticking out, like the kind of talisman you could attach to a key chain. She slid it into her pocket, feeling vaguely like Nancy Drew. She'd give it to Ruth when she talked to her. Maybe it was a clue.

In the barn, Cam stood with hands on hips, staring at Albert's old rototiller. "You're going to start for me now, Red, aren't you?" Albert had named it after its original color, of which only traces still remained. Cam wanted to call it Rust Bucket but didn't think she should risk getting in its bad graces. Her uncle had tried to explain his tricks with the machine. She checked the oil and gas. She pushed the throttle level to the fastest setting and persuaded the lever into the choke position. Now came the part she hated. She grasped the rope handle with the rope snaked between her middle fingers, set her feet in what she hoped was a strong stance, and pulled.

Nothing. No whir of the small engine. She let the rope back in and pulled again. Silence. Ten pulls and twenty curses later, Cam glared at the obstinate metal beast, then turned and grabbed her weeding tools. Tomorrow she'd have to call Nick's Small Engine Repair and hope they had time for a tiller tune-up.

She weeded the lettuce rows and thinned the carrot and bean plantings for a couple of hours, then loaded six shallow two-quart baskets into the big-wheeled garden cart. The birds sang their version of the "Hallelujah Chorus" and the sun had already crested well over the trees in the distance when she arrived at the strawberry patch, stomach growling. She spent the next hour picking strawberries and sampling a few, too, glad it was an early season. Her cut hand hurt, but it didn't get in her way too badly. She was grateful the EMT hadn't needed to stitch the cut.

As she plucked, she thought about Ruth the night before. Her old friend had dutifully transcribed Cam's account of the day, from the pesticide encounter with Mike all the way to when she pressed 911. Cam had thought Ruth would be more sympathetic, more reassuring of Cam's innocence. But Ruth had maintained a somber expression and hadn't answered any of Cam's questions. She'd stayed 100 percent police officer. Cam wondered what it would be like to spend time with her once this business blew over. Could they regain their childhood closeness?

They'd both been stubborn in their way, but those ways had taken different paths. Cam, the childhood geek, the would-be scientist, liked to take risks in the name of experimentation. She had always tried to convince Ruth to make potions with her, to combine all manner of household liquids and watch what happened. Ruth, on the other hand, had a need for order, for following the rules. She had kept the two of them out of trouble when they forayed into alcohol and drug ventures as teens. After only one drink or one toke, Ruth had abstained. She'd kept Cam safe until it was time for her to return to Indiana for the school year.

Cam sat back on her heels. The baskets were nearly full. She gently took a final big deep-red strawberry by its top and savored tiny bite after tiny bite of the sweet, juicy flesh. Jake was going to love these. She carried the baskets back to the barn and set them on the ground in the shade. She grabbed a quick breakfast in the house, then spent another couple of hours weeding around nascent tomato plants and planting a second crop of bush beans, now that the soil was fully warmed. As she worked, she thought about the creep factor for customers of buying food from a farm where someone had died a violent death. If it seriously affected her budding business, she was in trouble.

She managed to water the seedlings in the hoop house from the doorway without destroying them, although she wondered how long the tape needed to stay up and, more important, why the authorities weren't here investigating.

Cam's final task before she delivered the berries was to harvest rhubarb. She swung an empty bushel basket beside her. She approached the big, showy plants growing around the back side of the barn, a plot Marie had planted as a newlywed and had maintained all those years until her death.

The big, green, elephant-eared leaves, toxic to humans, flopped over as if they'd been picked and left to wither. But they were still attached to their cherry-red stalks. Cam frowned. She squatted at the edge of the patch, rubbing the leaves and smelling them. The stalks sagged like limp pieces of rubber. What had happened?

There weren't any holes in the leaves. Cam looked around. She didn't see any vole tunnels nearby. The rhubarb leaves weren't chewed off, like the woodchucks loved to do with less poisonous foliage. Cam couldn't see any fungus. The plants had been fine the day before. They'd been fine! They shouldn't be sick. It was spring, their healthiest season. She had been counting on a big cutting to take to Jake today and to the farmers' market on Tuesday. Rhubarb and strawberries were a big sell in June, when so many other crops weren't yet ready. Cam examined the plants, her eyebrows knit into a straight line.

Maybe a spray had drifted over here on the wind. But from where? Cam gazed down the long row, then spied a white coating on most of the plants. Her throat tightened. Had Mike already done his damage before he'd been killed?

She walked down to the first affected plant. She leaned down and sniffed. It had a chemical odor. It had to be a herbicide. How could it have happened that a poison used to remove unwanted plants had been applied to one of her prize crops? And applied heavily.

"Oh, Ms. Flaherty!"

That voice again. Cam whirled. *Great.* The reporter stood ten yards away in Tully's meadow, what passed for her neighbor's quarter-mile-long front yard. Cam doubted if Tully had given the woman permission. She looked uncomfortable standing in weedy grass up to the knees of her expensive-looking black pants. Her camera-person appeared to be focusing on Cam. How long had they been there? And now the poisoned rhubarb was going to be on television.

"We want to hear your side of the murder in the greenhouse." The drama in the woman's voice could have landed her on *Masterpiece Theater.* She walked toward Cam, extending a microphone attached to a black shoulder bag.

Cam opened her mouth to shout at them, then shut it again. She took a deep breath. "Five more feet and you're on my property.

Don't cross that line." Cam turned away and strode into the barn, fists clenched. Mike could have brought herbicide onto the farm, too. Or maybe it was the pesticide from the container she'd found, applied heavily. A chemical like that surely could destroy anything. She thought she'd thrown the container in the trash yesterday. It was time to check.

CHAPTER 4

It hadn't been Mike's pesticide. The jug still sat in the barrel in the barn when she checked, and it felt as full as when she'd tossed it.

Cam washed up in the house and changed into a green flowered cotton sundress and flat sandals to go into town. She told herself the butterflies in her stomach couldn't possibly have to do with seeing Jake. She checked her appearance in the tall mirror. She wanted to look nice but didn't want to appear as if she had dressed up for her strawberry delivery. She smoothed an errant tuft of hair. A fashion plate she wasn't, but it was a big step up from her usual outfit.

Downstairs, the mid-afternoon sun filtered through bright green leaves outside before it washed the room with light, a sight that normally cheered Cam. Between a murder, the reporters, and crop sabotage, though,

56

sunlight didn't have a chance. She looked at the telephone. She really should call the organic inspector and tell him about the rhubarb. But it had to be an isolated incident, and she hadn't found any other forbidden substance in the barn. That bed wasn't near any of the fields. Her organic certification was still in progress. If she reported a chemical on a crop, well, that could totally derail things. On the other hand, if she'd been filmed with the destroyed crop behind her, the inspector might be calling her after the evening newscast.

Cam frowned and then worried about adding frown lines to her face. She exited the house, careful to lock the back door. She ignored the calls from the street as she made her way to the barn. She laid the baskets of berries in the bed of the truck and covered them with a clean cloth, securing it with elastic cords. She turned Great-Uncle Albert's old vehicle around and drove down the driveway as fast as was safe. As she approached the clump of newspeople that included her persistent reporter, she leaned on the horn. Her heart raced. She really didn't want to hit anyone. And she really didn't want to talk to any of them, either.

The group scattered, leaving Cam scarcely

enough room to turn onto the road. She gripped the steering wheel with white knuckles. This was crazy. She hoped they weren't going to follow her.

She headed down to the wide Merrimack River and along its banks until she arrived in coastal Newburyport. Federalist mansions lined the main street, large houses that had belonged to sea captains, with widow's walks atop every roof. As she drove, Cam again saw the poisoned rhubarb. Who could have done it? More important, who would have done it, and why? Mike said he hadn't used the pesticide yet. Maybe the killer did that to her crop. Maybe Mike caught the person and was killed because of that. The problem with all these scenarios was the same. Cam had no idea of the motivation. Why ruin her crop? Why kill Mike?

Cam turned down a side street lined with smaller old homes built right on the road. Their age showed most around the window frames, which were no longer squared, and in the many times repainted clapboards. Tiny tidy gardens peeked out from the sides or backs of the homes.

Cam, her heart rate finally back to normal, parked behind The Market. She carried the baskets to the rear door of the restaurant, set them down, and pressed the bell until the door opened.

"Hi, Jake. Berry delivery."

The chef smiled as he took the baskets. He leaned down to kiss her cheek. He smelled of shampoo, citrus, garlic, and a trace of male sweat.

A zing raced through Cam. She could get used to this.

He stood upright, tossing hair from his eyes as he led the way into the kitchen, setting the baskets on a counter. "You look nice, Farmer Flaherty. How you can go from the field to the fashion page, I shall never know."

"Just be quiet," she said lightly, trying not to smile.

Jake sampled a berry. "Heavenly." He rolled his eyes and enfolded Cam in a bear hug.

Cam flushed at the delicious feel of her face against the shoulder of this solid white-clad man but said, "Let me go, Lurch!" And then wanted to bite her tongue. Calling someone the name of a monstrous TV character remembered from her childhood wasn't very complimentary. With any luck the Swede wouldn't know the reference.

He let go. "My customers will adore you in perpetuity. They will grovel at your doorstep. But no rhubarb to go with the strawberries?"

Cam's smile vanished.

"What is it, Cam? What's troubling you?" Jake put a hand on her shoulder.

Cam shook her head as she dropped her bag on the floor, pulled a tall metal stool next to a stainless-steel island, and perched on it. The fragrant kitchen was quiet now between the lunch and dinner rushes. Piles of chopped leeks and a bowl of scrubbed potatoes in water sat on the broad counter nearby. A young man in white chef's garb chopped tomatoes. Several large pots simmered on a ten-burner stove behind him. Cam tried not to look at the flames.

"Come on now. Tell me what's worrying you," said Jake as he emptied a big bag of lettuce and greens into a sink and ran cold water to cool and wash them. He looked over at her from under bushy eyebrows, his hands busy in the deep sink. "Tell, tell."

Cam slouched, with her elbows on the island. "I guess you haven't seen the news. There was a murder on my property last night."

"Murder? You're kidding, right?"

"I'm not kidding. My employee, I mean, the employee I had fired at noon, was the unlucky recipient of a pitchfork in his neck. My pitchfork."

"Who found him?" Jake looked at Cam. She pointed at her chest.

"You poor thing. Did they catch the killer?"

"Not yet. The police weren't even around today. I don't understand it. Oh, and I found herbicide on my rhubarb."

"No problem. We'll wash it off, and it'll still make great pie. And, you know, compared to murder —"

"You don't understand. The whole crop is ruined. I don't know how it could have happened."

"So you overapplied it, big deal. What's the fuss? Won't it grow back?"

"Jake, listen to me. It was real herbicide, not a product I can or would use. I don't even have any on the property." *Or won't once the trash gets picked up,* Cam thought. "It wasn't my mistake. Couldn't have been. And I could be decertified."

"I see."

Cam looked down at her hands. The skin was rough, and dirt still lingered under her fingernails. Jake was a chef. His hands were always clean. She smoothed the skirt of her dress several times, shoved her fists into the wide front pockets, reconsidered, then clasped one hand with the other in her lap.

"You know, my customers and me, we

don't care if you're certified or not. We don't care if someone is killed on your property — well, as long as you didn't do it." Jake laughed as he raised his eyebrows Groucho-style. "We love your vegetables. But I'll help you locate the scoundrel and his reasons. We will talk him out of this lunatic behavior and settle the matter like civilized people." He loaded the greens into an industrial-size salad spinner and began to rotate the top to dry the leaves. "And I'm sure the police will catch the killer any minute now."

"Sounds good to me," Cam breathed and tried to believe him. She leaned down to get her purse and then rose. "I'm going to take myself for a walk. I'll be back to eat at about five o'clock. That's not too early to sample your best cooking?" After Cam had met Jake earlier in the spring, she had started a ritual on Sundays of treating herself to his cooking. She never minded eating alone, and she had brought the latest Michael Pollan to read.

Jake shook his head. "See you in a few." He walked her to the doorway. He smiled, but his eyes were sober.

Cam focused on her computer screen the next morning. She had much work to do in the fields, but the message on her voice mail last night had said George Frost was coming by to talk with her this morning at nine, so she was catching up on record keeping, marketing tasks, and paying bills. After searching everywhere for small-farm management software and finding either nothing satisfactory or nothing affordable, Cam had written her own. It let her track what she planted and when, as well as costs, the weather, harvest yields, soil tests, business associates, barter-based sales, the works. It was a simple app, but it did the job, or it would when she got everything transferred over from the paper ledger system Albert had used. Maybe she should market it to other small farmers. One more thing to add to the to-do list. But more cash income couldn't hurt, so it would be worth the effort of improving the user interface and making it easier to navigate. She'd work on that in the quiet winter months.

Frost was late. Glancing out the window, Cam was glad the reporters weren't back. They'd been gone when she arrived home last night. It was a relief, but it made her wonder if they had information she didn't.

Returning to the computer, Cam clicked the SUBMIT button in the Harvest-to-Hand window. There, now Produce Plus Plus would be one of the farms listed on their mobile app. What would Great-Aunt Marie have thought about people looking up sources for local food on their cell phones? She probably would have chided Cam for not registering on the site earlier. Marie had always been ahead of her time.

Cam set up a link in the app to the farm's brand-new Facebook page. And hoped she could find time to keep up with all this publicity and marketing, when she really just wanted to grow food. She needed a Web page, too. Cam sighed, then had a thought. Why not get a CSA volunteer to set up the Web page? *Brilliant.*

She picked up a letter sitting on the desk. She'd almost been late with her last home owner's insurance payment. She logged into the company's Web site and set up automatic online payments, groaning at the amount. She squeezed her eyes shut and reopened them, but the monthly charge hadn't magically reduced itself. Well, she had to have insurance, and that was that.

Three short raps brought her back to the present. She strode to the door and flung it open.

George Frost faced her. Behind him stood another man.

"Morning, Ms. Flaherty. This is Pete Pappas with the state police."

State police? What was up with that? Cam looked from one man to the other.

"May we come in?"

"Sure." She held the door open for them. "But why are the state police involved?" She gestured at the table and pulled out a chair for herself.

Frost sat across from her, and Pappas, a diminutive man in an immaculate blazer and slacks, stood for a moment, looking around the room, before he sat with an air of reluctance. Preston sidled up to Chief Frost and snagged a couple of strokes, but when Pappas stretched his hand toward the cat, the cat twisted away and stalked off.

"When a murder occurs in a small town like Westbury, protocol calls for a state investigator to participate," Pappas said. "We have resources the local towns don't."

George Frost nodded but didn't look particularly pleased with the situation.

"I thought you would have been here yesterday," Cam said. "Don't you have to look for evidence?"

"We were here yesterday afternoon. You were out," Frost said. "We had several emergencies yesterday morning, not the least of which was a case of arson. Our fire department barely got a couple of children out."

Cam froze. Children in a burning house. She could almost smell the smoke.

Frost brought her back to reality. "We talked with several of your CSA customers. You stated on Saturday evening you had not had a fight with Mike Montgomery, correct?"

Cam nodded.

"A Mr. Ames and a Ms. Slavin remember it differently."

Felicity and Wes. Great.

Chief Frost continued. "According to them, Mike Montgomery threatened you."

"He was unhappy I fired him. I wouldn't call it a threat, though."

Pete Pappas raised his thick black eyebrows but didn't speak.

"They also mentioned a Lucinda who was there. We'll need her contact information."

"Sure. She's the president of the Locavore Club."

Finally Pappas spoke. "The what?"

"It's a group of people who like to eat locally grown food. Many of them are my customers."

Pappas rolled his eyes.

"If they want to buy my produce, it's fine with me."

"Let's have contact info for Lucinda, uh . . . What's her last name?"

"DaSilva. Capital *D*, capital *S*," Cam said to Chief Frost, who had pulled out a small notebook. Cam rose and moved to her desk. "I'll get it off my customer list."

"I'd like you to print out the entire list for me," Pappas said. "It's possible one of your customers saw or heard something relating to the crime."

Cam sighed. "All right." She sent the file to her printer.

"And we'll need you to come down to the Westbury station to take your prints," Frost said.

Cam stood. "Why? I didn't kill Mike."

"Purposes of elimination," Pappas said with a little smile.

"But he was killed with my pitchfork. My fingerprints are going to be all over it."

"We done here, George?" Pappas stood and drummed his fingers on the table.

Chief Frost nodded as he unfolded from his chair. "You'll be around, Ms. Flaherty, correct?"

"Of course I'll be around. I have a farm to run!" Cam heard the screech in her voice with horror. She cleared her throat and tried to calm herself. It wouldn't do to be antagonistic with men like this. "When do you need my fingerprints? Oh, never mind. I'll go down there in a few minutes." Might as well get it over with.

The men headed for the door. Preston appeared from nowhere and ambled toward them. Pappas paused. As he leaned down to pet the cat, Preston gave him a look and shot straight back where he'd come from.

"Oh, by the way," Cam called, "I need to get into my hoop house. I have seedlings that need my care, and . . ."

George Frost turned. "We took the tape down yesterday. You're free to go in and out now."

"But if you find anything we missed, you tell us." Pappas focused on Cam. "Anything at all. Do you understand?"

His arrogant tone rubbed Cam the wrong way.

"You don't touch it," he went on. "You don't tell anyone else. You call me. Here's my card." He pulled a business card out of his jacket pocket and proffered it.

"You can call me at the station, too," Chief Frost added with a rush, earning him a cold glance from Pappas.

Cam pasted a little smile on her face and nodded, glancing over at the kitchen counter. She'd forgotten until this minute about the disk she'd found the morning before. And now she thought she might hang on to it for a little while longer. She'd give it to Ruth. She trusted Ruth.

After she watched their cruiser pull onto the road, Cam trained a flashlight on the disk but couldn't see any identifying marks. She used the tip of a knife to flip it over and examined it again. It was dim and scratched, but the face and hat almost looked like the New England Patriots' logo. The letters *PM* were superimposed on the shape. Cam shook her head. She didn't know what it was. It could have been Mike's. It could have been the killer's. Or it could have belonged to any number of other people who had traipsed through the hoop house over the years, including Great-Uncle Albert.

When she got home from the station, Cam called Nick's.

After a brief conversation, she said, "What do you mean you don't have time to fix my tiller?"

"Lady, it's June. We got broken lawn mowers out the wazoo. I told you I can fix it next week."

Cam winced at the click and the subsequent dial tone. She pulled a book off the shelf where she kept gardening and home improvement tomes and trudged to the barn.

"I'm smart. I should be able to figure this out. Right, Preston?"

Preston answered by rearing up and rubbing his side along her leg.

Sunlight streamed through the clerestory window above the barn's back door. Cam had found the wide window at a salvage shop last fall and had installed it to add more natural illumination to the barn.

She sat cross-legged on the floor next to the tiller and opened *The Idiot's Guide to Small Engine Repair.* She wasn't usually an idiot, unless you counted social interactions, but when it came to rototillers, she was a dunce.

A few minutes later, Cam rummaged in Albert's toolbox for a socket wrench. She found one, as well as a socket. She pulled the little hood off the spark plug and tried to unscrew it. The socket spun around the white bolt-shaped base of the plug. Off she went to find a smaller one, which, of course, was too small.

"Just call me Goldilocks. This one has to be just right," she muttered to herself after selecting a third socket from the tattered bag where Albert had stored them. Cam extracted the plug after exerting pressure on the wrench. She carried it out the open door and examined it in the sunlight. Exactly like the book predicted, the business end was coated in black oil. She pulled a rag out of her pocket and wiped the plug clean as she walked back in. A thin file from the toolbox was the next weapon in the process. She slid it into the gap between the electrode set in its ceramic base and the bent-over hook of metal. She sanded a deposit off the metal. She didn't have a way of measuring the gap and hoped it hadn't changed from the last tune-up, which had to have been a decade or more ago.

Cam reassembled the works and checked the levers. She crossed her mental fingers and pulled. The machine coughed and almost caught, then died. She tried it again. It started.

Cam screeched as the tiller bucked toward her and knocked her to the ground. Her hands flew off the handlebars, and the tiller shut off.

"Crud. I left it in reverse." She got up and dusted herself off. "At least it started, right, Mr. P?" She rubbed her left hip where she had landed hard, then winced. The rubbing had opened the cut on her hand. Blood oozed through the bandage.

Preston eyed her from the doorway in a

stance that said he was watchful for additional crazy machines.

That afternoon, Cam pushed up from the ground. She dusted the dirt from her knees and checked the height of the sun. She didn't wear a watch in the fields but figured it had to be close to three o'clock. A breeze smelling of rain rustled the leaves in the tall trees at the back of the property. She dumped the bucket of weeds on top of the others in the garden cart. She'd been pulling them since lunchtime, but at least the lettuces had clean beds now. They didn't take well to the competition of weeds like purslane and dock.

She wheeled the cart to the row of three compost bins and dumped it in the one holding the newest, roughest ingredients. Cam narrowed her eyes at the far bin, which held the almost finished black gold that nourished her crops and maintained balance in the soil. A layer of fuzzy white coated the top.

Cam's stomach dropped. Was this more sabotage? She pushed the cart out of her way and took two quick strides to the compartment. She leaned in over the bin. She sniffed.

Beyond the familiar earthy scent of organic matter decomposing aerobically, Cam sensed a different kind of decay. She sniffed again. And exhaled in relief. It was only a bit of damping-off. Only an algae bloom.

Last week had been rainy, after all. Cam had been so busy getting ready for the first share day, she hadn't given that pile its final turning when it needed it. But at least it hadn't been attacked. That would have been the last straw.

"Mrs. Flaherty?" a high voice called from the barn area.

Cam whirled toward the front of the property. *Darn.* Now she was late to meet her newest, youngest volunteer. Before the girl and her father had left the farm on Saturday, they had asked Cam if Ellie could work with her on her Girl Scout locavore badge. Cam had tried not to show her reluctance when she agreed.

"Coming!" Cam loped toward the barn. Panting as she arrived, she said, "Sorry. I was out weeding and lost track of time."

"Not a problem." David Kosloski leaned against his car. Kosloski's tapping foot seemed to belie his words. The car was a big SUV of the sort Cam always thought more properly belonged navigating the desert than driving around an exurb like Westbury. His daughter bounced on her heels next to him, a notebook in her hand and an eager expression on her face. She wore a pair of denim shorts with a hot pink T-shirt. High-top sneakers matched the outfit.

"I'm Ellie," the girl said. "Thank you for letting me shadow you, Mrs. Flaherty."

Cam was suddenly both nervous and feeling ridiculous for feeling so. "Hi, Ellie, Mr. Kosloski."

"David. Call me David."

"David, Ellie, please. I'm Cam, not Mrs. Flaherty. Okay?" Cam did her best to smile. Why she'd gotten involved in this Girl Scout venture, she couldn't imagine. The family was already a customer. It wasn't like she needed another sale. "I'm looking forward to showing you the farm, Ellie."

The girl smiled again. "Me, too. I mean, I can't wait to see it."

"May I have a word with you?" David folded his arms, tilting his head toward the barn. "We'll be back in a second, Eleanor."

Cam followed him in, puzzled.

"I heard there was a murder here. Are you sure it's safe for my daughter to work with you?" Deep lines surrounded an unsmiling mouth.

Cam looked at David straight on. "Listen, I don't know who killed Mike Montgomery, but it must have been someone who knew him. It's always been safe here, and I'm sure it still is. But if you don't want your daughter alone with me, I'll understand."

"The police are on the case, I assume?"

Cam assured him they were.

"Do they have any suspects? Anyone in custody?" His hand jingled change in his pocket as he asked.

"Not that I know of. Although you really should call the local police and ask them. They must have a public liaison person."

"Never mind. Anyway, Eleanor doesn't know about the murder, and I'd prefer it stayed that way."

Cam nodded. "On my honor." The last thing she wanted to do was talk about violent death with a sunny child.

He strode outdoors. "I'll be off, then. Pick you up at five thirty, Ell." He waved and slid into the driver's seat.

Ellie ran around to the passenger door of the car and stuck her head in the window.

Cam looked over to see a woman in the front seat. Must be Ellie's mother. These people had a legitimate concern, she realized, feeling grateful they had decided to trust her with the girl.

Ellie stepped back and waved as the car backed down the drive. "I'm ready now."

She turned a determined face up at Cam.

"Let's get started, then. Want to show me your requirements?"

Ellie opened her notebook. " 'The locavore badge lets girls explore the benefits and challenges of going local,' " she read out. "I have to, like, find my local food sources, cook a simple dish with only local ingredients, make a family recipe substituting local foods, and then make, like, a three-course meal."

"Sounds like a lot to do."

Ellie looked up at Cam again. "This is the local food source part. It doesn't get any more local than this."

"That's right. Let's go visit the source."

"Sweet."

Sweet? That was what Great-Uncle Albert said when he liked something, Cam marveled. As they walked out to the fields, Cam said, "Have you been on a farm before?"

"Only to see Buffy."

"Buffy?"

"You don't know Buffy? The buffalo at Tendercrop Farm." The girl's voice expressed astonishment as only a preteen's could.

"Oh, that Buffy." Cam did know Buffy, or at least a previous incarnation of her, but only from her own teen summers, when they'd tried to entice the captive buffalo to ingest hash brownies, a project that now horrified her. "But have you walked around the fields or anything?"

"No. My mom has MS. We don't, like, really get out much as a family."

So that was why her mom stayed in the car.

"But when I told them I wanted to do my locavore badge, Dad found your farm and signed up. He likes to cook vegetables." Ellie rolled her eyes.

Cam found herself warming to this elfin creature, who she thought must be ten or eleven at the most. "And you don't like to eat them?"

"They're sort of disgusting." Ellie grimaced. "Well, I like carrots, and I like red cabbage. But raw, not cooked."

"That's a start. So what grade are you in at school?"

"I'm finishing eighth. I'm fourteen. I'll be a Senior Scout when I start high school, and the locavore badge is only for Seniors." Pride shone through her voice.

So much for guessing a child's age. Ellie was so tiny, Cam had assumed she was younger. Cam herself had been an ungainly beanpole who towered over her classmates at that age.

"Can I ask you a question?"

Cam nodded.

"Everybody's saying a man was killed here. On your farm. Is it true?"

Cam stopped walking. Of course, kids would have heard about it in a town this size. "Yes, that's true." She looked straight at Ellie, who also stopped. "But the police are working on it, and we're safe. It didn't have anything to do with me or the farm, really." Cam hoped that was true.

"Okay." Ellie resumed progress toward the fields. "We only have a couple of weeks of school left. Maybe I could help you here in the summer?"

"That's a possibility. We'll see."

Ellie raised her eyebrows and twisted her mouth. "That's what Dad says when he means no."

"Good thing I'm not your dad," Cam said, glad to see the smile this produced on the girl. "I can always use volunteers. We'll work it out." She gestured around them. "Now, do you recognize anything you see growing here?"

CHAPTER 5

Cam washed her hands in the kitchen sink. She gazed out the window at the yard and the barn beyond. The session with Ellie had gone better than Cam had expected. She was a curious, funny kid, not yet taken over by a typical teen's sullen reactions or rude back talk, and seemed genuinely interested in learning how plants grew. She had asked what the names of all the plants were. She had tasted each of the herbs Cam grew, and had seemed delighted at the citrusy taste of the lemon thyme and the aroma of a basil leaf.

Creaking open the refrigerator door, Cam surveyed its mostly empty shelves. Her stomach growled. She'd rather just pop open a Five Mile Ale and have dinner delivered, but in the interest of her meager bank account, she grabbed her purse and her cloth shopping bag and set out for the Food Mart.

The two-mile drive was over in a flash. She grabbed a plastic basket and walked the short aisles, selecting pasta and a couple of jars of sauce. Being a locavore was all very nice for her customers, but Cam knew this time of year would be a hungry one if she opted for that lifestyle. Last year's potatoes were shriveled or rotten, and even if she'd had a crop of tomatoes last September, she would have been too busy to spend the time canning or freezing them. Although she had salad and asparagus at home, such a meal didn't go too far to assuage the appetite of a working farmer.

At the sound of whispered voices, Cam looked up. At the end of the aisle near the checkout area, a stocky man and an equally stocky woman stood with heads together, staring at her. The woman reached down and put a protective arm around the shoulders of a young boy in a soccer uniform. He tried to wriggle away without success.

The bread aisle was right beyond them, so Cam kept on walking. The woman's eyes widened. She almost pushed the little boy ahead of her as she hurried out of sight around a corner. The man stood his ground, blocking Cam's path.

"Excuse me," Cam said, trying to ease past him.

"You're the farmer with the murder, aren't you?" He scowled.

"A man was killed on my land, it's true. It's very sad."

"You knocked him off, didn't you? Mike was our friend, you know."

Cam halted. She looked him in the eyes. "I'm sorry for your loss. I had nothing to do with Mike's death."

"We'll see about that." He snorted and turned.

His bicep sported a small tattoo. Cam gazed at the same symbol that decorated the disk from the hoop house. She whistled under her breath and kept on walking. She added a loaf of whole-wheat bread and a jar of natural peanut butter to her basket, barely seeing them. It seemed that certain of the townspeople thought she killed Mike. *Great.* She ended up at the meat and deli wall. Her hand was on a package of ground beef when someone called her name. She looked up.

"Hey, Stuart. I forgot you worked here," Cam said with a smile.

Stuart stood behind the deli case, a long stained white apron over his clothes. "How are things at the farm? Heard you had a touch of excitement over there the other night."

81

Had anyone not heard? Cam was willing to bet he learned about the killing in this very store and not on the local news.

"I wouldn't really call it exciting. Horrifying, more like. But Westbury's finest are on it, apparently. Did they call you?"

Stuart raised his eyebrows. "Why would they call me?" He gave a quick glance around the store, then looked back at Cam. They were alone in the aisle.

"Uh, they wanted to talk to all my customers." Cam gestured in the air with her free hand. "I don't know. See if anybody saw something suspicious, I suppose."

Stuart busied himself with a large piece of beef on the cutting board. He sliced a steak off it. "Get you anything?"

"Actually, yes. I'd like a half pound of the maple ham, sliced. And also of the sharp cheddar."

She grabbed a bag of chips and a jar of salsa from the shelves behind her while she waited. As Stuart handed her two packages wrapped in white paper, Cam said, "Then you didn't talk to the police?"

He shook his head. He picked up the bloody knife again and gestured with it in the air. "I don't much like police. They want to talk to me, they'll have to come find me."

■ ■ ■ ■

Cam's cell phone erupted with the *Star Trek* theme song as she drove home. She fished it out of her bag with one hand. She glanced at it to find the SEND button, then looked up and swore as a horn blared at her. She'd swerved toward the center line in that brief moment. She cursed the existence of cell phones but pressed SEND, anyway, and said, "Hello?"

"Cameron? Are you in front of a television?"

"Hi, Uncle Albert. No, I'm driving home."

"Well, you ought to take a look when you get there. Why didn't you tell me Marie's rhubarb was harmed? And what in blazes was it?"

Cam wished she'd never picked up the call. "I shouldn't be talking and driving. I'll call you back after I get home, all right? Thanks for letting me know." She didn't wait for his reply. She felt for the END button and pressed it without looking down.

Wonderful. Damn reporter.

Panic stung Cam like a prickly nettle the next morning. Produce was scarce in early June. The fields stretched out around her,

83

mute, unyielding, displaying rows of immature seedlings. The spring fragrance of fresh earth released by the early morning sunshine did nothing to cheer her. What had she gotten herself into by thinking she could learn how to farm in one short year?

She'd be unloading her truck at the Tuesday farmers' market in a few hours. But Cam was afraid she couldn't harvest enough to make the table look inviting to customers.

A twig snapped behind her. Her heart sped up to warp speed. She whirled.

"Hey, *fazendeira*!" Lucinda strode toward Cam.

"Hi, Lucinda." Cam let out a breath she hadn't realized she was holding. "What does *fazendeira* mean, anyway?"

"It means 'farmer.' "

"I guess that's me."

The Brazilian stopped in front of Cam. She shoved her hands into the pockets of khaki shorts. "The police called me." A tightness around her eyes gave a cast of alarm to her face.

"I know. They made me give them the whole list of CSA customers. I'm sorry."

"I didn't talk to them. I didn't pick up."

"I'm sure they just want to ask if you had

seen anything, you know, about the murder."

"I'm not talking to no cops."

Cam shrugged. "Whatever. They have a pretty long list to work through. I think they're barking up the wrong tree, though. They need to find the list of people who didn't care for Mike."

"Maybe I got an idea about that. But I'm not telling them. I tell you, and you call them, okay?"

"I guess." Cam didn't understand why Lucinda didn't want to talk to the authorities. But this wasn't the time to figure it out.

"That Mike, he was in with this anti-immigrant group called the Patriotic Militia. They don't like me, so I stay out of their way."

"Really? Do you think he was murdered because of that?" Cam pictured the disk she'd found in the hoop house. Maybe *PM* stood for Patriotic Militia. Mike must have dropped it when he was working in there.

"I don't know. But maybe, you know, you can maybe tell the police you heard it somewhere." Lucinda's eyes widened. "But not from me. Don't tell them I told you."

"I guess I can do that. But, listen, can we talk more about this later? I'm terrified I won't be ready for the farmers' market, and

85

it's only my third time there."

"Right." Lucinda's face relaxed. "Let's go. What do we pick first?"

"I don't know what else we can pick." Cam shook her head. "I've always been a gardener, and I thought I could handle farming. Now I'm not so sure, despite the course I took during the winter at the college. I think I might have bitten off more than I can chew."

Lucinda frowned. "What do you mean?"

"I mean I don't know if I have enough produce to take to market today. This farm deal might have been a bad idea."

"Too late now, Cam. Listen, I'm here to help you, right? So what do you already got, and how much do we need to harvest?"

"I'll show you." Cam led Lucinda along the path to the barn. "I already cut the asparagus. It's still growing like there's no tomorrow." Cam pointed to the asparagus patch, where feathery fronds waved in the gentle breeze.

In the barn, Cam showed Lucinda what she had laid out on the farm table, which looked much like it had Saturday morning. Bundles of asparagus she'd cut over the last couple of days. A big bag of spinach she'd cut earlier in the morning from the bed that had overwintered. Bunches of slim green-

and-white scallions. A dozen small heads of Red Sails lettuce. Cam squinted at the table of produce as if to squeeze more out of it.

"Hey, we're going to be okay. You got more food out there we can harvest." Lucinda folded her arms and locked her eyes on Cam's. "Remember I told you I read that *Animal, Vegetable, Miracle* book, about a family who only ate local food for a year. I told you I'm going to do the same thing for a year, like the Kingsolver family. I started Saturday, and I'm doing great."

"You told me. I guess you're going to be disappointed this week." Cam couldn't believe that, despite all her careful planning, the start of the farm year was already stumbling. She rubbed her hair, glad she kept it cut short.

"Wrong attitude, *querida.* Come on, I show you." Lucinda tucked her arm through Cam's and propelled her out into the fields.

They stopped at the herb garden. Mounds of oregano, thyme, sage, and rosemary showed new growth on their overwintered stalks. Tarragon pushed bright green slivers of leaves skyward. Cam had tucked several dozen young plants of basil, dill, and parsley among the perennials.

"What about munches of herbs? How many we need?"

Cam laughed out loud. "You mean bunches. Great idea. We can harvest some of the mature perennial herbs. Those annuals aren't ready for cutting yet."

"And those shoots of, what do you say, garlic? There in the field. They can be like, you know, green onions, but garlic."

"Oh, yeah. Spring garlic scallions. I can thin out the little shoots and make room for bigger bulbs. How'd you know about that?"

"Look, I grew up on a farm in Rio Grande do Sul. More south than here, but a farm is a farm. I know farms. Now, how about *flores.* I mean, flowers. I saw purple ones over there, yes?" She pointed back at the house and the large flower garden next to it.

"The Japanese irises. Nice. We can throw in a few of those antique narcissus, too. The flower garden was Great-Aunt Marie's prized project, rest her soul." Cam tilted her head at Lucinda. "You're good. Can I hire you? I need to replace Mike."

Lucinda turned away. "I pay for my farm share. I work here because I love it." Her voice dropped to a whisper. "Anyway, you don't want somebody like me for an employee."

Cam cocked her head, wondering if Lucinda said that because she was an undocumented immigrant. She certainly would like to hire Lucinda. As it was, the Brazilian seemed happy to volunteer to weed, turn compost, or whatever else Cam asked her to do. Lucinda was strong, smart, and funny. It was a pleasure having her around, and she got Cam to come out of her insecure, geeky shell a bit, not an easy task.

Cam mustered a smile. "So, shall we get to work? I need all the help I can get."

Lucinda turned back to Cam. She nodded, the glow restored to her light brown face. "Let's do it."

Cam drove fast along a back road paralleling the river. She looked over at the little magnetized clock she kept on the dashboard.

"Shoot, I'm going to be late. Picking took too long," she said aloud. "I hate being late." She drove her laden truck over a bridge, across a busy main street, and up a hill, to turn left at the Haverhill city park, with a sign on the corner that read WEEKLY FARMERS' MARKET, TUESDAYS, 12:00–4:00 PM. Colorful dancing cabbages and smiling tomatoes decorated the sign. It was right before noon as Cam backed into a space adjoining the park.

"Rats, Mrs. Boukis got the spot I wanted."

The vendor slots were on a wide sidewalk at the edge of the block-long park. Huge, old maples in leaf here and there shaded the walkway, which was transformed into a market every week. The spot Cam had snagged last week was under one of the biggest trees, so her produce didn't bake in the sun all afternoon, but she was too late. It had been claimed by an older woman who grew an acre of flowers and did a landmark business in mixed bouquets.

Cam hurried to unload a table and assorted containers of produce and flowers from the back of the truck. Certain farmers sold directly off the tailgate of their truck, but Cam preferred to set up a table, with bushel baskets and buckets full of flowers on the pavement at each end. She had a colorful cloth with bright vegetables printed on it to cover the table. An attractive display really seemed to draw customers, and the cloth helped. It also helped with the feeling of intimidation she had being around so many experienced growers.

Everyone else was busy setting up their wares, too. One big farm always used two slots and had its own colored canopy to protect the produce and customers from sun or rain. Another vendor was a widower with only a card table to sell from. An old friend of Great-Uncle Albert's, he was famed for his berries and could sell enough strawberries, raspberries, and blueberries to justify paying the market fee each week. He'd gone out of his way to welcome Cam, too.

"Hey, Rich. What's up?" Cam greeted one of the farmers, a robust retired opera star, as he strolled by. He sang a bit of an aria in response while he continued down the line several more spaces to his own. She'd met him last fall, after she had moved to Albert's farm and had come to this market as a buyer, not a seller. Cam saw him pull blue plastic bins of lettuce out of his truck and set them on a long white display table shaded by a simple but effective homemade white canopy. He grew high-quality produce and claimed to do it all organically.

Cam continued setting up. She wondered if any of these farmers could have been on her land lately. Who would try to sabotage her work? She couldn't believe that anybody would be so threatened by her few organic acres. As she worked, hands moving rapidly so she would be ready when the customers showed up, she was so busy thinking through the list of farmers present, she almost missed seeing Bev Montgomery approach. Cam was surprised she was out in public so soon after her son's death, even though Bev was the market manager.

"Ms. Flaherty." Bev was dressed in a worn green plaid shirt and green work pants. She sported a Celtics cap atop her iron-colored hair and sun-fatigued face. She looked beaten, and more.

"Mrs. Montgomery, I am so sorry for your loss."

"I might not have lost him if you hadn't fired him. He was a good boy." She glared up at Cam, shading her eyes with her hand against the noon light.

Cam was taken aback. "What did that have to do with his death?"

"He needed his job. He needed that stability. I'm holding you responsible. Maybe you killed him yourself." She stalked away down the line of tables.

Cam took a deep breath. She looked around, hoping no one had overhead. So it wasn't only George Frost who thought she might have tried to get rid of Mike Montgomery.

Cam finished setting up and walked briskly four spaces down the row, surreptitiously noting the prices other farms were charging for strawberries, lettuce, fresh herbs, and bunches of flowers this year. She stopped at Rich's table. "We're lucky it's an early season, aren't we?"

"Absolutely. Last year strawberries didn't come in until a week after this, and this year we've been selling them two weeks already," he said, turning toward her.

"Have a good market."

He nodded, gripping a cigarette between closed lips as he grabbed another bin from his truck with both hands.

Customers began to crowd around the vendors, so Cam hurried toward her own spot. "Can I help you?" she asked the older couple clutching a canvas bag. As she sold them a half pound of asparagus, she looked at the lettuce in the sun. This was awful. She hadn't even brought her big umbrella. Cam chastised herself for being late and losing the shady spot.

An hour later, with people clustering around most of the stands, Cam muttered, "I wish I had rhubarb. People see there isn't any on the table, and they don't buy the berries, either. They just walk on."

The market looked like a scene from another country. Shoppers of all ages carrying string bags and canvas sacks picked over produce and flowers. Newly arrived Cambodians and Haitians rubbed elbows with second-generation Italians, fourth-generation French Canadians, and Yankees whose ancestors had founded the city. A baker hawked crusty round loaves, long baguettes, and huge cookies. The market was a portrait in contrast to the sterility of a supermarket.

Cam busied herself answering questions about organic methods, bagging lettuce, and making change, moving fast. Well, at least she was making money, rhubarb or no rhubarb. She had her envelope ready for food-stamp customers who had swiped their EBT cards in exchange for little wooden "nickels" they could use to pay for produce.

A rattly pickup backed into a spot at the opposite end of the line of farmers from Bev Montgomery's. A short, squat man in dirt-stained overalls jumped out, creaked open the tailgate, and pulled a few bushel baskets of red stalks to the rear of the truck.

Cam focused on the newcomer. *What?* Albert had told her Howard Fisher didn't sell at this market. Wasn't he a pig farmer? And it looked like rhubarb was the only crop he was selling. Cam handed the thin man standing at her table his change for two bunches of herbs and a bag of red mustard greens and thanked him automatically.

The crowds perusing the farm tables thinned somewhat, allowing the farmers time to sit down, chat with each other, and tidy up their displays. She finally had a minute of peace in this crazy week. She consolidated two half-empty baskets of herbs into one and realigned the bunches of asparagus standing upright in water. Her thoughts turned to Mike Montgomery's death, and the feeling of peace vanished. She wiped her brow with her purple bandanna. The sun was still strong, although the light of the day had begun its decline. The humidity kept the heat intense.

"Organic strawberries, hmm? I'll take four pints."

"Chief Frost. You come into Haverhill to shop?" Cam said to the uniformed Frost. Or was he here checking up on her?

"Well, I had to see a person of interest over in this neighborhood, so I stopped down here. My wife, you know, is nuts about fresh stuff, and even nuttier about your natural food. Why, times she drives all the way over to Andover just to get groceries."

"Whole Foods?"

"Yup. It being her birthday tomorrow, I thought I'd better see what I could get. I don't know that I could find anything that would please her more than these berries."

Cam smiled her relief. At least he didn't seem to be here to interrogate her. "You'd better get some salad fixings and fresh lemon thyme for her, too."

"All right. She'll be pleased. Now, there's no poison in that salad, is there?"

"Poison?" Cam's voice squeaked. She cleared her throat. "I don't know what you're talking about." She gazed at him. Was he kidding or serious?

The chief folded his arms, regarding her. His eyes didn't smile.

"That'll be fifteen dollars," Cam said evenly. She eased the pint boxes sideways into small paper bags, placed them in the bottom of a brown paper grocery bag, and topped it off with the bags of mixed greens and herbs. She worked carefully, her face somber, thinking of the lifeless rhubarb. She should report it. But would he think she had poisoned her own crop? Cam handed the bag to Frost and took his money. She began, "You know, Chief, there was —"

"Why, George! What? Shopping from the competition?" Bev Montgomery suddenly appeared at Frost's side. Her green cap was pushed back on her head, her browned face flushed, her breathing slightly ragged, as if she'd rushed over. Bev avoided Cam's eyes, looking only at the police chief. "You get yourself down to Montgomery Farm's stand in a hurry. I saved you my choice Victoria rhubarb and a bunch of those turnips I know Hope likes." Bev Montgomery took Frost's elbow and led the officer down the line.

Cam would have to tell him later. Maybe. Rhubarb. It was everywhere. It seemed like everyone was selling it and talking about it except her. Frowning, she tucked the bills into one of the pouches of the cloth hardware store belt she used as a cash register, then rearranged the strawberries to fill in the gaps left by the ones she had just sold. Customers liked to see a full display so things didn't look picked over.

At around three thirty, business picked up again. Most farmers lowered their prices at the end of market. Growers hated to take product home and have to throw it on the compost pile. Cam knocked fifty cents off each pint of strawberries and marked the herbs and asparagus half price. Shoppers in the know, especially those with lower incomes, squeezed past each other to claim the well-priced, slightly wilted, but still tasty produce. Cam's last bunch of sage went to a young Hmong couple, the last asparagus to a stooped, white-haired woman, the last quart of strawberries to a harried-looking mother with a Jamaican lilt in her voice and young twin boys at her side, who handed

Cam five of the wooden Supplemental Nutrition Assistance Program tokens.

Cam's table was almost empty when she checked her watch. Four o'clock. She began to load empty baskets and buckets into the truck. Everybody around her also started to close down. She could hear Rich's booming voice in song again as he dismantled his display. Lonely leaves of discarded lettuce littered the sidewalk. Strawberry tops, still clinging to bits of red flesh, lay in the gutter where children, impatient for the sweet taste, had thrown them. Cam was about to pull into the street when Bev Montgomery appeared at the driver's side window.

"Here," Bev said, presenting Cam with a long plastic bag. Bev's worn hand held the bag gently. "Want some to take home? I didn't sell out, and I can't use it." Bev's faded blue eyes focused on the door handle.

Cam was tired from the day's work of picking and selling and emotionally fatigued from worry. She watched the older farmer. What was Bev doing? Trying to make up for accusing Cam of murder, and didn't know how? Or maybe rubbing it in that Cam didn't have any rhubarb for sale today. Bev couldn't possibly know what had happened to Cam's crop. Cam hadn't told anybody but Jake. Unless Bev watched television, of course.

Finally, Cam simply said, "Thank you, no. I've decided to go pure strawberry this year. See you next week." She steered the truck into traffic.

She glanced back in the mirror. Bev Montgomery still watched her, the bag of rhubarb hanging heavily from her hand. Cam should have taken it. Keeping the peace was important in a small town. She needed friends, not enemies. So far she'd been more adept at screwing up relationships than fostering them.

Chapter 6

Cam knocked on the doorjamb of room 116 at Moran Manor that evening. "Anybody home?"

Albert St. Pierre put a finger on the page he was reading and looked up. "For you, Cameron, I'm home." He waved her in with a thick, age-spotted hand. He would have looked like any other octogenarian in a red plaid shirt, relaxing in his recliner, except for the crutches at his side and the pants leg tucked up under his right knee.

Cam walked into the cozy room stuffed with books and photographs. "Your door is wide open, Uncle Albert." She kissed the old man's snowy-white hair. "Looks like you're home to just about everybody."

"Sit down, girl. You look tired."

Cam rubbed her forehead. "It was market day, so yeah, I'm tired."

"Now, tell me what in blazes you got going on up to the farm. Did they find whoever killed young Montgomery?"

"Not that they've told me. I'm afraid they think I did it."

Albert's pale blue eyes widened. "The devil you say! But why?"

Cam outlined the disagreement she'd had with Mike. She had called Albert earlier about the murder but hadn't given him much detail.

"So you had to let him go. Too bad. I thought having a steady job, doing honest hard work in the fresh air, might have turned the boy's life around. Bev asked me for that favor. And I owed her one."

"I'm sorry, Uncle Albert," Cam began.

He held up a hand. "Don't you go apologizing. You have your venture there. I gave the farm over to you to do what you liked with it. If organic meant you had to fire the boy, so be it. I'm not questioning you, Cameron."

"Well, the police have. I wish they'd focus on finding the real killer, though."

"Who's working on it?"

"Chief Frost has been asking questions. Plus a state police officer, a Pete Pappas."

"Pappas. I think I knew his father." Albert stared out the window into the still-rosy gloaming. "Ran a Greek grocery down to Ipswich, as I recall. We used to do joint

101

Rotary events with them. But I believe he's gone on ahead these five years now, don't you know."

Cam smiled. Her great-uncle had quite the turn of phrase.

Albert shook his head back into the present and focused on Cam. "Are you safe out at the house? All by yourself, I mean?" He frowned at her.

"I think so. I have good locks, and this afternoon, on the way home from market, I picked up a motion detector floodlight for the back and installed it."

"How'd a girl like you learn electrical?" Albert cocked his head.

Cam knew he was more curious than challenging. She flashed him a wry smile. "One of the few good things I picked up from Tom. He was always fiddling with lights, plugs, and wires. He didn't mind teaching me when I asked. It's not so complicated if you're careful."

Albert nodded. "What do you think happened with Marie's rhubarb, anyway?"

"I wish I knew." Cam cocked her head. "Wait, how did you know about it? Did the reporter mention it on the news?"

"Oh, no, but it was in the background. I knew those plants didn't look right."

"It was a herbicide. I'm sure of it. But I

have no idea where it came from or who applied it. I'm mad about it, I'll tell you."

"I'm sure you'll figure it out." He wagged a finger at her. "To change the subject, hear anything from your parents?"

Cam shook her head. "I got a postcard from Kathmandu a month ago." Her peripatetic anthropologist parents were academics who had spent much of their lives living in far-flung locales, researching the culture of peoples out of the mainstream. "I can't remember where they're headed next."

"It's too late now, but I wish they'd been more settled. You know, when you were little."

"Me, too, I guess. Although then I wouldn't have had summers on the farm." She smiled.

"True enough." Albert gazed at her. "You started coming up when you were what? About six?"

"I think so. Summer after first grade is what I remember."

"Yes. It was because of the . . ." He watched Cam. "Do you remember?"

"What my parents called 'the incident'?" Cam shuddered.

"That's best left in the past, I think. Now, what do you think of this gal who's running for Teddy's Senate seat?"

To citizens like Albert, the Massachusetts Senate seat Edward Kennedy held until he died would always be Teddy's seat. She chatted with Albert for another thirty minutes about the political primary season, life in the assisted living complex, the farm, a recent piece of news.

"I wrote letters yesterday to our congressman and both senators. It's an outrage."

Albert might have been old, but his rabid liberalism had not dimmed. He'd always been vocal about his sense of justice and injustice, and he acted on his beliefs.

Cam nodded, then yawned as she rose. "I'd better get going. It's a busy season." If anybody would understand a farmer's life, it would be Albert

He nodded. He held out his arms.

Cam embraced him. She brightened. "Hey, how about I spring you Friday night? Those customers of mine, the Locavore Club, are holding a Locavore Festival. Local food, local wine and beer. You can be my date."

Albert nodded slowly. "I suppose. Do me good to get out of here, I guess. This locavore business is kind of silly, though, don't you think? I remember when all we ate was local, because that's all there was, except for maybe a few oranges trucked up from

Florida."

"It's a date, then. Hey, I'm curious. Why did you owe Bev Montgomery a favor?"

Albert gazed up at Cam for a moment. "We'll get into that another time, my dear. It's not a fast tale to tell."

Cam looked around the barn the next morning. She thought she had everything ready for Volunteer Wednesday. Despite Lucinda being such an eager helper, the workload at the farm was more than Cam and Lucinda combined could manage. Starting a weekly volunteer day was an idea Cam had read about on the Web site for the Massachusetts chapter of the Northeast Organic Farming Association, NOFA/Mass. She liked the concept and hoped she could find enough jobs for both the skilled and the unskilled. Hiring another farmhand wasn't easy and wasn't cheap. If this worked, maybe she wouldn't have to.

"Hey, Cam!" Alexandra strode in. "I know I'm early, but I couldn't wait to get my hands dirty." Today the tall young woman sported a denim work shirt tucked into short cutoff jeans. A yellow bandanna was tied around her head, letting her hair spill down her back, and a pair of work gloves stuck out of her back pocket. "Where do we start?"

The aura of fresh air surrounding Alexandra made Cam smile. Even in her early twenties Cam hadn't been so open and energetic. "Hang on a minute. Let's wait until a few others show up. I can give a quick orientation to everyone at once."

Alexandra nodded. "So did you think any more about us using the farm as our CSF pickup site?"

"No, but that would be fine. What day do you want to do it?"

"Can we do Saturdays? That way we can pick up the fish when we come for our shares."

"No problem."

"OMG, that's solid. Did you want to sign up, too?" Alexandra pulled a flat phone out of a pocket. "Here," she said, pressing a few buttons. "Here's the information." She extended the device toward Cam.

Cam laughed. "I'll check them out online later, but thanks." Then she had a thought. "Alexandra, I don't suppose Web programming is among your talents, is it?"

"I'm not bad. I created the Locavore Club site. HTML is easy, really."

It was easy for people like Alexandra and herself. But Cam didn't have time to tackle it. "I want to set up a site for the farm. Would you be interested?"

Alexandra agreed.

"Great. Let's figure out a time to meet, and I'll sketch it out with you. Maybe before you leave today?"

Alexandra frowned. "I have an appointment later on. What if I stop by tomorrow morning?"

"Sounds good."

Felicity bounced in, sloshing water out of a jar full of flowers. "Am I late?" She beamed. She wore black work pants tucked into green rubber boots. Her braid wound around her head like a queen's. "I'm so excited to get to work on a real farm. I have a little garden at home, you know, but nothing on this scale. Wes had to work, or he'd be here, too. Oh, and I brought your chart."

Cam sighed. "Can we talk about that later?"

"Sure. But it's interesting. You're a Scorpio, which explains why you like writing software. Scorpios like to get deep into things. But your moon is in Taurus, so that's why you're attracted to farming and earthy things."

"Interesting," Cam said, mentally rolling her eyes. She'd thought she was interested in farming because Albert had offered her the opportunity right when she needed to escape the city and Tom, too.

"I also brought a few flowers from my garden in this jar." Felicity proffered the pint canning jar filled with fragrant narcissus. "I thought it would be nice to set up a little memorial at your hoop house for poor Mike Montgomery. You don't mind, do you?"

"A memorial?"

"Yes, you know. To honor his memory."

Alexandra held out a striking hand-drawn card in a plastic sleeve. "I have something for it, too. Felicity called me about the idea, so I sketched a message of peace." The sketch was a near-professional drawing. It portrayed neat rows of green crops stretching back toward a hill, with an idyllic blue stream wandering along the side and a full basket of harvested vegetables in the foreground.

"That looks very peaceful, Alexandra, although I'd say it's a lot more than a sketch," Cam said. "You're very talented."

"I just diddle around with drawing."

"A memorial to Mike is fine," Cam said to the women, who walked out of the barn with their offerings. Cam probably should have thought of that herself. But hadn't.

Several other shareholders drifted in,

including Stuart, as Felicity and Alexandra reentered the barn.

"I don't work until this afternoon, and this sounded like more fun than weeding through Monster.com for a real job." Stuart shifted a small knapsack on his back.

"Glad to have you," Cam said.

"Hi, Stuart," Alexandra said, folding her arms. "Hey, so I hear you and my sister broke up."

"Yeah, not exactly."

"Really? That's what Katie told me." Alexandra raised one eyebrow.

"She *tried* to break up with me, okay?" Stuart's voice was gruff.

So that was the subscriber Stuart had referred to earlier.

"Anyway, don't we have work to do, Cam?"

To Cam's ear, he sounded like he wanted to be anywhere but there. Cam nodded and gathered the group. After eyeing up everyone's relative strength and assessing their experience levels, she assigned each person a task. One rather out-of-shape-looking couple got the easiest job, tying the tomato vines to their stakes. Alexandra appeared to be the biggest and strongest, so Cam gave her the compost to turn. Cam asked Felicity and another woman to cut greens. The rest

Cam assigned to weed.

A man whose name Cam didn't remember spoke up. "I heard there was a murder here last week. Is the killer still at large?"

"Yes, are we safe here?" an older woman asked amid a quiet chorus of volunteers talking among themselves.

At large? The first speaker must have watched too much old television. Cam mustered her most confident farmer face. "The local and state police are hard at work. I am quite sure you're all safe. The killing wasn't directed at me or at the farm, so we have nothing to worry about. I want to thank everybody for coming to help. Now, let's get started."

Cam picked up the wheelbarrow handles and led them out to the fields. She showed the volunteers in each group where to focus their energies, doled out hand hoes and weeding tools, and demonstrated the tomato-tying technique to the retired couple. Cam handed Alexandra the spare pitchfork, since the police had confiscated the murder weapon, and showed her how to accomplish her job.

"The basic concept is that compost needs regular doses of air mixed in so it can break down. You should sprinkle it with water every few minutes, too."

"Got it, boss."

Cam walked back to the barn to get the garden cart. She paused at the hoop house. Someone had added a few sprigs of herbs next to the small memorial to Mike. Cam rounded the corner of the hoop house to see Ruth Dodge walking toward her down the drive.

"Ruthie! How nice to see you. What's happening?"

Ruth, in jeans, T-shirt, and sandals, smiled at Cam. "I'm off duty and thought I'd stop by and see how you were doing. You holding up?"

Cam nodded. "Pretty much. I wish you'd find the murderer, though. It's making a few of my customers uneasy."

"I'm sure we will soon. Detective Pappas is the best."

Cam wrinkled her nose. "He's obnoxious. I can't imagine him getting people to tell him anything."

Ruth pulled her mouth. "I guess he comes across that way. But he really is good at what he does, Cam. I should know. I worked with him before I came back to Westbury. So what's with all the cars here?" She gestured toward the drive.

"Volunteer Wednesday. Got a bunch of shareholders giving me free labor. It's good.

I need the help."

"Well, I'm here. Want to put me to work?"

Cam agreed. She led Ruth into the hoop house and halted, shuddering. "That's where I found him." Her feet refused to take another step. *There must still be blood in the gravel.* She scanned the ground and instead saw scraped-up mounds of gravel and bare dirt.

"Cam?" Ruth laid a hand on her shoulder. "They cleaned it all up, you know. It was a terrible thing to happen on your farm, but you need to let it go by."

Cam took a deep breath. "I'll try."

"Now, show me what to do."

Cam explained about applying water gently to the seedlings, then said, "I'll be right back."

She wheeled the big garden cart out to the weeders. She told them to throw the pulled matter into it and she'd empty it later. She didn't see Stuart anywhere. *Odd.* Where was he? She shook her head. Maybe he'd gone off in the woods for a minute to take a leak. Cam made a note to tell her volunteers about the small bathroom in the corner of the barn. She strode back to the hoop house and surveyed Ruth's work.

"Nice job, girlfriend." Cam moved up and down the rows. "Enough water but not too much. You've got the touch."

"Thanks. It's not really that hard."

"Here's what's next," Cam said. She showed Ruth how to gently separate the seedlings in the cells that held two or more tiny lettuce plants, and how to replant them in a new flat, so there was only one plant per cell.

"I'm not going to hurt them?" Ruth asked.

"Lettuces are pretty hardy, even tiny like this."

They worked together in silence for a few moments.

"So when was it that we stopped seeing each other, Cam?" Ruth straightened and looked at her old friend.

Cam raised her eyebrows. "I went to your wedding, what? Seven years ago?"

"Eight. I was a child bride." Ruth smiled, but her mouth had a wistful cast to it.

"Twenty-three isn't exactly childhood. Anyway, then I started the job in Boston. And you seemed busy with Frank. How is he, anyway?"

"*He's* fine. I'm not so sure how *we* are."

"But you have the girls. They must be five by now?"

Ruth looked out the door. "Natalie and Nettie are the joys of my life." She looked back at Cam with full eyes. "The best thing that ever happened to me."

"So what's wrong?" Cam moved over to stand next to Ruth.

"Frank and I aren't doing so great."

"Oh, I'm sorry."

"Cam?" A voice sounded from the path outside the hoop house. "We need your help out here!"

Cam gave Ruth a quick hug. "We're going to take a bottle of wine to the beach one of these days. And you're going to tell me everything."

Ruth agreed.

"I'll be right back. Gentle with those lettuces."

Cam exited the hoop house, nearly colliding with Felicity.

"What's going on?"

"Oh, dear." Felicity looked toward the fields and then back at Cam. Worry etched her brow. "Well, I think you should look at one of the fields."

Cam walked back with her. "What did you see?"

"I don't know. You asked us to cut arugula, but it doesn't look right."

If this was more sabotage, Cam wasn't sure what she'd do. They passed the weeders, who were rapidly filling the cart. Steam rose from the compost pile that Alexandra turned, forkful by forkful, into the adjacent bin.

"See?" Felicity pulled at Cam's sleeve.

An entire row of leaves lay limp on the ground, still attached to their roots, but nearly lifeless. A pale, granular substance coated them. Droplets of water stood up from the green.

"Oh, no!" Cam knelt to smell the crop. On a hunch she wiped a bit of the white substance off with her finger and tasted a grain of it. "Salt?" She frowned and shook her head in disbelief. "How did salt get onto this crop?"

"We got a good cutting from the other row, though." Felicity's voice was hopeful. "You can use that, can't you?"

"At least salt isn't grounds for being decertified, but it's ruined the bed." Cam looked up at her. "Did you see anyone out here? Were any of the other volunteers working on this bed before you? I could swear it was fine yesterday."

Felicity shook her head. She glanced over at the other volunteer, the man who had asked about the murder. He also shook his head.

Cam rose. "I'll pull the bed. Can't sprinkle it down, or it will get into the soil. It's not that serious." She hoped that was true.

"Some kind of mistake, I guess." She wanted to put on a good front for the customers, but inside she fumed. Whoever thought they could come onto her land and try to wreck her life was going to have to deal with her.

She'd left the wheelbarrow at the back of the hoop house, near a wooden fence where Albert and Marie had trained up sweet peas. A whiff of their fragrant blooms instantly transported Cam back to her childhood summers. This year she'd chosen to plant pole beans in the rich soil at the base of the fence as a way to utilize all possible space for producing food.

Stuart strode toward her as she approached the spigot, his arms full of vines.

"I cleaned up that fence area for you." He gestured with his chin toward the greenery he held.

Cam stopped short. "You what? Those aren't weeds! That's my pole bean crop."

"Oh, crap. But that's a fence. Those aren't poles."

"Did anyone tell you to weed there? What do you think you're doing?"

"Sorry. They looked like weeds. I was only trying to help."

"Sorry?" Cam's voice rose.

"Fine." Stuart dumped the mess of greens on the ground. "Look, I said I was sorry,"

116

he spat out. "Thanks a lot for your under-
standing, Farmer Cam." He stalked toward
the driveway.

Cam bent over the beanstalks. Tender
roots stuck up out of clumps of soil, their
tiny white nitrogen-fixing nodules already
apparent. Beans didn't transplant well.
She'd never be able to get these back in the
ground and growing again. She'd have to
replant. One more setback in a really bad
week.

As Cam gazed at Stuart's retreating back,
Ruth emerged from the hoop house a few
feet away. She looked at Stuart, at Cam,
and back at Stuart as he climbed into his
rusty car.

"Stuart Wilson?"

"Yeah."

"Everything okay?"

A dead man, wrecked rhubarb, salted arugula, and ruined bean plants were a long
way from okay.

Chapter 7

As the last of the volunteers drove away, Cam sank into a lawn chair, discouraged and hungry. Sure, she'd gotten a lot of help. But dealing with people tired her. Plus the business with the arugula and Stuart pulling up the pole beans was very disturbing. She'd mentioned the arugula and the rhubarb to Ruth, who had walked out back to check. Since she was in casual clothes and didn't act like a police officer, Cam didn't think Ruth had alarmed the volunteers. Cam had had to pull all the arugula plants, scrape as much salt as she could from the top layer of dirt, and then rake out the soil, hoping to disperse the rest of the salt.

Maybe this whole venture had been the wrong decision. Writing software was so much more straightforward. She could just give the farm back to Albert and take herself back to the city. He could sell the land. She could find another cubicle job.

Cam shook her head, hoisted herself out of the chair, and aimed herself at the kitchen. It was time to refuel, not time to reverse a major life decision. She still had an afternoon's work ahead of her. From the look of the dark thunderclouds forming to the west, it might be a short afternoon.

She grabbed a peanut butter and banana sandwich and poured a glass of beer. The first swallow went down way too easily, and she took a second. As Cam ate standing at the kitchen counter, she flipped through the seed catalog. She needed to reorder pole bean and arugula seeds and thought of a couple of other items she could add to the order to get it up to the minimum for free shipping.

Next to the toaster, Cam caught sight of the talisman she'd picked up in the hoop house that morning. Sunday seemed like weeks ago, instead of only three days earlier. She should have given it to Ruth today. Well, she'd be seeing her again.

Cam placed the seed order online. She took a moment to check the farm's e-mail. She frowned at one missive, with a subject line of "Must pick up elsewhere," and clicked open the message.

"Can't come to the farm Saturday to pick up share. Too dangerous. Pls deliver to police station parking lot. Thx."

What? She wasn't about to start hand delivering shares. Cam's blood pressure rose like an outdoor thermometer in August. She checked the sender. It was the man who had questioned her on the farm's safety at Volunteer Day. She tapped out a reply, then paused to read it over again.

"We are sorry you feel the farm is too dangerous, but we cannot accommodate delivery and hope you feel able to pick up your share on Saturday at the barn. Please know the authorities are doing all they can to arrest and prosecute the murderer."

Was her message too abrupt, too unaccommodating? Cam shook her head. She worked hard enough as it was. She clicked SEND and headed back to work.

On her way to the fields she stopped in the flower garden. A blue glass globe rose from a short pole. Marie had tucked all kinds of small statuary and embellishments into the array of perennials. Cam plucked the globe from the ground and carried it to the memorial in front of the hoop house, where she stuck it in the dirt next to the other objects. It was the least she could do.

She spent the next couple of hours starting broccoli seeds and other late-season cabbage-family crops in the hoop house, trying to place just one tiny seed in each cell of the flat she'd filled with her own special seed-starting mix. Two flats of lettuces were ready to be planted out, which meant an hour of kneeling, poking holes in the soil with her five-dowel dibble, gently inserting a two-inch seedling in each hole, and smoothing and tamping the soil around the stem.

Cam usually found transplanting meditative, despite the strain on her back, but today her concern about the ruined arugula bed stuck in her brain. She worried about these seedlings, too, as she placed them in the earth, gingerly so she wouldn't reopen the cut on her hand. She hoped a malicious act wouldn't cut their lives short. As she worked, she mentally flipped through the morning's volunteers, considering each as the culprit and rejecting each one. Except maybe for Stuart. But she thought he had his heart in the right place. She shouldn't have been so severe with him about the pole beans. He really had been trying to help. And she didn't think he'd actually sprinkle salt on her crop.

It must have been an outsider. But who? Maybe someone had come onto the land when she'd been out at the farmers' market the day before or visiting Albert later that evening. She always parked the truck in the middle of her driveway, making no secret to the public of when she was home and when she wasn't.

Cam had just finished transplanting when she heard a giant clap of thunder. A drop of rain plopped on the back of her neck, then two more. Suddenly the skies let loose, and along with them, a flash of lightning. She grabbed the dibble and the empty flats and ran for the barn.

After Cam cleaned out the flats and stored them, she leaned against the open doorway of the barn, watching the rain. Nothing was better for the crops than a good natural watering. A thunderstorm was even better, since lightning somehow channeled nitrogen from the air into the soil, or at least that was what Great-Uncle Albert said. She hoped she'd cleared out enough of the salt. Whatever was left was getting well watered into the ground. She'd have to ask Albert how long she would need to keep that bed fallow. With such a small acreage, she couldn't afford too many unplanted beds.

When the lightning seemed to have moved on with the wind, and the rain settled into a steady downpour, Cam raced to the house. She arrived on the back porch as a car turned into the drive from the road. Who could it be? Fear stabbed at her. She started to open the door. She hoped she could she lock it in time. Then she saw.

It was Lucinda's little blue Civic. Cam breathed her relief, not sure why she'd been frightened in the first place. She waved to Lucinda, who dashed for the porch.

"Good rain, no?" Lucinda said, shaking the water out of her hair.

"I just finished planting out lettuces. It's perfect. Come on in."

Inside, Cam handed Lucinda a clean hand towel and used one herself to mop off her face and hair.

"Missed you this morning," Cam said. "But a good-size group showed up."

"I thought I told you I had to work. Mrs. Kosloski wants the house cleaned every Wednesday morning, no exceptions."

Cam raised her eyebrows. "You clean for them?"

"They're one of my steady jobs. They have only the one child, so the house doesn't usually need much." She rolled her eyes. "You should see the lady executive with four boys. Whoo. What a mess all the time. She doesn't do anything around the place, and she doesn't make her sons do anything, either."

Cam extracted a glass jug from the fridge.

"Glass of beer? It won't keep, and it's local."

"Sounds like an excuse to me, but sure. *Obrigada.*"

Cam poured two glasses, set a bag of chips on the table, and poured salsa into a bowl. She sat across from Lucinda, raising her glass.

"Cheers. How do you say that in Portuguese?"

"*Saúde.*" Lucinda clinked her glass with Cam's, then took a sip. "Hey, this is good. What's it called? Five Mile Ale? Five miles from where?"

"It's the Ipswich Ale Brewery's local beer. Most of the ingredients come from Massachusetts farms, and at least one was grown within five miles of the brewery."

"We should get this for the Locavore Festival."

Cam agreed. "Great idea. I learned about it from Jake."

Lucinda frowned. "Jake from the Market?"

Cam nodded. "He serves it there. You know him?"

Lucinda hesitated for a moment, then said, "No. Just heard about him."

"So were you a house cleaner in Brazil, too?" Cam asked, then sipped her drink.

Lucinda snorted. "No way. I was head

librarian at the university."

Cam must have shown her surprise, because Lucinda continued, "I was a big . . . What do you call it? Big cheese."

"Then why . . . ?" Cam spread her hands out, palms up.

"Long story." Lucinda's face clouded. "I had to come here."

"Can't you get work as a librarian here?"

Lucinda shook her head. "Might as well tell you. I came here on a tourist visa. I don't have no green card. I applied for one, but it takes years. Meanwhile I'm illegal, undocumented. Nobody hires me like that. Only cash jobs, like cleaning." She glanced at Cam and then looked away. "Now you'll probably kick me off the farm, too."

"No! Why would I do that? Anyway, it's not illegal for you to buy vegetables or to volunteer. It can't be." That must have been why Lucinda had said she couldn't work for Cam for money. Too bad. And why she didn't want to talk to the police, either.

"Funny, you know?" Lucinda looked wistful. "At home, *legal* means 'cool.' 'Awesome.' 'Great.' Now I'm the reverse of that. But I didn't come over to tell you that." She brightened. "I think I have an idea about your murder man."

"Really?"

"The one who killed Mike. You know, so you can tell police." She leaned toward Cam over the table. "I heard some big cheese around here is also undocumented, and these guys, they know he's illegal. I told you Mike was in that Patriotic Militia. I think Mike was their dirty guy. Do you say 'dirty guy'?"

Cam thought for a moment. "You mean he did their dirty work?"

"Yeah, yeah. So maybe this big guy killed Mike because he was going to go public."

"Well, who is this big cheese?"

Lucinda shook her head. "I don't know. I hear stuff, you know, from other Brazilians."

Cam sat back. "You have to tell the police, Lucinda." Was Lucinda being honest with her? She was so evasive.

"No!" Lucinda's eyes widened. "I'd get deported. I can't go back."

"Why not? I don't think you would be sent away, not for offering information on a murder case."

"You don't know American cops. They're pigs." Lucinda narrowed her eyes at the rain-streaked window, as if a bad memory stood right outside.

Cam decided to change the subject. "So how's eating only local food going?"

Lucinda whistled. "I'm kinda hungry.

126

Potatoes are all from last year. They taste bad. I got local cornmeal, and I heard about a farm out in the western part of the state that grows rice, but I didn't get any yet. I got enough vegetables and meat, plus strawberries, but it's kinda tough." She looked longingly at the chips and salsa.

"Oh, darn. Sorry about that, Lucinda." Cam swept the snacks off the table and set them on the kitchen counter. She opened the refrigerator and poked around. She turned to Lucinda. "Want some asparagus?"

Lucinda laughed. "You're funny. No, I'm okay. Anyway, you're coming to the festival Friday, right?"

"Of course. It's okay to bring Uncle Albert, isn't it?"

Lucinda assured her he would be welcome. "It's going to be a great event," she went on. "Alfalfa Farm Winery is coming, and I'll call this Ipswich beer place, see if they can come. The Cape Ann CSF is bringing smoked bluefish samples. You'll have a table, plus other farms around here are going to be there. You giving out samples?"

Cam groaned. "I guess. What am I going to hand out? Lettuce leaves?"

"You could give them strawberries, like one each."

Cam frowned. "They are bearing well this

year, but I have to make sure I have enough for share day on Saturday."

"How about little bunches of herbs? You have lots of herbs out there. And if it gets you new customers, it's worth it."

"Good idea. I can tie them up like little nosegays. I'll make up a display basket of other produce, too. And I guess it's about time to get business cards printed."

They chatted for another hour, avoiding topics like immigration and murder suspects. By the time Lucinda left, the storm had blown through. The descending sun shone through the treetops against dark clouds as they retreated, casting the farm in a buttery glow like in a painting.

Cam heated up leftover quiche. She brought the plate and a glass of wine to the computer desk. Setting aside her concern about the sabotage for a moment, she decided to see what the Internet had to say about the Patriotic Militia. If what Lucinda said was true, this bucolic town might be harboring a sinister underlayer.

She sat back thirty minutes later. Plotting ways to destroy the government was patriotism? The site shouted in all capital letters about liberty and the freedom to own assault weapons. It warned that the American way of life was being destroyed by the social justice mentality, "a combination of Communists, Marxists, and Socialists who want to turn the country into a dictatorship." The anti-immigrant and racist vitriol in what she read disturbed her dreams all night long.

Chapter 8

"Knock, knock," a voice called from the porch the next morning.

"Hey, Alexandra. Come on in," Cam replied. She rose and welcomed the young woman. "Thanks for coming. Can I get you coffee?"

"No problem. And no coffee, thanks. The closest place growing it is a thousand miles away. Not exactly local. I heard they raise it in Iceland. But in greenhouses warmed by volcanic steam."

Cam picked up her mug, wondering if she should feel guilty. "I don't know. I am happy to supply you guys with local food, but if I didn't have my coffee, I wouldn't be able to get out there and grow anything."

Alexandra laughed, then turned serious. "Hey, so some guy named Pappas talked to me. He thinks I might have killed Mike Montgomery. What's up with that?"

Cam eyed her. "You did happen to describe the actual murder a few hours before it happened. In the company of others."

"I didn't mean I would do it." Alexandra snorted. "That's crazy. Just because I don't think pesticides are good for us doesn't mean I would actually kill someone." She curled a braid around her finger.

Cam sat watching her.

"Cam! Do you think I'm a murderer?"

"No." Cam hoped she meant it. Alexandra certainly had the height and strength to have been able to do it, not to mention the passion. "I simply want the state police to find the real killer."

"Me too." Alexandra gestured at the computer. "So how do you want to do this?"

"Well, while I've written HTML before, I don't have time right now and I'm not artistic at all, so you wouldn't want me to design anything. I put together a paper mock-up." Cam showed Alexandra several sheets of paper. She'd sketched out the home page, a payment page, an events page, and a couple of others. "It's not very complicated."

"Let's add a volunteer page, too, and maybe a comments page. Can I add a link to the Locavore Club site somewhere?"

"Yes, on all counts."

"I think you want a clean look, an easy-to-read sans-serif font, and farmey kinds of colors. You know, greens and yellows and reds. Do you have any photos or artwork you want me to use, or should I look for free graphics?"

"I don't really have anything," Cam said, frowning. "We could go out and take pictures, at least of crops that are bearing now." *Except for rhubarb,* Cam thought. The plants still hadn't recovered. She hoped they weren't permanently damaged.

"Let me handle it. My phone has a wicked awesome camera in it. Now, show me how I can access the hosting site. We'll have to buy your domain name, too, unless you've done that."

Cam shook her head. She should have, but planting and growing had filled her days to overflowing.

"What do you want, www.produceplusplus .com?" Alexandra asked.

The two huddled at the computer for a few minutes. Alexandra straightened. "I think I'm good. I'll put together a draft site, but I won't publish it until you've approved it. What about a logo? Do you already have one?"

Cam sighed.

"I guess not. You're going to want to maintain your brand across your online presence and your printed materials, too."

"You're right. I hadn't thought of that." The list of what Cam hadn't thought of was growing by the minute. "Did you study marketing?"

"Nope, history. I like this stuff, though. Maybe I should have gone into marketing design. Let's sketch out a logo." She quickly drew a basket overflowing with vegetables and a stylized field in the background. "How's that?"

"I like it." Cam sat back. "You're here two mornings in a row. You don't have a job?"

Alexandra shook her head. "My college degree didn't get me far in the employment market. If I knew what I wanted to do next, I'd go to grad school. But it's okay. I get along pretty well with my parents, and they actually love having me back home." She rolled her eyebrows. "Not so sure about my sister. And the 'rents and me have had to work out a few issues about, like, my not having to report in every hour when I'm out at night."

"I'm sure," Cam said. "Did I overhear that your sister goes out with Stuart Wilson?"

"She used to. She broke up with him because he had anger-management issues. At least that's what she told me. And then she seemed to be going out with another

133

guy, but I never met him. We don't really talk that much."

"Is she older than you?"

"Yep. Okay, gotta run." Alexandra swept out, calling through the screen door, "I'll be in touch."

Cam walked to the door in time to see Alexandra ride off on her bicycle, braids flying. Cam scanned the skies, today a perfect paint-box blue. The storm had blown through and left the world looking clean and hopeful. It was a good morning for working. She had put in a couple of hours picking strawberries before her appointment with Alexandra and still had more work to do. Always more to do.

A truck rumbled up the driveway.

"Hey, Ms. Flaherty! Where do ya want me to dump it?" A scrawny teenager stuck his head out the window. "It's me, Vince. With the, you know, manure?"

Cam groaned. She'd forgotten all about the manure delivery. Her day's workload had just doubled. She grabbed a check and tip money from the house, then instructed the boy to back the truck up to the compost area. Cam walked alongside him to make sure he didn't swerve over one of the herb beds on his way.

He dumped the load of composted cow

manure, then climbed out of the cab. "I heard you, like, had a murder here. Did you see the killer? Dude, it must have been exciting."

Cam shook her head. "That's not the word I would use." Neither *exciting* nor *dude.* She thanked him and handed him the check as well as five dollars for himself.

"Thanks, Ms. Flaherty. Let Pop know when you want more. Those cows never stop, like, sh . . . I mean, going."

Cam waved him off. She groaned at the pile, then trudged to the barn for a pitchfork. No time like the present.

When she came in for lunch, Cam scrubbed her hands. She was exhausted from shoveling manure into the wheelbarrow, adding it to the future lettuce beds, and repeating. It added organic material and nutrients to the soil, but working with manure was heavy going. She was going to have to hire another farmhand. She had no idea who, though, or even where to look.

She checked her e-mail. Alexandra had already created a lively logo and had sent Cam several versions of it in different resolutions. Alexandra had also sent a link to an online printer. When Cam clicked it, an order form for Produce Plus Plus business cards and refrigerator magnets opened. It was already filled out and included two magnetic signs for the doors of her truck, too. She shook her head, wondering at the efficiency and expertise of her young volunteer. Outsourcing the marketing part of her business was a smart move. Cam would definitely pay Alexandra for doing this work.

She added overnight shipping to the order, filled in her credit card information, and clicked the SUBMIT ORDER button. Now she'd have business cards to hand out at the festival. Everywhere she drove she'd be advertising the farm. She could give each CSA customer a refrigerator magnet. Cam smiled. She could imagine Felicity hosting a dinner party featuring the farm's produce and then excitedly showing her guests the farm's magnet. Hey, if it brought in new customers, all the better.

After scarfing down a cheese sandwich and a glass of nonfat milk, Cam was about to head back out to the fields when she spotted the disk she'd picked up in the greenhouse. She focused on it for a moment, then picked up the phone. She left Ruth a message, inviting her for dinner. "If you can get away from the family," she said at the end. "Or bring the girls if you want to," Cam hastily added. She rooted around in the freezer, finally drawing out a package of nonlocal chicken. She checked her recipe file and then checked the fridge. If she ran out to the store, she could make a strawberry cheesecake, too. And might as well do it now, while her hands were clean. She could still get in a few more hours in the fields this afternoon if she hurried.

As she pushed open the screen door, the house phone rang. Cam glanced at it, looked out at the sunny afternoon, then turned back to answer it.

"Hi, Uncle Albert. What's up?"

"Wondered if you'd mind driving me to the wake this afternoon."

"Wake?"

"Mike's wake. Surely you planned on going."

"Right." Cam shook her head. How had that gotten off her radar? "What time?"

"It's from four to eight down at the Mc-Claren Funeral Home. You know, next to the church. I'd like to be there at the beginning."

"I'll pick you up at three forty, then." She disconnected. There went her work afternoon, since she wasn't about to cancel the dinner with Ruth. But she could hardly miss Mike's wake, either, although it wasn't her favorite kind of outing. All those somber people to negotiate, all those polite things to say.

Cam helped Albert out of the truck and made sure his crutches were in place. The handicapped-parking placard he'd hung from her rearview mirror gave them the best spot in the lot.

"Early yet," Albert said, gesturing at the empty parking spaces. "I'm sure it'll fill up later."

"Was Mike well liked, Uncle Albert?" They proceeded slowly up a zigzagging ramp.

"You wouldn't say that, particularly. But Bev is, generally speaking."

A black-suited woman held the door open for them amid a rush of cold air. As they entered, she pointed to the Rose Room. Cam took a deep breath. She flicked a spot of cat hair from her black skirt and hoped the businesslike purple blouse wasn't too bright. She wasn't very well equipped with mourning clothes.

Bev stood at the end of a line, preceded by two younger men and a woman about Cam's age. Sprays of flowers decorated a blessedly closed coffin to Bev's right. What looked like a high school graduation picture of Mike sat on an easel. A younger, tidier, handsomer Mike than the one Cam had known only for the few months he'd worked for her.

Cam and Albert took their places at the end of a short line of people who moved along, clasping the hands of family members and murmuring condolences.

"Are those Mike's siblings?" Cam whispered to Albert.

He nodded. "He was the youngest."

She followed Albert along the line, uttering what she hoped were appropriate condolences, until he reached Bev.

Propping himself on his good leg, Albert reached out an arm to embrace his old friend. "Too young, my friend, he died too young."

Bev returned the hug and closed her eyes for a moment. When she reopened them, she focused on Cam.

The chill in the look had nothing to do with the air-conditioning.

Bev looked back at Albert. "Thank you for coming, Albert. Don't you wish life was back like it was before? You farming, my Mikey working for you, Marie still with us?"

Albert put his hand back on his crutch. His smile was a sad one. "But we can't turn the clock back, can we? My Marie, she's resting in peace. That I know. And Cam-

139

eron here is a good farmer, or will be when she gets her feet under her."

Cam shot a sharp look at him. When she got her feet under her? It sounded like Albert thought she wasn't doing a good job yet. *Great.*

"I've moved on, Bev. You will, too, in time."

Bev gazed from Albert to Cam and back, her face expressionless.

"I'm so sorry for your loss, Bev," Cam murmured, then realized she'd already said that to her at the market earlier in the week. Was she never going to get the hang of the right thing to say at the right time? It seemed to come so easily to others.

Bev's smile as she turned to the next visitor was unconvincing.

Albert turned to the coffin. He rested on his crutches in front of it with head bowed. He crossed himself. He touched his fingers to his lips and then to the coffin.

Cam waited, arms by her sides. Her parents weren't involved in any church, and while Cam had usually accompanied Albert and Marie to Saint Ann's in the summers, as an adult Cam didn't feel called to keep up the practice. Working with plants under God's blue sky was enough religion for her.

Her head snapped toward the doorway

when she heard raised voices in the hall. One of the black-suited staff quickly closed the door, but not before Cam saw Bev Montgomery's eyes widen. If Cam wasn't mistaken, that was Stuart Wilson out there, raising the ruckus.

Curious about what Stuart was doing yelling at a wake, she whispered in Albert's ear, "I'll be right back." She slipped out the side door she had spotted and strode down the hall to where it turned. She peeked around the edge. Sure enough, two large attendants were escorting Stuart out the door. He was still yelling.

"I only wanted to pay my respects!"

One of the black suits made sure Stuart was well out the door. The other walked in Cam's direction.

"You don't get to pay your respects drunk and angry, buddy." He shook his head, looking back at the doorway. "And you especially don't when the family doesn't want you here."

Stuart had been laid off from his job, just like Cam had been. The golden marketing whiz she had known didn't seem to be taking the fall from grace very, well, gracefully.

"So, Tina, if you hear of anything, will you let me know? I'm kind of wondering if I made the right decision with this farm thing." Cam left her number on her friend's voice mail and hung up. Her friend Tina was still employed at the old company, still head down in a cubicle, writing software. If the job market started looking up, she'd be the first to know. It wouldn't hurt for Cam to keep her options open. For now, she had a dinner to pull out of a hat.

Ruth arrived right at six o'clock, bearing a bottle of wine. Cam, wearing a striped apron over her shorts and T-shirt, greeted Ruth at the door, then rushed back into her kitchen, which was adjacent to the dining area.

"Sorry. I'm in the middle of Chicken Ezekiel. And there seems to be a step missing in the instructions. That drives me crazy."

Ruth let out a deep, throaty laugh. "Still cooking by the recipe, are you?"

"Well, yeah. Doesn't everybody?" Cam waved a spoon at Ruth.

"No. But it doesn't surprise me that a geek does."

"Geek status fully acknowledged."

"And you always wanted to have procedures to follow. Remember the meal we made for those boys?"

Cam nodded. "I was dating Robbie — if

you can call doing our math homework together dating — and you invited . . . wait . . . Was it Paolo? The Italian exchange student?"

Ruth rolled her eyes. "He was gorgeous, and taller than me. Which was saying something."

"And we cooked coq au vin from Julia Child, right? We had to steal wine from your dad's stash for it." Cam sniffed. "Oh, crud!" She whirled to the stove, where she gave a furious stir to a Dutch oven on the stove top. "Close one. Almost burned the onions."

"Smells great, Cam. Can I open this for us?"

Cam nodded in the direction of a drawer. She had to stop talking and start focusing on this dinner, or it would be ruined. She added the pieces of chicken she had cut and dried on a clean dish towel to the pan and stirred again.

Ruth extended a glass of red to Cam, who lifted it and clinked Ruth's. "Here's to old friends."

Cam returned the toast and sipped. "Now, let me concentrate for a minute." She sipped again before setting the glass down. She added cut-up tomatoes to the pot, then minced garlic, kalamata olives, and fresh rosemary from the herb garden. She stirred, set the lid on, and maneuvered the pot into the warm oven.

"There. Now I can relax a little." Cam wiped her forehead with the apron as she returned to the table. Sinking into a chair, she eyed Ruth. "Sit down. You're making me nervous."

Ruth obliged, but her cheery mood seemed to have vanished. She didn't meet Cam's eyes.

"What?" Cam asked. "It's like a dark cloud just came and sat on your head."

"I probably shouldn't have come."

"Why not? We can't be friends, at least on your day off?"

"Cam, there's a murder investigation under way. They haven't told me much directly, but I don't think they've eliminated you as a suspect."

Ruth must know she couldn't have killed someone. Cam shook her head. This was getting ridiculous. "It's making me nervous, you know, that a murderer is running loose out there." She drummed her fingers on the table. "Oh! I just remembered. Look what I found in the hoop house the morning after the killing." She rose and reached toward the kitchen counter.

In a flash Ruth was at her side and had encircled Cam's wrist with her own strong hand. "Don't touch it. It could be evidence."

"Ouch! I wasn't going to. I was just showing you. I even picked it up with a tissue," Cam said.

Ruth released Cam's hand but sighed. "Next time call the station. It's better if we process things like this in the proper way from the start. It probably can't even count as evidence now, but maybe we can get a print off it." Ruth leaned over and peered at it. "Any idea what it is? Or whose it was?"

"I don't know. There's a logo of some kind and the letters *PM*. See?"

Ruth's eyes widened, then narrowed. Her face grew pale. She blinked at the disk. She shook her head like she was trying to rid herself of a pest. "Sort of. Got a sealable bag?"

Cam extracted a bag from a drawer and handed it to Ruth, who managed to scoop the disk into the bag without touching it.

An insistent rapping sounded at the back door. Cam slid past Ruth. She addressed the door. "One second." Whoever it was didn't have much patience. Cam peered through the curtained glass top of the door and frowned. Him again. Cam looked back at Ruth. Preston sidled up and rubbed against Cam's leg.

"It's your favorite statie," Cam said.

"Detective Pappas himself." Since he was here, she could take the opportunity and tell him about the two instances of sabotage. Which she probably should have done much earlier, except that Pappas made her feel like she and her farm were under attack. He did not project a helpful "We'll find the murderer, so don't worry" kind of vibe.

"Wonderful." Ruth did not sound enthusiastic. "Go ahead. Don't make him drill a hole in your door with his knuckles."

As Cam opened the door, Preston streaked out past her. "Hi," Cam greeted Pappas. She suddenly couldn't think of a single other thing to say.

"Evening, Ms. Flaherty." Pappas, now in a crisp oxford shirt with pressed blue jeans and brown loafers, glanced beyond her. "Hello, Officer Dodge." He raised one eyebrow.

"Um, can I help you?" Cam asked, not sure of the protocol. Should she offer him a glass of wine? Or stand here at the door?

"May I come in?"

His tone was the most polite Cam had heard from him yet, but it reminded her of the ominously polite pitch Tom used to use when he was furious. She stood aside and gestured him in. He walked up to Ruth, who stood at the counter, next to the transparent bag with the disk.

"Officer Dodge, that looks interesting." Pappas eyed the disk.

A repeating electronic *ding* from the kitchen sped up in frequency. Ruth glanced behind her and then at Cam.

"That's my timer. Excuse me." Cam fled farther into the kitchen to switch off the annoying digital timer, wishing she could find Marie's old-fashioned wind-up device, which merely rang with a pleasant little bell tone when the time was up. She opened the oven and stirred the stew. She strained to hear what Ruth and Pappas were saying, but they had their backs to her and spoke in low tones. Cam replaced the lid, shut the oven door, and set the timer for another thirty minutes. She filled a big pot with water and set it to boil. Drying her hands on her apron, she turned back to them.

Pappas was holding his hand out.

"I can sign this in at the station," Ruth said, keeping hold of the plastic bag with the disk in it.

"I'd rather take it now." Pappas glared at her. "I am the detective in charge."

Ruth glanced at Cam. "Yes, sir." She handed the bag to Pappas.

"Now maybe you can tell me why you are here out of uniform."

"Sir, Cam and I are childhood friends. I'm off duty, and she invited me for dinner. So I'm here." She raised her chin and looked down at the detective at the same time.

Cam opened her mouth and began, "Yes, we're . . ." but stopped when Ruth held up her hand in a halt gesture. All right, Cam would let her work it out. It was Ruth's job, after all.

Cam decided to match Pappas's manners with her own. "Can I offer you a glass of wine, Detective?" She mustered her sweetest smile.

He frowned, as if trying to figure out if she was kidding or not. "Uh, no thank you."

"I suppose you came by to tell me you found the killer?" Cam raised her eyebrows.

Ruth, in turn, raised hers.

"No, I'm afraid not." Pappas seemed about to interrogate when Cam interrupted.

"Too bad. No clues?"

He looked like he was about to shake his head when he caught himself. "Why don't you fill me in on this clue right here?" He held the bag up in front of Cam's face. "Before I charge you with withholding evidence."

Could he? "Let's all sit down, shall we?" Cam gestured to the table. At the look on

Pappas's face, she added in a hurry, "And I'll tell you all about it."

After Cam related how she'd found the disk, she asked, "What do you think it is, Detective?"

"I couldn't say."

Couldn't or wouldn't? Cam figured it didn't really matter. She glanced at Ruth. Her friend's face was nearly expressionless.

"You can be sure we'll check it out, though. I'm curious why you neglected to turn it over when Chief Frost and I visited you several days ago," he continued in the superpolite voice, and his icy eyes bored into Cam's.

"It slipped my mind. I'm very sorry," Cam lied.

"Don't do it again. Now, what I originally stopped by to ask you concerns several of your customers. I understand an Alexandra Magnusson threatened Mike Montgomery on Saturday. Why didn't you tell me about that?"

"It slipped my mind." He was going to think she was an idiot with a Teflon brain. "Finding a dead body has done a number on my memory. But, anyway, Alexandra didn't threaten Mike. She was upset about anyone anywhere using chemicals on food crops. She's kind of an idealist."

"Ms. Slavin related that Ms. Magnusson said she would knock Mike down and run him through with a pitchfork. Did she say that?"

"Well, yes, but Mike wasn't even there anymore. She's passionate about the environment. That's all."

"You know what I'm passionate about? I want to find Mike Montgomery's murderer. To do that, I need all the information you have. If there is anything else you aren't telling me, I'd appreciate knowing it now."

Cam swallowed and shook her head.

"Now, about Ms. DaSilva. We can't seem to locate her. Are you quite certain you provided us with her correct contact information?"

"I think so. I printed out my customer list for you, didn't I?"

Pappas nodded.

"That's the only information I have on her. She lives in Salisbury." *Strange.* Surely Lucinda had given Cam her correct number and address. Cam realized she'd never needed to call the Brazilian, and she certainly had never gone to her home. Then she thought about the tremor in Lucinda's voice the day before, when she'd spoken about being undocumented and not wanting to talk to the police. Maybe Lucinda was not answering her door or her cell on purpose.

Cam realized Pappas, now standing, had spoken. "Excuse me?"

"Officer Dodge filed a report about sabotage on your farm. I wondered why you didn't tell me that, either."

"I meant to. Really." Cam hadn't felt this guiltily uncomfortable since being called on while daydreaming in class by her strict sixth-grade teacher, Mr. Aguirre.

"Maybe you can file an insurance claim against the lost crops." Pappas raised his eyebrows. "I'll be going. If you happen to hear from Ms. DaSilva, I'd appreciate it if you would ask her to call me. You still have my card, I trust?"

Cam nodded as she stood. "Do you want me to show you where I found the disk? It was in the hoop house."

Pappas looked like he'd tasted a sour lemon. "It's a little late for that." He shook his head. "If you happen to find anything else, please call me immediately, instead of conveniently forgetting. Enjoy your dinner, ladies." Pappas let himself out.

Cam whistled. She turned to Ruth. "You're the quiet one. A wooden nickel for your thoughts?"

Ruth narrowed her eyes at the door. "He

doesn't seem as nice as he used to."

Cam snorted. "Nice? He doesn't seem so nice to me." *Probably compensating for being so short,* she thought but kept it to herself.

Her stomach growled out loud as the melded aroma of chicken, olives, and rosemary wafted their way.

Ruth laughed as Cam headed for the kitchen. "I'm hungry, too. Tell you what. Let's not talk about the murder any more tonight. What do you say to that?"

"Fine with me." It wouldn't make an uncaught killer go away, but it would be nice to take a break from thinking about it.

CHAPTER 9

A steel-gray sky and air heavy with humidity greeted Cam the next morning. She hadn't slept well. She brewed a strong pot of dark roast coffee and took the first sip, grateful for its power to bring her into the world of the living. She carried the cup out to the back stoop. Only a good downpour would vanquish the oppressive stillness, but the forecast on the local station had included words like *stalled front* and *low pressure.* This weather could be with them for a while.

Cam pulled a list out of her back pocket. Last night before bed she'd jotted down what she had to accomplish today. The list of chores for the morning stretched down the page. Besides the usual farm tasks of weeding, planting out seedlings, harvesting, and general maintenance, she had the Locavore Festival to plan for. All those little bundles of herbs to cut and tie up for the samples. And tomorrow was the next CSA pickup day. Cam shook her head. *Better get to it.* In the kitchen she threw the rest of the coffee into a travel mug, grabbed a granola bar, and headed for the barn.

As she worked, she thought about her dinner with Ruth. They'd sipped wine, Ruth cutting herself off after one glass so she could drive home safely. They'd talked about their childhood summers and Ruth's unhappy marriage. They discussed Cam's ex, Tom, and how his breaking up with her had probably been for the best. The chicken was tender and rich with the olives and herbs, and it went perfectly with a plate of rotini, followed by a green salad fresh from the farm. They sat in the circle of their friendship and savored its uncomplicated warmth. They avoided the dark questions of the present.

Cam walked around the corner of the barn to check on the rhubarb. She knew this week's crop was ruined, but she hoped to rescue Great-Aunt Marie's antique plants. Pulling on gloves to protect her cut, she wheeled over a heaping cartload of finished compost. She carefully spread it along the row, tucking the black gold under the wide leaves and gently digging it in with a hand fork. The organic material should bind with the roots, preventing more toxic substances from being taken up. Cam was heartened to see the stalks and leaves starting to gain more turgidity, beginning to stand up again.

As she surveyed the crop, she didn't have much faith that the police would be able to figure out who had executed the destruction of it and the arugula. How would they? Cam promised herself she'd set up a database with the names of anyone who could even remotely have wanted to do her or Mike harm. She'd add the dates and times of day when when she knew people had been on the farm or when she'd been away. If she ever got a minute free to do that. She problem-solved best when an issue was all laid out in cells and probabilities, so she'd have to make time.

For now? Work called.

A few hours later, Cam headed to the house for a bite of lunch. She had just stepped onto the empty drive when Lucinda suddenly emerged from around the corner of the barn in front of her. Cam yelped.

"Lucinda! You scared me."

Lucinda put her finger to her lips as her eyes darted around, coming back to Cam's face. "Shh. Anybody else here?"

Cam frowned, shaking her head. "No. Why?"

Lucinda grabbed Cam's arm. She pulled her into the barn.

"Where's your car?" Cam asked. "Where are we going?"

"Be quiet. Listen, the cops are looking for me. I had to hide my car down the road. I sneaked in from the other field."

Cam gave Lucinda her best stern look. "Girlfriend, you have to talk with the police. It's illegal for them to ask for your papers. Anyway, you didn't do anything wrong."

Lucinda looked away for a moment.

"Did you?" Cam asked, pressing.

Lucinda shook her head, her face stretched tight. "But them? They like to be big macho *policia.* They are going to deport me. I told you!" Her deep brown eyes pleaded with Cam.

"No, they won't. I'll vouch for you. Maybe I can be, like, your sponsor." Cam laid her hand on Lucinda's arm. "Detective Pappas was here last night, looking for you. The longer you wait, the worse it's going to look."

Lucinda nodded. "I know. I hid in my apartment when he came to the door. One time he was there on my porch, and I drove right by. It's terrible, like I'm being hunted."

156

"You need to talk to him about that militia thing. About what you know. Listen, let's call him now. I'll be right next to you. Would that help?"

Lucinda nodded slowly. "I should be getting ready right now for the festival tonight. I wish I could turn over the clock, you know?"

"You mean turn back the clock. I know the feeling. But we can't."

"Cam, I really don't want to talk to that man."

"Lucinda, you are too naive about this. I can't make you, but I strongly encourage you to contact him. You'll be all right."

"You don't know that." Lucinda shook her head. "How can you?"

"Come on. Let's go in and call before we both lose our nerve."

Cam finished packing the truck for the Locavore Festival and checked her watch. Five o'clock. Just enough time to clean up before she had to head over to get Albert and then make it to St. John's Hall, the church function room the locavores had reserved for the event. She had given up on the idea of herb samples — too much work — and had picked a flat of strawberries, after all.

In the house, she poured the last glass of

beer from the jug and took it upstairs with her. After taking a quick shower and running a brush through her hair, Cam stood in front of her closet. Overalls or party clothes? Business attire or casual chic? It was a business event, after all, but it was a party, too, and Jake was going to be there. She settled on a sleeveless green silk blouse with her best jeans. She ran a hand down them as she turned in front of the mirror. All this hard work had taken a few pounds off. Cam was tall enough that she had to worry more about getting too thin than about putting on weight. She drained the beer, then added a pair of tomato earrings and a necklace strung with little silver farm implements, which her mother had sent her after she'd heard about the farm venture. Cowboy boots would finish the outfit, even though sandals would be cooler.

She leaned into the mirror and applied a little eye shadow and lipstick, grimacing at her chipped front tooth. Her fourth-grade experiment in walking the halls of her school with her eyes closed to prove how well she knew the school hadn't played out too well when she marched right into a metal pole. She'd lived with a marred incisor ever since.

As Cam drove to pick up Albert, she

thought about Lucinda's call to Pappas. Lucinda had hung up, looking relieved and a little suspicious at the same time. She told Cam that Pappas had asked her a few questions, but he hadn't raised the issue of Lucinda's immigration status.

Cam managed to ensconce her great-uncle in the front seat of the truck without incident. She folded his wheelchair and laid it in the back.

"Big night out for the old guy," Albert remarked as they headed onto the road.

Cam glanced over at him. He gazed straight ahead, but a smile flickered under eyes creased with humor.

St. John's Hall was hopping. Green and yellow balloons festooned the entryway, and one of the trucks parked outside sported a bumper sticker reading THINK GLOBAL, EAT LOCAL. Albert lowered himself into the wheelchair, which Cam had brought around to his door.

"I could have brought my crutches, you know."

"I know. I thought we agreed the chair would be easier, especially if they haven't provided seating."

Albert sighed. "You win, young lady."

Cam handed her display basket to Albert. "Carry that on your lap for me?"

At his nod, she pushed the chair up the ramp zigzagging along the side of the building, meeting the front stairs at the wide-open doorway to the hall.

"There you are," Jake boomed. He strode toward them in clean chef's whites and a multicolored skullcap with a flat top. "Let me take that for you."

Albert kept his hand firmly on the handle. "I have it, young man. Who might you be?"

Cam laughed. "Uncle Albert, this is Jake Ericsson. He's a chef and a customer. Jake, Albert St. Pierre. I learned almost everything I know about farming from him."

"Except how to use pesticides," Albert snorted.

"Or why not to," Cam said.

Jake extended his hand. "Nice to meet you, sir. I hope Cam will bring you to eat at The Market one day soon." His wide smile lit up the room.

Albert shook Jake's hand. "We'll see." He squinted up at Jake. He didn't return the smile.

Cam made a note to ask Albert on the way home what he thought of Jake.

"So where's my spot?" Cam asked Jake as she surveyed the room. Long tables lined the periphery, most of them already set up with various local wares. A woman attached a sign reading WARREN'S GROVE APPLES to the front of a table. A color poster showed bushels of shiny heirloom apples, and apple products filled the tabletop: jars of apple butter, packets of dried apples, bottles of apple cider. A Locavore Club banner hung at the end of the room, above a podium with a microphone, and people were starting to mill around, browsing from table to table. "Am I late?"

"No. I think folks are eager for this, though. Hungry, you might say." Jake leaned his face close to Cam's.

She inhaled his scent, today a heady combination of aftershave, a hint of the sea, and a peppery smell. Cam looked into his eyes, hoping her blush wasn't too notice-able.

Jake winked. He straightened and gestured with his head toward an empty table. "You're over there."

"Here." Albert handed Cam the basket. "Take this, and go get set up. I plan to check out every vendor." He executed a neat reverse turn and wheeled himself away.

Cam spread a colorful hot pepper cloth over the tabletop, then set up her basket. She made sure the bouquet of herbs in a vase was as nicely arranged as the bunch of flowers she'd cut. She pulled a few bits of outer skin off the garlic scallions and fluffed out the three heads of lettuce, tucking the red looseleaf between a dark green head of Bibb and one of a lighter green oakleaf. She fanned out the business cards, which had arrived in the afternoon mail.

Before she headed back to the truck to get the strawberries, grateful again it was such an early season, she took a moment to greet the vendors on either side of her table. One was a grain farmer from the western part of the state. His table held cloth bags folded open to show wheat berries, cornmeal, and a couple of grains Cam couldn't identify. Plastic sacks of flour were lined up neatly behind them. A basket of miniature corn muffins looked so delectable, Cam's stomach growled. On the other side was the Herb Farmacy from Salisbury. Their table featured small pots of dozens of varieties of herbs, all neatly labeled. Samples of four kinds of mint leaves were attractively arranged in small bowls.

Cam greeted a woman dressed in no-nonsense khaki pants and shirt who sat behind the table, and introduced herself. "I heard about your farm. I've been meaning to get up there for a visit."

The woman handed her a card and told her she was always welcome. "It's a good season so far, being early and all."

Cam agreed.

"You know, you should join us at the Newburyport Farmers' Market. It's thriving. Lots of vendors, lots of eager buyers. Sundays, nine to one."

Cam said she was already committed to the Haverhill market but would consider it.

As she left the hall to get the berries from the truck, she ran into David and Ellie Kosloski, who were coming in.

"Hey, Cam," Ellie said. "I am so going to report on this for my badge."

Cam greeted her and her father. David's expression was one of reluctance, but to his credit, when Ellie beamed up at him, he returned the smile and let himself be tugged by the hand into the hall. At her truck, Cam unloaded the flat of strawberries.

A deep voice behind her startled Cam.

"Need a hand?" Wes Ames held out his arms.

"I'm good, but thanks, Wes." Cam looked around. "Where's Felicity?"

"Inside. She's been here for a while already. Decorating and such."

Cam followed him up the stairs and laid the flat on the floor behind her table. She arrayed a shallow bowl full of berries on the table and propped up a little sign she'd made that read ONLY ONE APIECE, PLEASE, hoping it didn't make her look stingy. She stepped back to check the table.

"Oh, crud." She'd forgotten the farm sign she liked to hang from the front of the table. Well, the business cards would have to do.

Cam surveyed the hall. The far corner had accumulated a crowd. When she saw Felicity stroll away from it, holding a plastic beer cup, Cam realized why. One table housed the Ipswich Ale Brewery. Next to them on one side hung a sign for Alfalfa Farm Winery. On the other side was Mill River Winery. One of the two wineries was apparently David Kosloski's preference, since he now carried a clear plastic cup of red wine. And on the other side of the brewery, Cam spied a sign for Turkey Shore Distilleries, makers of a historically correct rum. She had heard of the outfit but had never gotten the chance to try the rum.

The atmosphere in the room was festive. The central area was filling up fast, with people old and young visiting tables and sampling local foods of all kinds. Cam spied Albert in a cluster of men near the beer table. *Good.* He'd found cronies to hang with. She decided to dash over to the Market's table and grab a little plate of whatever Jake was offering. The thought of physical proximity to the tall chef made her body thrum with excitement.

"Felicity?" Cam waved at the petite woman passing by. She was dressed in a flowing purple dress, with a brilliant turquoise scarf draped around her shoulder.

"Hey, the table looks great, Cam. Isn't this wonderful?" Felicity sipped her beer. "Have you seen Lucinda?"

"She's not here?" Cam's mouth dropped open. This was Lucinda's event.

"No. In fact, I had to call my brother to open up for us. She was supposed to have gotten the key from him."

"Your brother?"

"He's the sexton here."

"That was lucky. Listen, can you watch my table for a minute? I need to ask Jake a question. Try to make sure people take only one strawberry if you can. So we don't run out."

Felicity nodded. "Sure."

"I'll be right back."

Cam decided to grab a drink before she visited Jake's table. She searched all the faces she passed for Lucinda's, but she didn't seem to be in the room. Harm could have come to Lucinda. It had been only a week since the murder. Thoughts of violence pushed into Cam's brain. Or maybe the

Brazilian had been detained. Cam had no idea if the INS was active in Westbury, it was such a backwater. The recent push across the country to make the local police report immigration violations had to make undocumented workers like Lucinda nervous.

The Turkey Shore table had the smallest crowd, so Cam steered in that direction. She introduced herself to the burly, rosy-cheeked man behind it.

He smiled at Cam. "I'm Mat. Can I offer you a sample of the White Cap or the Tavern Style rum?"

"I'd love a little. How about the Tavern Style? But, wait, it can't be local." Cam paused before tasting the small cup of amber liquid. She eyed Mat. "I mean, you don't get your molasses from around here, do you? Sugarcane doesn't grow in Zone Six."

He shook his head. "Louisiana." He glanced around. "Don't tell," he whispered, with smiling eyes under raised eyebrows. "It's not a secret, really," he continued in a normal voice. "Lucinda let me display, anyway, since the rum is locally made."

Was there anybody Lucinda didn't know? Cam sipped the rum. "Ooh. Nice. It's so smooth, like bourbon, almost." She ran her tongue against the back of her teeth, savoring the buttery feel and catching a hint of vanilla. "Thanks. I'll spread the word." She downed the sample and waved as she moved toward Jake's table, the warmth of the rum spreading through her. She cast her eyes around the crowd for Lucinda.

"Hey, watch where you're going!"

Cam thudded into someone. "I'm sorry!" Cam said. "Oh, hi, Stuart." She stepped back with a sheepish look that turned to chagrin when she saw the spilled beer near the hem of his pants. "Sorry about that."

Stuart cleared his throat as he pulled a handkerchief from his pocket. "Don't worry about it."

Anybody could make a mistake. "And while I'm apologizing, I might have overreacted about you pulling those pole beans."

"I'm over it. But did you lose something just now? You were walking around like a woman on a scavenger hunt." He frowned up at Cam as he leaned down to pat the spill with the handkerchief.

"I'm looking for Lucinda. Have you seen her? She planned this whole event, but she doesn't seem to be here."

Stuart focused on the wet spot on his leg. "Can't help you." He did not look up.

"All right. Hey, I am sorry. I'll try to pay

more attention to where I'm going." He seemed more rational, at least, than he had been at the funeral home.

An eager group stood in front of the restaurant's table. Cam paused. Jake stood motionless, an empty plate in one hand, with a somber look on his face. She followed the path of his eyes, which blazed at Stuart in the middle of the room. Cam cleared her throat.

Jake shifted his eyes to Cam. He didn't smile. "You know that guy?"

"He's a customer. And we worked together, sort of, a few years ago. We were both at the same company. Why?"

Jake shook his head. "He's not my favorite guy. He's been into the restaurant. Let's just say he's not the easiest customer I've ever cooked for." He mustered a smile, but it didn't look easy. "Want food?"

Cam nodded. "Hungry. Thanks." She accepted the plate after Jake filled it. "What do we have?"

"Local shrimp ravioli in a reduction of Alfalfa Farm Winery's pinot gris with local sun-dried tomatoes from last year, Sunrise Dairy's butter, and your own lemon thyme. It's been getting rave reviews."

A server gestured to Jake to answer a question from one of the many samplers. Cam thanked him and took her plate back to her table. She also thanked Felicity and managed to snag a bite of one of the ravioli before a white-haired couple demanded her attention. The ravioli definitely earned their rave reviews.

Several hollow-sounding taps came over the PA system. Cam glanced at the podium.

"Can I have your attention, please?" Lucinda stood behind the mike, her curly hair twisted up in a messy knot, with wild strands escaping all over.

Cam let out a breath. Her volunteer was present, she was alive, and she looked fine, if a bit disheveled.

Lucinda sounded breathless as she called out, "Greetings, locavores!" A deep magenta blouse brought out the warm tones of her skin. She wore matching lipstick that flashed when she smiled broadly to the gathering. She went on to welcome the crowd. She spoke for a moment about her Kingsolverian plan to eat locally for a year. She then urged people to sample from every table.

"We all need to encourage our local sources of food. With that, I'm happy to introduce one of our biggest supporters, Farmer Cameron Flaherty. Cam, come up and tell us about your farm."

Cam gulped. Her? Oh, no. Public speaking was not on her list of favorite activities. It wasn't even at the bottom of the list. She tried to catch Lucinda's eye and shook her head with energy, but the crowd had started clapping. Heads turned to look at Cam. She spied Irene Burr, who caught her eye and nodded with raised eyebrows, encouraging Cam to speak. Lucinda clapped at the mike, too.

"Farmer Cam of Produce Plus Plus, where are you?"

Cam sighed. That had to be a rhetorical question, since between her height and her red hair, she was sure Lucinda knew her exact location. Where Lucinda had been was another question, one Cam hoped to get answered before the evening was out.

Striding to the podium, she glanced over at Jake. He winked at her with a wicked smile. *Wonderful.* Now she also had to perform in front of a guy she had a crush on. As she stepped onto the small platform, the toe of her boot caught and she nearly fell. Lucinda reached out a hand.

"Gotcha, *fazendeira,*" she whispered.

"Thanks," Cam whispered in reply as she shook her head. She swallowed hard and began to speak, leaning over at an awkward angle to reach the microphone. She told them about Great-Uncle Albert and Great-

Aunt Marie and how Albert had offered her the farm. Lucinda jumped up next to her and straightened the mike neck with a smile. She hopped off the podium again.

Cam spied Albert, still in place near the beer table. The crowd had moved aside in front of him, presumably so he could see.

"That's Albert St. Pierre right there." She waved at him. "He taught me about the soil and how to nurture it so plants will be healthy."

When Albert raised a hand in return, a wave of applause swept the room.

Cam continued. She spoke for a moment about organic certification. She described the CSA and lauded the Locavore Club's decision to sign up early. She finished by thanking the crowd.

"I'm a geek farmer. What can I say? If the food I grow makes you happy, that's good. And really, why buy from far away when you can eat what comes from your local area? I have to confess, though, that personally I am not giving up coffee." The audience laughed, to Cam's relief.

"Back to you," Cam said as she turned to Lucinda. But Lucinda wasn't there anymore. "Okay, enjoy the evening."

As she stepped down, a woman a bit older than Cam pushed past her and took the mike. "I hate to pop your bubble, folks, but you've got your heads in the clouds. Eating locally is all very nice, but it's not an efficient way to feed the world's population."

A hiss arose from the audience, and someone in the back booed. Cam wondered why this person was even at the festival if she was so anti-locavore.

The woman, whose tidy blouse and slacks contrasted with unkempt blond hair, started to speak again. A man hurried toward the podium.

"Clarice, honey. Come down from there," he murmured, extending a hand to her. She complied as he said in Cam's direction, "Sorry. She's not well." He put his arm around the woman and led her to the door.

Cam shrugged as she headed back to her table. The woman was probably right, but this wasn't exactly the right venue to start a debate on the topic. People kept stopping her to say hello or ask a question about the CSA. It was slow going.

"Nice speech." Ruth Dodge patted Cam on the arm.

"Hey, Ruth! Thanks. Nice to see you."

"Good speech, right, girls?" Two little girls stood on either side of Ruth. One wore a striped top, a short denim skirt over striped tights, and little hiking boots; the other a pink sundress and purple sandals. "Can you say hi to Ms. Cam?"

The girls said "Hi" in unison.

"You've gotten so big," Cam said, smiling at them, then thought she must sound like an old lady aunt. "Ms. Cam?" she said with raised eyebrows to Ruth.

"It's how they address their preschool teachers. Respect and informality combined. Seems to work."

"You guys having fun?" Cam squatted down to their level.

"I am. I'm Nettie." The girl in stripes pushed back a cap of dark curls from her forehead. "We're not the same, even though we're twins," her tiny voice asserted. It sounded like she'd been practicing the statement.

"Of course not. And you're Natalie, right?" Cam asked the girl in pink. Blond curls framed her face like angel hair.

Natalie nodded and looked away, hugging Ruth's knee.

Ruth ruffled Natalie's hair and mouthed "Shy" to Cam.

Nettie's face broke into a wide smile. "Daddy!" She flew at the man who had appeared at Ruth's side. He scooped up both girls, one in each arm, and kissed each in turn. He was taller than Cam and Ruth and wiry, with a scrawny brown ponytail. A feather earring hung from an earlobe. He wore old jeans and an untucked cowboy shirt, the kind with snaps instead of buttons, sleeves rolled up to his elbows.

"Cameron, right?" He greeted Cam without looking at Ruth.

Cam returned the greeting. "Haven't seen you since the wedding, I think."

Frank Jackson nodded, busying himself with his girls. Nettie demanded they go explore, while Natalie nestled into his shoulder like that was the only place she'd ever wanted to be.

Ruth reached out a hand to his other shoulder, but he shrugged it off.

Cam watched the hurt on Ruth's face be replaced by a mask of public good nature. Frank teased Nettie and stroked Natalie's hair. Clearly, he loved his kids, but he and Ruth were just as clearly having issues.

Cam froze. His left arm, the one around Natalie, sported a tattoo. She narrowed her eyes, as if it would improve her eyesight. She didn't need to. The tattoo depicted the same symbol as the one on the disk she'd found in her greenhouse.

CHAPTER 10

Cam shifted her eyes quickly. She watched Ruth watch the father of her children instead. It suddenly seemed important not to let Frank know she was interested in his tattoo, which had to be from the Patriotic Militia. She did know she was intensely curious about the image on his arm. It had to mean that Frank was part of the militia. Ruth had reacted to the logo on the disk, but she hadn't told Cam her husband was involved with the organization. And she hadn't told Pappas, either, as far as Cam knew. She worried about what Ruth had gotten herself into. It was time for that walk on the beach with her friend. And soon.

Nettie was out of Frank's arms and pulling him with her little hand across the hall, so Cam excused herself. "I have to get back to my table. Bye, Frank, girls!" she called after them, then lowered her voice. "Let's talk soon, Ruthie." Cam squeezed

Ruth's hand.

Her eyes on her daughters and her husband, Ruth nodded. She returned Cam's squeeze before she let go and followed them.

Cam headed back to her table. Stuart appeared at her side, holding two full plastic glasses.

"Wine?" He extended one toward Cam. "Alfalfa Farm Winery."

"I should be bringing you beer instead, to make up for the one I spilled on you." Cam accepted the glass. "Thanks."

"No problem. Wanted to make sure you know there's no hard feelings about pouring beer on me." Stuart laughed. "I was walking by, and they handed me two glasses for the price of one."

"I thought the samples were free." Cam smiled back. "Cheers."

Stuart raised his glass. "Let me know if you need another." He winked before he strolled away.

Alexandra was standing at the table when Cam returned. "I told Felicity I'd mind the space for you. It's been busy. I put out a sheet for people to leave their e-mail addresses on." She wore a green-and-blue rayon dress, a garment Great-Aunt Marie might have worn, that looked like it came from an antiques store. Except on Alexandra it was stunning, and not an everyday house-dress.

"I appreciate it, Alexandra." An image flashed in Cam's mind. An image of Alexandra standing over Mike's limp body with a pitchfork raised above her head, a pitchfork aimed at his throat. Cam shuddered.

"Are you all right?" Alexandra cocked her head and drew her brows together.

Cam shook her head a little. "I'm fine. Looks like we had lots of takers."

The young woman must have refilled the strawberry bowl several times, since the flat on the floor was nearly empty. The array of business cards was almost depleted, too. Cam dug the box out of her purse and displayed another couple of dozen.

"Hey, Alexandra. Is Katie coming?" Stuart materialized next to Cam.

Alexandra frowned. "Stuart, really. You need to leave her alone."

"What, little sister can't put in a good word? We had a nice thing going there for a while." Stuart sounded like he'd been sampling a little too much from the wine and beer tables, pronouncing *nice* as "naish." "Maybe now the competition's gone. . . ."

"Forget it, Stuart. She's moved on." Alexandra put fists on hips. "And, anyway, why would she listen to me?"

Stuart's smile turned to hurt. "Thanks a lot." He stalked away.

"Sounds like he wants your sister back. Anyway, thanks so much for filling in." She smiled at Alexandra. "Go enjoy yourself." Cam shooed her away and banished the image of Alexandra as murderer, too.

The next hour passed quickly. The burst of publicity from Lucinda brought all kinds of interested eaters who wanted a slice of Cam's time. She didn't think she could fit any more customers into the CSA this year but urged folks who asked about it to come to the farmers' market instead or even drop by the farm itself.

Lucinda breezed by several times. She wore black capri pants with her blouse and stylish black espadrilles. She didn't stop to talk, though, giving Cam a little wave of her hand as she worked the crowd. Bright spots burned on her cheeks, as if from the energy of the event.

"How's business?" Pete Pappas materialized opposite Cam.

Why was he at the festival?

"May I?" He gestured to one of the last strawberries.

"Sure. Business is booming. You're lucky to get one of those." Cam pointed to the strawberry. "Are you interested in local foods?"

"Not in the slightest. But it's my job right now to be interested in your farm." His smile was thin and didn't include the least scrap of warmth.

Cam returned the smile.

"Cam! Great speech." Ellie Kosloski stood next to Pappas, her father behind her. "I can't wait to come and help tomorrow morning."

Pappas raised an eyebrow. "More of your volunteers?" He nodded at Ellie and David.

"David and Ellie Kosloski, this is Detective Pappas. Detective, two of my shareholders. Ellie's doing her Girl Scout locavore badge, too."

Pappas nodded. "Mr. Kosloski. We've spoken on the telephone."

David nodded in return. He met Pappas's eyes briefly. Ellie waved at someone across the room and led her father away.

"Young Peter!" Albert's voice boomed from Cam's side.

Pappas's startled look was the first time Cam had seen him surprised.

"I knew your father. Spiros was a good man." Albert extended his hand. "Albert St. Pierre. I'd get up, but . . ." He gestured toward what was left of his leg.

Pappas shook Albert's hand. A smile drew across his face, under eyes tinged with sadness. "You knew my *babás*?"

"Yes. Spiros and I ran Rotary events. You know, getting money for winter coats for poor children. Bringing the kids up from the hot city — from Dorchester or Lowell — to the country for the summer. Why, we used to host them at the farm." Albert turned to Cam. "You remember, don't you, Cameron?"

Cam shook her head. "Maybe it was before I started coming. I was usually alone there. I mean, the only child. That's why I hung out with Ruthie."

"I daresay you're right. It must have been in my younger days."

Pappas ran a hand through his hair. Cam hadn't noticed the gray in it before. It was almost a week since the murder and still no arrest. He was in charge of the investigation. She imagined that could cause gray hair to sprout in anybody.

"I remember older children staying with us when I was little," he said. "They helped out at *Babás's* store."

Albert nodded. "Say, my niece here says you're the man in charge of finding who stabbed poor Montgomery on my, I should say *her,* farm. Haven't found the killer yet?

180

Mike's mother is getting worried you might never."

"We haven't made an arrest, sir." Pappas glanced at Cam. "Yet. We could be getting close, however. I should have asked to interview you earlier, since the victim was your former employee. My oversight. When would be a good time to talk?"

"No time like the present. Cameron, we're not leaving soon, are we? It's still hopping here."

Cam looked around. It was still hopping. She checked her watch. It was eight o'clock, but the hall remained full. The discordant notes of a tuning fiddle drifted over from the corner and then morphed like a butterfly into a full-fledged bluegrass tune, accompanied by a banjo and a guitar. Looked like the hopping was ramping up.

"No, we're not going soon."

Pappas gestured toward the doorway. "How about a breath of air?"

"I wouldn't mind it," Albert said, deftly turning the chair. Pappas followed him out.

Tapping her foot to the tune, Cam watched them go. Albert had mentioned Mike's mother to Pappas. Wouldn't Cam love to be a fly on the handle of his wheelchair to hear what Great-Uncle Albert knew about Bev Montgomery. What he hadn't wanted to tell Cam the other night. And then Pappas's comment "We could be getting close." If it was true, she might be able to breathe easily again.

Cam swung around at the swell of a crowd's worth of rhythmic clapping. A contra dance had materialized, complete with a caller in a swirly black skirt and red cowboy boots. Lucinda, squired by Stuart, sashayed to the music down the middle of a double row of people and then back. They separated and danced alone down the outside of the rows, Lucinda twirling as she went, Stuart doing fancy maneuvers with his feet. They took up positions facing each other again at the far end. Stuart smiled at Lucinda, who returned it with a five-hundred-watt beam. The rest of the dancers and half the observers clapped in time to the music.

Cam turned back to her farm table. The Herb Farmacy woman was packing up. Wes and Felicity had joined the dancers. Cam tidied up the cards and the display, removing the empty strawberry bowl and the note about taking only one, now facedown and forlorn on the cloth. She hummed along with the band, swaying to the music as she worked.

Suddenly a large warm arm encircled her waist. "Want to join the contra line?" Jake asked. His eyes twinkled under a mock frown. "Dare we?"

Cam flushed, loving the feeling of his arm but thinking this was a very public place to be seen so close. "Uh, I don't dance." She twisted away and faced him, smiling.

"You were, Farmer Flaherty. I saw you." Jake's double-breasted white shirt bore evidence of serving, and his hat was now askew as he returned her smile. The smile lines around those pale eyes countered their icy blue color. An escapee lock of hair over his brow gave him a boyish look.

"That wasn't dancing." Cam shook her head. "Besides" — she gestured around the room — "too many people here." She raised her eyebrows, hoping he would understand.

"Maybe we'll dance in private one of these days. What do you think?" Jake leaned his face close to hers until she could feel his heat.

Cam thought she would very much like to dance in private with this man. She took a deep breath. "How about I cook dinner for you tomorrow night?"

Jake gestured at his shirt with both hands and gave her a rueful look. "I'm a chef, remember? I cook all the nights but Monday and Tuesday. Even tonight I had to talk my sous-chef into being the big boss for an evening."

"Monday it is, then. On the farm. Six o'clock?"

Jake nodded. "I'll bring the dance music." He smiled over his shoulder as he strode away.

The tune changed to an even livelier one. Cam packed up the rest of the display and folded the cloth, tapping her foot. The dancers had formed two circles mostly defined by gender, one inside the other, women on the inside, men on the outside. The men's circle moved at the caller's instruction, so the partners changed with every call.

"Now, ladies and gentlemen, you be sure to introduce yourself if you don't know your new partner when he or she shows up," the caller announced.

Alexandra looked like she'd done this before, decorating the basic moves with flair and energy. Ellie and her father danced in the circles, too, Ellie holding her own with men twice her size and three times her age as the outer circle moved.

While Cam watched, David Kosloski came face-to-face with Lucinda. She smiled at him as he leaned toward her and seemed to say something. Lucinda's eyes widened in a look of alarm. Her smile vanished. She spoke, then dashed out of the circle and toward the propped-open back door.

Cam checked the clock as she lay in bed. Midnight thirty. The unmoving, moisture-laden air pushed down like a blanket. Even a sheet felt too hot, so she sprawled uncovered, wearing only a long T-shirt softened to the texture of silk by years of washing.

The heat kept her awake. Her stomach was a little queasy, too. Thoughts chased each other around her brain as she lay there. Lucinda had acted so oddly tonight. Showing up late to her own event? Very strange. Absent when Cam finished her little speech? A little weird. Zooming around like she was high during the event? Okay, normal. But tearing out of there, with alarm written on her face, right after seeing David Kosloski? Just plain odd, and a little scary. The two must know each other, since Lucinda cleaned the Kosloski house. Maybe Cam should call her, but it seemed like too much effort right now.

Then Pappas taking Great-Uncle Albert outside so Pappas could grill him, or maybe it was Albert getting information out of Pappas. Cam hadn't been able to find out which, since Albert had fallen asleep on the drive home.

She grabbed her stomach and groaned.

All of a sudden she had a lobster thrashing around in her gut, claws and all. She raced down the stairs to the bathroom, arriving in the nick of time. Her head pounded as she lost her dinner in first one direction and then the other, like she was being turned inside out. When the attack seemed to be over, she washed her hands and rinsed her mouth out. A shudder rippled through her, and she wondered if she was going to be sick again. Looking in the mirror, she was shocked at how pale her face was.

Cam inhaled deeply and let the air out. If this was from what she'd eaten at the Locavore Festival, it wasn't very good advertising for local foods. She padded out into the dark parlor and sank into an armchair. She shook her head. Unless others reported getting sick, she didn't have any way of finding out what had caused her own distress. It could be a flu bug, she supposed. Or maybe it was mixing beer with rum with wine. How many times did she have to tell herself not to do that?

Exhausted by the quick ordeal, Cam thought she could probably sleep now. It was warm and a little claustrophobic down here in the dark. She checked the door and windows, then climbed the wide pine stair treads, which dipped in the middle from centuries of farmers going up to bed. The wood was cool under her bare feet and was lit only by the ambient light from the uncovered windows upstairs. At the landing she paused and leaned her elbows on the windowsill at the front of the house. The Strawberry Moon shone fuzzy around the edges from the moisture in the air. Crickets fiddled while she watched fireflies swell to light and then dim again as they danced around the antique lilac.

Cam heard a noise. She froze. What was that? She heard it again. Not a sound produced by the natural world. A clunk, a kind of metallic noise. She peered out as best she could. The yellow glow of the streetlight didn't reach into the dark areas next to the house or the hiding places under the lilacs and forsythias filling the space between the road and the house.

She shivered. Someone might be out there snooping around the house, spying on her. Or trying to break in. Or doing more damage to her crops.

Cam shook her head. She told herself to get a grip. She was a competent adult with a smarter-than-average brain. She knew the doors were locked downstairs and the windows were open only at the top. What she needed was a plan.

She tiptoed into her room. She exhaled with relief when she saw her cell phone by her bed. She threw a work shirt on over her sleepwear and pulled on a pair of shorts. She unplugged the clock radio that sat on the bedside table and slid back into the hall. She plugged it in at the receptacle directly under the front window. She set the radio on the windowsill, speaker facing out, switched it to a talk show, and turned the volume up as high as it would go. Flipping the lights on in the other rooms upstairs completed the plan. Let whoever it was think she wasn't alone.

In her bedroom at the back of the house, Cam sat on her bed in the dark. The motion-detector floodlight she'd installed could finally come in handy tonight. If the intruder moved to the back, he or she would have no place to hide.

She waited about twenty minutes. The floodlight did not come on. She heard no more noises. She switched off the radio and the room lights. Tomorrow was share day, and dawn would come in a few short hours. If someone wanted to break into her house, well, let them try. As sleep started to dance around the edges of her consciousness and the beginning scene of a dream projected its images, an idea came to Cam. She told herself to remember it in the morning, then slid into oblivion.

"Here you go, Ellie." Cam handed the girl a pair of scissors and a basket. "Clip the greens right above the ground. They'll grow back, and in two weeks we'll have another whole crop of mesclun."

"I'm all over it." Ellie knelt in the path next to the greens bed. "Thanks for, like, letting me help."

"Hey, I need all the help I can get. The thanks are all mine, girlfriend."

Ellie cocked her head and frowned, then started cutting.

"Is that an odd thing for a grown-up to say?" Cam asked.

"Yah, duh. I mean, well, *we* don't say stuff like that."

Cam smiled to herself. She hadn't hung out with fourteen-year-olds since she'd been one herself. She was glad Ellie wanted to help harvest on share morning. And, frankly, that Ellie's father hadn't stayed to help, too. He was a little odd, that one.

She checked her watch. Ten after nine. No Lucinda. She had told Cam she would come early to harvest again, like last week. Maybe Lucinda ran into trouble after she raced out last night. Cam shook her head. She had too much to do to worry about it. She set to work pulling lettuce heads, roots and all, then plunging them into the wide galvanized-metal basin she'd filled with water. She wiped her forehead with her wet hand. The air was as hot as yesterday, even this early, and as humid, too.

Cam looked over at Ellie. "I'd better get you a bin to soak those in instead of the basket. They'll wilt in a minute in this heat, and we need to keep them fresh. Be right back."

Ellie nodded, singing a song to herself under her breath.

Cam took a closer look. The girl had an earbud in one ear whose wire snaked down to the pocket on the bib of her overalls. The youth of today. Actually, Cam knew a lot of people her own age and older who were never without their minuscule music devices. As Cam walked to the barn, she reflected on what an aberration she was. For her, listening to the birds in the trees and the breeze in the leaves was a lot nicer music than anything that came out of a little metal square.

She rummaged through the corner of the barn where she kept big containers until she found a plastic storage bin Ellie could rinse the greens in. Cam glanced over at the farm table and wrinkled her nose. In three hours the table had to be full.

"Oh, crud! I forgot to make a dish for the shareholders to sample," she said aloud. A misbegotten plan if there ever was one. The printed recipes would have to suffice this week. And every week, for that matter. *Let them make their own dishes.* Cam ran to the house, glad she'd thought to type up a half dozen recipes before the season started.

She stopped short, with her hand on the door. A small galvanized metal bucket sat on the stoop. It held dozens of cut red carnations in water. A little metallic ladybug stuck to the outside. The array was gorgeous, but where had it come from? Somehow she had missed it this morning. She must have opened the door wide and not seen it. A metal bucket — that could have been the sound she'd heard in the night. The sound of kindness, not malice.

Cam picked the bucket up but didn't see a card or any other indication of who her secret admirer was. Thinking the flowers had to be from Jake, a rush zipped through her. She carried the bucket in and set it carefully on the table.

She fired up the computer and sent Rosemary-Roasted Lamb and Asparagus Frittata to print, thirty copies each, then raced back to the barn. She'd left Ellie alone long enough as it was.

When Cam got back to the greens bed with the bin and the end of the hose, Ellie was not there. She dropped the bin and swore. Ellie's basket was full, with the scissors laid neatly on top. Cam looked in every direction. She couldn't see Ellie. Cam hadn't been gone very long. She was suddenly cold, her veins infused with ice water.

"Ellie!" she called as loud as she could. The air seemed to have become silent except for her call. Cam didn't hear the birds, the leaves, the road traffic. Nothing. If the girl had come to harm, Cam would not forgive herself. She cupped her hands around her mouth and called again, in the direction of the woods skirting the back of the property this time.

"Hi, Cam! I'm over here." Ellie waved in the distance.

Cam's heart rate started making its way back to normal. She closed her eyes for a moment's gratitude to whatever goddess was out there. She reopened them to see Ellie sauntering toward her.

"Where were you?" Cam tried to keep the worry out of her voice.

"The basket was full and you weren't back, so I thought I'd look around. I was walking down the row of tomatoes when I saw a flash of light from the edge of the woods, like the sun was reflecting off something shiny. I already got my science sleuth badge, but I wanted to, you know, check it out, anyway."

"So you're all right?"

Ellie shook her head with a little frowning smile. "Yeah. Why wouldn't I be?"

"I didn't see you and —"

"And you thought maybe the murderer was back?" Ellie put one hand in her pocket as she raised her eyebrows. Her other hand she kept behind her.

"No!" At Ellie's frank gaze, Cam said, "Well, yes. Crazy, huh?"

Ellie nodded. "Want to see the thing I found? It looks like a gadget I read about in a novel about covert operations." She glanced around. "Maybe there's a spy organization operating undercover."

"Maybe," Cam said, indulging the bookish teen. "Let's see."

Ellie started to bring her hand out from behind her back, then looked beyond Cam. "I'll show you later."

"What? Why not now?"

Ellie pulled her hand back. She shook her head, stuffing whatever it was in her back pocket. "Hi, Lucinda," she called.

Cam whirled. Lucinda strode toward them, hair flying. "Sorry, *fazendeira*. I was detained."

"Oh, no. What happened?"

Lucinda laughed, but it was a weak imitation of her usual peal. "No, not like that. I mean, I'm late. But I'm here now. Hey, Ellie."

The girl waved.

"Okay, what do we got to do?" Lucinda gazed at Cam. Her eyes were watery, with smudged circles under them.

Cam wanted only to sit her down, get answers to what had happened last night, find out why she was late, make sure she was safe. Of course, maybe she'd had too much to drink, or mixed her drinks like Cam had. Instead of getting into it, she asked Lucinda to fill the bin with water for Ellie. She directed Ellie to dump the greens into the water and cut enough more to refill the basket. She pointed Lucinda to the asparagus beds and took herself off to the perennial herbs to cut and bundle rosemary and thyme for today's shares. They'd be lucky to get the harvest done and organized by noon. As she knelt to cut, she wondered for a moment what Ellie had found. It was probably an object Ellie's teen imagination had embellished a story for. But why had she wanted to keep it secret from Lucinda?

CHAPTER 11

Cam surveyed the farm table. The three of them had barely made the noon deadline.

"No, we didn't," she thought aloud. She turned to Lucinda. "Flowers! Can you . . ."

"I'm on it." Lucinda, still looking like she'd eaten a rotten eggplant, grabbed scissors and a bucket and headed for the flower garden.

Cam thought of another forgotten task. "Ellie, greet anybody who arrives, will you? I need to get the recipes from the house."

At the girl's pleased nod, Cam loped across the yard. She grabbed the printouts and cut the sheets in half with a little too much speed. She shook her head at the rough slanted cuts, but she was out of time. She had just locked the back door when a rumbling in the drive made her whirl.

A panel truck crunched the gravel as it drove slowly toward the back. Cam tried to hail the driver with a wave, but she didn't wave back. *Now what?* Cam shook her head, then followed the truck to the barn.

Great. On only her second share pickup day, the entire entrance to the barn was blocked. Who was this?

The passenger door slammed, and Alexandra strode around the front of the truck. "Hey, Cam! Good timing, right?" She gestured to the idling truck, a delighted smile lighting up her face.

"I don't know. Is it? What's going on?"

Alexandra's smile vanished. "You don't remember? It's the CSF. People are going to pick up their fish shares at the same time as their vegetables. You agreed to it." She frowned into Cam's eyes.

Cam nodded slowly. Of course. What a week it had been. "You're absolutely right. Sorry I forgot. But you know, this isn't a very good place for the truck. You need to move it. How about in the parking area?" She gestured to a graveled area off the driveway and closer to the road.

"Sure. No prob." Alexandra turned to the driver, still ensconced in the cab. "Bev, let's move it over there." She pointed down the drive.

Cam took a closer look.

Bev Montgomery gripped the wheel. She jammed the truck into reverse and backed down the drive.

What was Bev doing driving a fish truck? Cam wondered if she was going to ask to see where her son was killed. It had to be painful for her to be here, where Mike had met a violent death. At least there was the memorial to him. Maybe Cam should offer to show her.

A pain shot through the hand Cam had cut that night. She looked down. She still gripped the sheaf of recipes, now wrinkled from the force of her hand. She told herself to get a grip on her own world instead.

"Cam, want me to put those on the table?" Ellie looked up at Cam.

"Sure. Thanks. Anyone arrive yet?"

Ellie shook her head as she sauntered back into the barn, humming, earbud firmly in place.

Cam watched her go, then turned back to the truck. Bev now stood in the open back, next to a container that looked like a big refrigerator lying on its back. A large cooler sat on the truck bed next to her. On the ground, Alexandra busied herself with a clipboard. Community-supported fishery. Cam sighed at the excess of community.

"Hello, Bev. I didn't know you fished, too."

"I don't." The older woman pulled on

long, thick rubber gloves and rummaged in the container.

"What's your relation to the CSF, then?"

Alexandra piped up. "It's her brother. He's one of the supported fishermen. And fisherwomen."

Bev nodded but didn't meet Cam's eyes.

So much for getting information out of Bev. Her perky young spokeswoman was obviously going to cover for her. Cam resolved to keep trying.

"Is this your first time at the farm, Bev?"

Bev gave Cam a sharp glance. Now Cam had her attention.

"Of course not," she snapped. "Your great-uncle and I go way back." She opened her mouth to continue, then apparently thought the better of it and snapped it shut.

Cam saw Bev's clenched jaw working and decided to leave well enough alone. "Thanks for bringing the fish." She turned to Alexandra and nodded at her clipboard. "Are those the shareholders?"

Alexandra nodded.

"If there is fish left over, I'd love to buy a piece, since I never signed up. What kind of fish do you have, by the way?"

"Whole cod."

Cam had no idea how to cook a whole fish, but that was what the Internet was for, wasn't it? "Well, I'll take one if anyone doesn't claim their share."

Alexandra rolled her eyes in faux ecstasy. "It's to die for."

Cam sincerely hoped not. There had been enough of that at the farm already to last the rest of her natural lifetime.

Several shareholders streamed up the drive, including David Kosloski. Cam greeted them and welcomed them into the barn, bracing herself for several hours of being social.

"I'm sorry I missed the first week." Irene Burr, in expensive-looking slacks in a cream color and a shimmering blue silk shirt, waved a manicured hand. "I was in Morocco, picking up some rugs. This all looks wonderful."

Cam took a moment to show her the setup. "Careful of the dirt." She gestured at the roots on the radishes and smudges on the farm table. "I wouldn't want you to ruin those nice pants."

The woman laughed and began to fill her cloth bag.

"Hi, Dad!" Ellie strolled over to her father. "Look what we have today." She gestured in a broad sweep at the produce displayed on the table. "I cut the mesclun and did a bunch of other stuff, too."

David put his arm around Ellie and walked to the table. "It's beautiful, honey."

Ellie helped her father fill two cloth shopping bags with their share. They were at the barn door when Ellie said, "I'll meet you at the car, Dad. One sec." She hurried back to Cam.

"Cam," she whispered, beckoning Cam to lean down to her level.

Cam obliged.

Ellie looked around, as if to be sure no one was listening. "This is the thing I found in the woods." She drew it out of her back pocket and extended it in a closed fist.

Cam received it and closed her hand around the object, a little cylinder. She was about to examine it.

"No! Look at it later. You know, when you're by yourself." Ellie pursed her lips under a knit brow.

"Okay," Cam promised as she slipped the object into her pocket. She didn't have time to either study or consider it now, anyway. "Hey, thanks for all your work this morning. It really helped. You're very competent."

"No problem. I mean, thanks. I'm, like, learning a lot." She strolled toward the door, then turned. "Have a wicked good weekend," she called.

Cam waved her hand in reply. Just then

Wes and Felicity rounded the corner into the barn. In contrast to Felicity's bubbly spirit from all of Cam's previous encounters with her, today her face was stern, angry. Wes hurried along beside her, one hand on her elbow, speaking in a low voice.

Felicity twisted out of Wes's touch and halted, facing him. "I think we should tell her. She deserves to know." Her voice was shrill. She turned back to the middle of the barn. Catching sight of Cam, she instantly transformed into a smiling shareholder.

"Ah, Cam, there you are. We were just talking about you."

Wes removed his glasses and pinched the bridge of his nose.

"Hi, Felicity, Wes. How are things?" Cam gazed from one to the other.

Felicity glared at Wes, then smiled at Cam. "Oh, I forgot." She drew a cloth bag out of her market basket. "Here. I brought bamboo plates for your samples." She extended the bag toward Cam.

Ouch. "Well, we have a change of plans on that. Thank you so much, Felicity. But I realized it was just too much work to both cook and harvest every Saturday." Cam waved a hand at the table. "But I still have the recipes, and you know, people can cook their own versions. What do you think?"

Felicity drew the bag back, gazing at Cam in silence for a moment.

Cam's heart fell. This little woman had been one of her most enthusiastic customers so far, and helpful, too. Cam hoped she hadn't lost her loyalty, and wondered if it had anything to do with Felicity's argument with Wes. Cam tried to muster a smile encouraging of agreement.

"I think that's a wise business decision, Cam. Don't worry. I was thinking maybe we could start monthly farm potlucks, anyway, everybody sharing their shares, so to speak. What do you think?"

Cam's relief must have been painted all over her, because Felicity laughed.

"You don't need to cook for us, really! We need you to grow food for us. We can do the cooking. Isn't that right, Wes?" For the first time since Cam had met her, Felicity didn't look at Wes to confirm her statement.

Wes didn't speak.

"Thanks. Great." Cam filled the gap. She looked directly at Wes, but his eyes were on Felicity, who had moved on to the produce table. "Everything all right, Wes?" Cam asked in a low voice.

"Phew," he said, exhaling. "Life ain't easy sometimes, Cam." He shook his head, then took a deep breath. "Nothing a little loving-kindness can't cure, though." He moved on to help Felicity assemble their share.

Cam watched Wes. His touches were subtle but caring, a little stroke to Felicity's hair, a gentle caress of her shoulder as she selected flowers. Cam's longing for a man like that struck with a physical jolt to her gut. She had thought she had it in Tom, but in the end had realized she'd been reading caring into his behavior, when it was really only his self-interest pushing through. He'd been sweet enough when he wanted something from her. When she didn't serve his purposes, he had easily become brusque and distant, both psychologically and physically. In the end, he had rejected her. Claiming it was because she'd moved to the farm had been all so convenient for him.

Cam shook her head. What was she doing, reliving a failed relationship right here in the barn among a half dozen customers? She told herself to get back to business.

She approached Wes and Felicity. It looked like they were finished selecting their produce. "Are you picking up fish today, too?"

Felicity nodded. "Wes grills the cod whole. It's to die for."

Cam flinched. *Not again.*

Felicity must have noticed, because she said, "I'm sorry, Cam. That was a stupid thing to say. Forgive me."

Cam nodded. "No problem."

"What I meant was, it's totally delicious. The fish is so fresh, it's just the most tender seafood you've ever eaten. Are you getting a share?"

Cam replied that she was in line in case of a no-show. "Do you have a recipe, Wes?"

"I'll e-mail it to you."

Cam thanked him. "See you on Volunteer Day, then." She looked at Felicity.

"I'll be here." Felicity turned to Wes, her face instantly transformed to taskmaster firm. She folded her arms. "Wesley, don't we have information for Cam?"

Wes sighed. He gazed at Felicity. "You know I don't want to get involved."

"We don't have a choice! You can't just stick your head in the ground like a Yankee ostrich." Sparks shot out of her eyes.

"All right." Wes faced Cam. "That detective was snooping around again. Pappas. He was at our door this morning. I don't like the authorities on my property. Felicity thinks we should help them. But why help somebody you don't trust?" He looked around the barn, which for the moment was empty of anyone but the three of them, then focused on his wife. "But I talked to him, anyway. He was asking questions about Lucinda."

"Oh, no. But why was he asking you?" Wes didn't trust the police. Cam wondered why not and hoped it wasn't because he was part of the militia, too.

"I suppose because we're all in the Locavore Club. Felicity and Lucinda were the force that organized it in the first place."

"What kind of questions did he ask?"

"I gathered there might have been an incident last night, after the festival, perhaps." Wes looked down at Felicity for confirmation. She nodded.

"Why did you think that?"

"Pappas asked a lot of questions about when the festival ended, where Lucinda had gone, that kind of thing. But we told him we didn't know anything. Which is the truth."

"Oh, crud." Cam spied Lucinda at the back door of the barn. She lowered her voice. "Thanks for letting me know. I appreciate it."

"Let's go get our fish, honey," Felicity said to Wes. Peace apparently reigned again in the Ames-Slavin household.

"I'll come along. I need a little fresh air." All of a sudden the barn, the customers, the murder investigation, the entire farm constricted Cam's lungs so she could barely breathe.

At the doorway, Cam glanced back at the farm table. Lucinda stood behind it, one hand neatening the bundles of asparagus. The other gripped her forehead like it hurt, bad.

Cam inhaled deeply in the sunshine. She leaned against the doorway, watching Bev extract a plastic bag full of an entire fish from the container. She scooped ice from the cooler into another bag, added the fish, and handed it down to Alexandra, who gave it to Wes. Alexandra checked their names off her list and then slid a couple of sheets of paper out from under the list.

"Here's an explanation of the fishery practices and a couple of recipes for cooking the fish. Oh, and that Web site there . . ." Alexandra pointed to a spot on the top sheet. "It has a link to a video on how to fillet fish."

"Wes already has a filleting knife. Don't you, dear?" Felicity asked her husband.

Cam sensed Bev's eyes on her and glanced up at her standing in the truck. Her hostility was a knife in the air. Cam almost ducked. She hadn't done anything to deserve that. True, she hadn't been overly welcoming to Bev — she really should have accepted that rhubarb at the close of market — but she had reached out. Maybe offering to show her the memorial would help.

"How many more we got?" Bev barked at Alexandra.

Always serene, Alexandra answered, "Three, Bev."

"Well, I need to get going. I have my own farm to see to, you know."

Alexandra gazed up at her for a moment, then turned to Cam, extending the clipboard. "How about if I leave you the last three fish in the cooler of ice, along with the list, Cam? Anybody doesn't claim their fish, it's yours."

"No problem," Cam agreed. She moved forward to accept the list of subscribers from Alexandra.

Alexandra turned back to Bev. "All right? Then we'll be done. I have a few other commitments this afternoon, too."

"Let's be gone, then. I'd rather be with my own kind, anyway." Bev's glare this time wasn't at Cam but beyond her.

"Just one sec while I pick up my share." Alexandra grabbed her cloth bags from the cab of the truck and strode into the barn.

Cam eased around, following Bev's gaze. Lucinda stood in the entrance to the barn. And her look at Bev was equally unfriendly.

Lucinda wasn't Bev's "own kind"? What did that mean?

Cam checked the old clock on the back wall of the barn. Two forty-five. Fifteen minutes until she could be done with today, at least the public part. She looked at the share-holder sign-in sheet. Stuart Wilson was again the only one who hadn't shown.

She sank into a lawn chair next to the farm table, the last bunch of asparagus forlorn in its bucket of water, the last of the mesclun looking a little tired at having been pawed through for more than two hours. Cam had been pawed through, too. She slouched, her feet in their muddy work boots extending in front of her, crossed at the ankles.

The complications of the day elbowed each other for her attention. Wes and Felicity telling her Pappas was curious about where Lucinda had gone last night. Well, where had she gone in such a hurry, right in the middle of the dance? What had happened to pique Pappas's curiosity? Cam hadn't gotten a chance to ask Lucinda this morn-ing, and she had left an hour ago, during the busiest pickup time. Bev Montgomery had been so unpleasant to Cam, for no reason she could think of. Alluding to her past with Albert. Glaring at Lucinda and maligning her, really, with that talk about "her own kind." Cam found thinking about all of it more exhausting than the physical work of farming.

A sweet whiff of the antique narcissus mixed with the pungent spring garlic and with the smells of the barn: old hay, honest dirt, machine oil, and dust-filtered sunlight. She inhaled deeply and closed her eyes, folding her hands over her stomach. Time to just be in the present. Farming was what she'd wanted, after all, complications be damned. Life could be a lot worse.

At the slamming of a door, her eyes flew open. Stuart dashed into the barn, stopping when he saw her.

"Sorry. Late again."

"No, you're good." Cam nodded at the clock, then gestured at the table. "It's all here for you."

"Oh, hey, I forgot my bag. Do you have a couple I can use?"

Cam rose and dug several plastic grocery bags out of the assortment she kept in a box under the table for just that reason.

She sat again and watched as Stuart bagged the mesclun. She winced when he loaded heavier items on top of the tender greens in the bag. His hand shook slightly as he extracted the flowers from their water.

"Looked like you had a good time at the festival last night, dancing and all." Cam smiled at him.

Stuart laughed. "Uoh, I'm not too bad at it. I used to go to Cambridge Contra every week. I really get into dancing."

Cam raised her eyebrows.

"My old dad would be turning in his grave if he knew, though. Would have called it a sissy thing to do."

"Really?" Cam didn't dance, but it was because of her uncoordinated, gawky moves when she tried, not because she didn't believe in it.

"Yeah, he was military all the way. Didn't believe in dancing, flowers, none of the finer things in life. Gave my mother grief, I can tell you."

"Any idea where your partner lit out to?" Maybe Stuart could tell her about the rest of Lucinda's evening.

Stuart hefted the bundle of asparagus for a moment before adding it to his bag. "My partner?"

"You were dancing with Lucinda. Then, during the big circle dance, she split all of a sudden. I didn't see her again."

He rubbed his hair with one hand, then wiped his forehead. "I don't know. I stayed for the dance. Well, gotta run." He didn't meet Cam's eyes. He lifted the bag he'd just filled. "Thanks." Stuart strode out of the barn.

Cam waved in a wasted gesture. Had he seen Lucinda again after the dance? That was the question she should have asked him. The question he was probably trying to avoid by clearing out like he'd just been called to a fire. And she was pretty sure he wasn't one of the Westbury on-call firefighters. Well, hey, maybe they'd gone home together. Which was their business, not hers.

She caught sight of a full bag on the floor and sighed. Looked like half of Stuart's share was hers now. Shifting in her chair, she felt the object Ellie had given her press into the top of her thigh. She pulled it out of her pocket, wondering why Ellie had wanted to keep it a secret. It looked like a little flashlight. Cam switched it on and aimed it around the barn, but she couldn't see any light. She turned it to look at the lens but didn't see light there, either. What the heck was it, and what was it doing on Cam's farm?

She walked out to the daylight. She held the object close. The black rubbery case bore a small logo that read PursueTech and what looked like a product code. "IR four-fifty SuCov," Cam read out. She looked around, as if in another universe the owner would walk up the drive, claim the cylinder, explain why he or she had left it on Cam's farm, apologize, and leave.

Since that wasn't going to happen, it was clearly time for a cold beer, lunch, and the Internet, in that order. She grabbed the one unclaimed fish from the cooler and headed for the house. The Internet would also help with what to do with a whole fish, head and all.

CHAPTER 12

After lunch Cam set to researching the fish first. The plethora of recipes and filleting advice overwhelmed her. She gave up for the moment, wrapped the fish in plastic, and stowed it in the back of the freezer. What she really wanted to do was find out what IR 450 SuCov was.

Cam surveyed her monitor a few minutes later. She propped her elbows on the desk, chin in both hands. She had found the object on the Internet, all right, but was having trouble getting her mind around it. The IR 450 SuCov was an infrared light. SuCov stood for Super Covert. It was a tool the military, or the paramilitary, for that matter, used with night-vision equipment. According to the description on Pursue-Tech's Web site, the beam was invisible unless you wore the kind of goggles that worked on that spectrum. And if you did, the device provided high-power illumination.

Cam looked at the little cylinder next to her keyboard. She reached out a hand and rolled it back and forth. This object, Ellie's innocent-looking "gadget," was a tool for sneaking up on people, for spying, for communicating with fellow undercover agents, whoever they were. Ellie had guessed right. Someone had been using it on her property, had dropped it in her woods. She glanced back at the screen. PursueTech was just what it sounded like. The company sold high-tech tools used in pursuit of the enemy. This particular tool cost 160 dollars.

Cam whistled. The owner had to have bucks to spend so much on a flashlight, and he or she might be part of the Patriotic Militia. But whose light was it? People had been covertly searching her property at night, and she had no idea who or why. Or which enemy they were after. If anyone out there thought Cam was a bad guy, they were seriously misguided.

But a true bad guy was still out there. It was time to do a stint of armchair sleuthing.

Half an hour later she'd set up a database of everything she knew relating to Mike's murder. She examined the rows and columns. People who knew Mike. Other farmers who might be feeling the stress of competition with Cam's product. People who might be connected with the Patriotic Militia. Immigrants like Lucinda. People Great-Uncle Albert knew. Time of day Cam had seen any of the players or knew where they had been. Even all the subscribers. But finding a connection between motive, victim, and perpetrator seemed impossible.

What had she missed? Well, alibis for Saturday late afternoon, but that was the domain of the police.

Preston reared up on his hind legs to rub his head against her knee. As Cam scratched his brow, she said, "Mr. P, this is getting me nowhere. I don't know who disliked Mike. I have no idea who this shadowy militia is. The farmers I'm in competition with aren't mean or violent, as far as I know. Uncle Albert couldn't have had any enemies. What else should I be thinking of?"

When Preston didn't answer, Cam decided to hack together a Python utility script to dig through all the data and display it graphically in a Web page. Twenty minutes later, she narrowed her eyes at a flowchart with colored lines connecting names, times, and relationships.

But software didn't do any good if it didn't have data to work with in the first place. And she'd never encountered a software engineer who could predict how someone would act under X amount of stress or Y amount of pressure. Just for the heck of it, she poked around on the Internet, trying to find psychological predictive software. She finally came up with a document called the DSM-V, which looked like it was a catalog of all mental disorders. It was searchable, but it wasn't what she needed.

Preston mewed in his tiny voice and rubbed her knee again.

Cam drained the last bit from her glass and saved her work. The next time she picked up a bit of information, she could always enter it into the database and regenerate the display.

She checked her e-mail. She opened a message from Lucinda, asking if Cam wanted to join her at the free outdoor concert in Newburyport that evening. Lucinda wrote that they could bring food and wine and have a picnic supper. Cam looked at the time. She stretched and thought about sitting home alone versus being out in public and having to be social. The former was definitely her path of least resistance. The latter? Sometimes one was called to a higher purpose. She fired off a reply and headed for the shower, plotting how she could delve deeper into Lucinda's secrets, and maybe somehow into the secret of Mike Montgomery's death.

Cam scanned the crowd. Families sprawled on picnic blankets on the grass between the Firehouse Center for the Arts and the river. Near the temporary stage, a contingent of senior citizens waited expectantly in fabric lawn chairs. A young couple stretched out on their sides on a cloth, the man feeding the woman morsels of dinner. Two boys dashed by Cam, nearly clipping her as she searched for Lucinda. She saw a familiar hand waving from the slight rise on the right and headed that way.

"You snagged a nice spot," Cam said when she arrived. The hillock afforded a better view of the stage and of the wide Merrimack beyond. Lucinda sat on an Indian-print bedspread.

She greeted Cam. "Sit down. Plenty of room."

Cam set her basket down and sat cross-legged next to Lucinda. "Thanks for asking me, Lucinda. I was all set for another Saturday night at home alone."

"This band is good. I know the drummer. He's Brazilian."

"What kind of music do they play?"

"Cajun. Fun stuff." Lucinda stretched her legs out in front of her and leaned back on one elbow.

Cam extracted a chilled bottle of white wine from Jewell Towne Vineyards, two plastic cups, and an opener from her basket. "Wine? It's from just over the border in New Hampshire." At Lucinda's nod, she opened the bottle and poured for each of them.

"*Saúde.*" Lucinda extended her cup toward Cam's. "Cheers."

Cam returned the salutation and sipped the wine. It went down cool and easy. A breeze cooled the air, too, this close to the water. She closed her eyes for a moment.

A high-pitched sound blasted. Cam winced and opened her eyes again. Down on the stage the band was setting up and testing amplifiers. Lucinda drew several containers out of her bag, as well as a couple of plastic plates and forks. "Hungry?"

Cam nodded. "I brought green salad. That's all I have that's local yet."

"Good. I made tabbouleh. Got cracked wheat from the grain guy at the festival and used goat cheese from that farm in Topsfield and your mint." She leaned close to

Cam and whispered, "I cheated on the olive oil. Don't tell." Lucinda sat back and laughed.

"Listen, I don't care if you cheat or not." Cam proffered her salad. "The few fine things in life we can't produce here? I'd cheat, too, if it meant I couldn't have coffee, chocolate, or olive oil."

She filled her plate and began to eat, as did Lucinda. A seagull landed on the blanket next to theirs, vacated a minute earlier by a woman and a little girl who had headed hand in hand toward the boardwalk along the river's edge. The bird tugged at an open bag of chips with its beak until a chip fell out. It pecked at it and then flew off, chip secured. Lucinda reached over and flipped a corner of the blanket over the bag.

"You see why seagulls are so fat around here," a male voice said.

Cam twisted her head to look up. Wes Ames stood there. "Hey, Wes." Cam looked around. "Where's Felicity?"

He pointed to the other side of the crowd. "Her sister is visiting, and they're chatting up a storm. I'm just stretching my legs before the music starts. Hi, Lucinda." Wes squatted down. "The band is supposed to be good."

Lucinda nodded with her mouth full. She

chewed and swallowed before she spoke. "They're *fabuloso.* You know, really good."

Wes stood. "I'll let you ladies eat in peace. Enjoy the concert."

"Hang on a minute, Wes." Cam drained her cup and set her plate down. "I'll walk with you. I need to go find the facilities before the music gets going. Back in a flash, Lucinda."

Lucinda, taking another bite, waved them on.

As they walked, Cam said to Wes, "Can you tell me any more about what Detective Pappas asked you this morning, Wes?" The question came out way more bluntly than she'd intended, but it was too late to take it back. She despaired of ever learning the smooth dance of communication, which everyone else seemed to have mastered.

Wes looked straight ahead. Furrows creased his brow. "He asked us if we'd seen Lucinda leave. He wanted to know if she'd come back to the festival later or if she'd called us." He walked a few more paces, then burst out, "I hate it when the pigs come to the house. The cops lost my respect in the sixties and never earned it back."

Cam raised her eyebrows but kept her mouth shut. He was just an old hippie like her parents. Except then they'd become

221

itinerant academics. She realized she didn't know Wes's profession, but now wasn't the time to ask. She strolled in silence next to him. They walked slowly, weaving through locals out for a summer evening, dads pushing strollers, teenagers hanging on each other.

"I told him we hadn't seen her. I barely know Lucinda, you realize." Wes looked over at Cam. "Was she involved with the murder? Pappas seemed pretty suspicious of her."

"She wouldn't kill someone. I'm sure of that." Cam shook her head, then caught a wave of dizziness from having chugged her cup of wine. She took a deep breath to steady herself.

Wes kept his silence.

"Lucinda has been acting a little strange lately," Cam said, hoping to draw him out.

"I heard an interesting tidbit. Our neighbor saw a story about the murder on the news, and he said Mike was tight with that anti-immigrant group."

"I know. Lucinda actually told me that. Think that's why Pappas suspects her? That the militia was going to turn her in?"

Wes shrugged. "I couldn't say. Why don't you just ask the detective?"

Cam laughed. "Oh, that's way too obvious. But, anyway, I doubt he's going to tell me about his thought process."

Wes agreed. The walkway split, and Cam said good-bye as she followed the left branch to the portable johns the city had set up.

"See you next week," Wes called.

Cam answered with a wave. She stood in line for the toilets behind two teenage girls who must have bought out the makeup aisle at the drugstore. Cam glanced to her left. The setting sun lit up the river so it looked like God had poured rose-colored dye into it. Cam's thoughts were not on the natural beauty of the Merrimack, though. Somewhere in the universe was the person who had slammed Cam's pitchfork into Mike's neck. Cam wondered if she was deluding herself, thinking she could find a murderer. Maybe she should just let the police do their work.

Cam and Lucinda joined the rest of the audience on their feet during the last of several encore tunes. It was toe-tapping music, and lots of people danced. But the concert had been too loud for Cam to get a chance to ask Lucinda about the night before. When the song was over, Cam packed up the corkscrew and the now-empty bottle and cups.

As Lucinda stuffed the bedspread into her bag, she said, "I'm gonna go meet Jorge, the drummer. Want to come out with us for a drink?"

Cam checked her watch and groaned. "It's already ten thirty, Lucinda. I'm a farmer, remember? I need to get home. But I wanted to ask you a question before you go."

Lucinda gazed at the stage. She twiddled one long silver earring between her fingers in a fast little movement. "What is it?"

"Why did you cut out so suddenly during the dance last night? It looked like David Kosloski spoke to you and then you split. What did he say?"

"Oh, nothing. It was just about working for him." Lucinda didn't look at Cam.

"Really? It looked like you were upset by what he said."

Lucinda turned to Cam. Her eyes flashed. "Listen. You're very nice. But you've never been in trouble. You don't understand. Just leave it alone. Okay?" She gestured into the air with one hand.

"Did it have anything to do with Mike's murder? I need to know, Lucinda. It's been a week since he died. The police don't seem to be doing anything."

"Oh, they're doing something. Harassing

me is what they're doing. I think they're following me. And you know why I was late this morning?" Lucinda stuck her hands on her hips and glared at Cam. "They came and searched my apartment. Had a warrant and everything. I told them they wouldn't find nothing. In fact, I left them there, told them I had to get to the farm."

"Lucinda. You could have told me."

"Ellie was there this morning. I didn't want to get into it. I don't know what they were looking for, but I know I'm clean. I didn't kill Mike Montgomery, Cam. But they'd rather blame it on an immigrant than find out the truth."

"Pappas did say last night he thought they might be getting close. But every day that goes by, the killer is still out there. It's starting to spook my customers, and, well, funny stuff has been happening on the farm. It makes me uneasy."

"What kind of funny stuff?" Lucinda's angry look dropped away, and the glare was replaced by a look of intense curiosity.

Cam told her about the rhubarb and the arugula. "And I found this weird flashlight thing in the woods. Actually, Ellie found it. It turned out to be an infrared flashlight. You can only see the light from it if you're wearing night goggles. Who would be wearing night goggles on my property? And why?"

"Has to be that militia. Isn't that the kind of thing they do? They go around pretending they're at war. Mike could have dropped it."

"On my farm? But why? He worked there. He didn't have to skulk around at night." Cam took a deep breath. "It all makes my head swirl. Listen, I'd better get going. Go find your friend. I'll see you in a couple of days."

Lucinda nodded. "I'll come help you harvest for the market Tuesday."

"Sounds good." She watched Lucinda make her way toward the stage. Cam headed along the paved path toward her truck. The crowd had already thinned out, with parents taking tired children home and senior citizens boarding the van back to their assisted living residence. The younger adults wandered in the direction of the several bars in town.

As Cam rounded the corner of the Firehouse, she heard raised voices. She stopped still. Two figures faced each other under a tree. The direct illumination from the streetlight didn't reach under the canopy of leaves, so Cam couldn't see who they were, but she thought she recognized one of the

226

voices. It sounded like Frank Jackson. She stepped quickly behind an enclosure that had to house a trash Dumpster. Cam was fine with the smell of rotting vegetables, but the acrid tang of a chemical cleaning solution made her feel sick.

She pressed her back against the rough pickets of the stockade-fence enclosure and stuck her head out only far enough to be able to hear.

"Hush. You can't go around shouting like a crazy person," one of them whispered in a harsh tone.

Cam's arms grew a crop of goose bumps. Her eyes, adjusting to the dark, could now make out the other person's shape. It was tall and thin. Her eyes widened. A ponytail was silhouetted against a bit of light from across the street. It could belong only to Frank Jackson. What was Ruth's husband doing out here arguing with a woman?

"I just think it's time to take action," the man returned. "Why are we still messing around with plans, with surveillance?"

Yup, Frank's voice. He spoke with the kind of heavy local accent the mayor of Boston had. But who was he talking to?

"We have to be careful, Frank," the whispered voice said. "We have a plan everybody agreed on. Now, let's stick to it."

Frank shook his head. As Cam saw him turn toward her, she was horrified to feel a sneeze coming on. She made a quick decision. Stepping out from around the enclosure, she sneezed out loud and kept walking toward them as if she'd never stopped. She would never know what their plan was, but it was better than being caught snooping. She struggled to keep the surprise from her face when she saw the whisperer was Bev Montgomery.

"Hey, Frank. How's it going?" Cam kept her voice calm, level. "Hey, Bev."

"What are you doing here, Cam?" Frank's voice wasn't so calm.

Cam was about to respond when the Bev spoke.

"I'll bet she likes Cajun music, right, Cameron?" Bev mustered a smile.

"Wasn't it a great concert?"

Bev nodded. "If you like that kind of music," she added.

"You don't?" Cam asked.

"Not to speak of. I was just passing by." Bev looked at her wrist. "Getting late. I'm surprised you're not home, getting your beauty sleep, Cam. Or figuring out what to plant next. Say, do you succession plant greens? You know, like arugula?" She cocked her head at Cam.

Cam returned her gaze. Was this a message or an innocent question from a colleague? "I replant every two weeks. You?"

Bev turned away. "You think I grow those fancy greens?" She shook her head and made a sound like "sshhee." "I grow the traditional New England crops," she said, facing Cam again. "*My* customers don't want anything else."

Cam shot a glance at Frank. His hands stuffed in his pockets, he jiggled his right leg, looking away at the street.

"Well, have a nice night. See you at the market, Bev." Cam squeezed past them on the path, since neither had moved. "Say hi to Ruthie, Frank."

Bev kept her silence. Frank grunted.

After she'd walked a few yards, Cam glanced back. The two seemed to have resumed their quarrel. When Frank looked her way, Cam continued her brisk walk, hoping she'd played the innocent in a convincing fashion. So Bev thought growing varied greens was a fashion trend. *Fine. Let her.* Cam's customers loved her mesclun salad mix. But Frank? Cam worried for Ruth and her daughters' safety.

CHAPTER 13

Cam was up with the birds the next morning. She took a moment to trim fresh ends on the carnations and top up the water. That ladybug on the side was a clever touch, dressing up the metal bucket into a vase. She still couldn't figure out who had left them. She stood with hands on hips for a moment, wondering if she should worry about random flowers being delivered to her house, and then snorted at her own paranoia. How dangerous could a bunch of dianthuses be? It was probably just a misdelivered gift meant for some lucky recipient down the road, although she thought florists usually affixed their own card to a delivery.

She downed toast and coffee and strode out to the barn. A quick storm had blasted through the stalled front overnight and had shoved it out to sea. The air smelled fresh, and objects stood out with a clarity that seemed to match Cam's brain. The heavy thoughts of suspicion and worry from the week had lifted with the barometric pressure.

"It's probably temporary," Cam told Preston as he trotted along beside her. "The murder isn't solved, after all. But I'm glad to feel a little lighter this morning."

Preston stopped, sniffed the air with perked ears, and sped off into the middle of the flower garden.

Cam spent the next several hours weeding, planting, raking, doing the work of a farmer. She purposely did not think about anything except her labors.

Glancing at the angle of the sun, Cam pulled her cell phone out of her back pocket. Yup, eleven o'clock. Replacing it, she paused for a moment at the now wilting memorial to Mike. Rain had streaked Alexandra's drawing despite its clear plastic cover, and the flowers were past their prime. Cam's mood darkened again as she turned on the hose next to the hoop house and spent half an hour watering and tending the trays of starts. The lettuces, a tray each of red looseleaf, pale green butterhead, variegated summer crisp, deep green romaine, and rusty oakleaf, looked healthy for the most part, their fourth pair of true leaves already forming. Cam frowned at the tray of broccoli for the fall crop. The leaves looked too pale, and most of the seedlings weren't as big as they should be. There must be an imbalance in the starting mix, which occasionally happened. She measured nitrogen-rich fish emulsion into a watering can, filled it with water, and hand-fed the seedlings.

Cam turned off the hose. She sniffed. Fire. There was a fire somewhere. A chill ran through her. She scanned the horizon. Sure enough, smoke arose toward the south. Her throat thickened with the old panic. A vision of her ever-absent mother sprang into her mind. She worried the hem of her shorts with her right hand as she had her rag of a blanket when she was six.

A resident of the semirural community could be burning brush in their back field. Or maybe a house had caught on fire. Maybe a house with a small girl in it. She shuddered. No sirens kicked in, though. No flashing lights sped by on the road.

Cam took a deep breath. She told herself once again to get a grip. She headed toward the house for lunch and had her hand on the back door when her cell rang. She checked the display. Pressing SEND, Cam said, "Hey, Ruthie. What's up?"

"How about that walk on the beach this

afternoon? I'm off, and Frank's taking the girls to the new Muppet movie."

"Love to," Cam said. "Plum Island? Want me to pick you up on the way?"

They agreed on meeting at two o'clock, and Cam disconnected. She had just enough time to pick Sunday strawberries for Jake. She scarfed down a quick peanut-butter sandwich. Ten minutes later she was kneeling in the strawberry patch. Luckily, the season was turning out to be a good one, with the sizable patch yielding early and often. She knew Albert and Marie had had years when either the temperatures or the weather left them with pitiful picking.

The call from Ruth brought Frank to mind. The vision of him, both last night and at the festival, kept rerunning on the screen of her mind. He unsettled Cam. He had to be in the militia. And now it looked like Bev might be, too. They had talked about a plan. Frank wanted to move forward, to take action. Bev wanted to stick to what they had apparently agreed on as a group. Cam resolved to get the story from Ruth. If she even knew about it.

Waves crashed against the steep cant of the beach. Ruth and Cam trudged barefoot along the water's edge. Cam's knit skirt blew around her knees in the ocean breeze, and Ruth had rolled her pants up. Two children ran screaming with delight across their path, and a football soared overhead and then splashed in the water. On a sunny Sunday in June, after the long New England winter and cool spring, everyone wanted to be on the beach, although the water temperature was still frigid by Cam's standards.

"Sit for a minute?" Ruth said after they'd walked for half an hour.

"Sure." Cam trudged up the dry sand until she stood next to the bluff with its scrawny sea grass that looked like an old man's hair. She plopped down, her eyes on the Atlantic. A tern circled and then dive-bombed its prey, coming up with a fish wriggling for its life clamped in the narrow beak. Cam leaned back on her elbows and sighed.

Ruth sat a couple feet away from Cam, pulling up her knees and wrapping her arms around them. "Sounds like the world's on your shoulders." She peered at Cam's face under her blue hat.

"Wouldn't you feel burdened if a man had been killed on your property and the killer was still out there walking around?"

"I'm in the business, remember? Some murders get solved. Some don't."

"Can you at least tell me what's happening? Is Pappas getting anywhere?" Cam cleared her throat when she heard how whiny her voice sounded.

"They're not really telling me much. I'm back to the work of Westbury's finest. You know, speed traps, checking lapsed inspection stickers, doing the D.A.R.E. program at the Page School. Really exciting police work." Ruth removed her sun visor, wiped her forehead, and replaced it.

"I guess I'll have to give our esteemed detective a call and see if he'll tell me anything." Cam shoved her toes into the dry sand and wiggled them in the warmth, soaking up the summery feeling. "So I saw Frank last night."

"Yeah, he was out." Ruth watched a seagull trying to drag lunch out of an abandoned knapsack. "Where'd you see him?"

"Near the Firehouse. I went to the outdoor concert with Lucinda. Frank was talking with Bev Montgomery. It sounded like they were arguing about some plan. Why would they be arguing?"

It was Ruth's turn to sigh. "You don't really want to know."

"I do. Does it have to do with the tattoo on his arm?"

Ruth nodded without meeting Cam's eyes. "He's gotten deeper and deeper into the Patriotic Militia. I think it's awful." She turned to Cam. "They're nut jobs, all of them. But it's not illegal." She spread her hands. "Until they carry out an illegal action, that is."

"Has he always been part of the group?"

Ruth shook her head. "Not when we got married. As far as I know, I mean. We've just kind of slid apart since then, though. I don't really have a handle on how it happened, Cammie. I guess I've been so busy with my own career. That and the girls."

"You didn't take his last name. Did that bother him?"

Ruth nodded with a fierce motion. "You bet. What made it worse was that we had daughters. We'd agreed to give sons Frank's last name, Jackson, and to give girls mine. When the twins were born, though, he wasn't very happy about the decision."

"What does Frank do for work?"

"He's a carpenter. He's a very skilled cabinetmaker, but lately he's just been working on houses with another guy. Who I think is also in the militia." Ruth shook her head. "He's not bringing in much money, either."

"Lucinda told me the militia is very anti-immigrant. Do you share those views?"

Ruth snorted. "Of course not. I almost wish they'd do something illegal so we could break them up."

Something illegal would mean Ruth might have to arrest her own husband. Cam picked up a handful of sand and let it stream slowly through her fingers. "That disk I found in my hoop house. The PM must be for Patriotic Militia."

Ruth nodded. "I didn't want to tell you."

"Were there fingerprints on it?"

"I haven't heard. Pappas is keeping a lot to himself."

"If Mike was a member, maybe he just dropped it in the hoop house. Right?"

"Could be." Ruth sat up straight and crossed her legs. She dusted the sand and talk of militias from her hands. "How about lunch? How does Greek salad sound?"

"Excellent. All I ate today was toast and peanut butter."

"And we have a fine red wine to wash lunch down with. Speaking of illegal." She glanced around and clicked her tongue. "I don't see any authorities, do you?"

"Not a one."

"I'm warning you, it's a nonlocal salad." Ruth held up her hands. "Don't shoot me!"

Cam laughed. She'd had enough with

serious talk for today. "Forget those loca-vores. I love their business, but they take themselves a little too seriously."

Ruth handed Cam a plastic container and a fork, then unscrewed the top of a wine bottle and poured red wine into two red plastic beer cups. She took another salad and fork out of her pack and put the bottle back in.

"Here's to old friends." Cam held the cup up.

Ruth tapped it with her own. "Friendship all the way."

The ocean sparkled, the sun shone, and the company excelled. In the back of Cam's mind, though, thoughts of murder never left. She wondered if Frank was the killer, or somebody else in the militia. But Mike had also been in the militia. Frank wouldn't have had cause to kill him. Would he?

Cam shook her head, as if to shake those thoughts out and let them vanish on the breeze. She was on the beach with a good friend on a lovely afternoon. That should be enough. For now.

Glancing at her watch, Cam rang the bell of The Market's back door again. It was already five o'clock, later than she had planned. The beach lunch and walk had stretched out, and the time had gotten away from her.

"There you are." Jake had opened the door. He held it, frowning at Cam. "I thought you'd be here earlier."

"I did too. Sorry, Jake. I have your berries, though." Sun and wind still warmed her cheeks, and sand crunched between her toes.

"I thought I was going to be making a reduction with them a couple of hours ago." He folded his arms.

"I hope I didn't ruin your menu for the evening." This was the first time Cam had seen Jake upset with her, instead of his usual smiling and flirting self. A man that big being mad was a little intimidating. "I was walking on the beach with a friend. And then the traffic leaving the beach was horrendous. Do you want the berries?"

He sighed. "Of course I do." He propped open the restaurant door with a nearby concrete block.

Cam led the way to the truck, glad she'd laid the boxes of berries in her big cooler with cold packs. They wouldn't have fared well sitting in a hot truck for hours in the beach parking lot. Jake hoisted the cooler and carried it into the kitchen.

"Are you eating here tonight?" Jake asked

as he unloaded the boxes.

Cam stretched and yawned. "No, I don't think so. I had a late lunch. . . ."

"On the beach. With your friend." Jake turned to Cam. "What's his name?" His gaze was level and somber.

Cam returned the look. "His name?"

Jake turned away again. "Maybe we'd better cancel that dinner for tomorrow night, Cameron."

"What?" Cam was speechless, or almost. Then it hit her. She laughed. "Who do you think I was on the beach with?" The man was jealous. She couldn't believe it.

"I'm sure I don't know, and it's none of my business. You show up late. Your cheeks are all rosy. I just assume you were on a date."

Cam reached for Jake's arm. "Listen. I was walking with my old friend Ruth Dodge. My cheeks are rosy because it was sunny and windy and I forgot to reapply sunscreen. And I want to cook dinner for you tomorrow. All right?" She tugged on his sleeve until he faced her. "Okay?"

He nodded, the little crinkly lines around his eyes back again. "I'll be there. And, Cam?"

"Yes?"

"I'm just a regular old stupid male." He

raised his eyebrows in a sheepish look.

"It's cool, Jake. I'm going to head home. See you tomorrow at six?"

"Six."

As Cam drove home, though, she wondered if it was cool, after all. Was Jake just being a stupid male, and should she be flattered by his jealousy? Or maybe she just shouldn't mix work with pleasure. Cam didn't need any more complications in her life. But life wasn't simple. That much she knew.

She climbed the back steps of her house to find Preston waiting on the landing. He posed like the Sphinx next to the flowering shrub with its dainty pink blossoms and gracefully bowed branches.

"Hey, Mr. P. What's up? Didn't want to use the cat door?" She leaned down to pet him. "Well, come on in the people door. I know I'm spoiling you, but why the heck not? That's what I say." Cam unlocked the door and let them both in. She left the inner door open so the breeze could blow through the screen door, but she made sure to lock it. Not that an old wood-framed screen door would keep anybody out who wanted to get in. It was hard to imagine anyone forcing their way in on such a lovely summer afternoon, though.

The message light on the phone was blinking. Cam dialed the message number and listened. It was Detective Pappas, asking her to call. He sounded impatient and said he had also called her cell. Cam dug her cell phone out of her bag. Sure enough, the little message icon had appeared on the screen. It must have been while she was on the beach. She'd left her bag and phone locked in the truck.

She dialed Pappas's number, but it was his turn not to pick up, so she left a message that she was returning his call. She topped up Preston's food and refilled his water bowl. He turned his large eyes up to her and mewed. She petted him a few strokes while he ate. Such a funny cat.

After Cam stowed the salmon fillet she'd picked up on the way home in the fridge, she wandered into the living room with the Sunday paper. The end-of-day sun slanted on the old floorboards like a splash of amber paint. She stretched out on the couch and began, as she had since childhood, with the comics.

Cam started awake. It was dark. Disoriented, she rubbed her eyes and sat up. The newspaper slid from her lap onto the floor with a gentle whoosh. She glanced into the kitchen, where the LED on the stove shone its blue-green time into the dimness. Eight thirty. She must have needed to catch up on sleep.

Cam switched on the lamp and retrieved the jumbled sections of paper. The Metro-North section was on top. She straightened it out. The second headline down on the right caught her eye.

POLICE STYMIED IN FARM MURDER.

Cam groaned. Now it was the Farm Murder, and the story shouted out to the greater Boston area that hers was the farm. She read on.

"Well, at least they say I'm cooperating." Cam snorted. "Of course I'm cooperating!" *But you haven't solved it,* she reminded herself. She threw the section on the floor and got up. She was about to hit the computer when she realized how hungry she was. The lunch on the beach had been a long time ago.

She fixed herself a grilled ham and cheese and took it to the computer table with a glass of milk. She checked her e-mail. Alexandra had written, with a subject line of "Web site up and running. Please check."

Cam smiled. She clicked the link in the message, which was attached to Alexandra's name, and there it was. Produce Plus Plus Farm. The young woman had done a stellar job. Cam clicked through the pages, jotting down a few notes about minor things for Alexandra to fix.

She opened the file she'd named Find-TheKiller. Her spreadsheet stared at her. Was there anything new she could add since Saturday? *Sure.* Frank was definitely in the militia. And it looked like Bev was, too. Cam tapped in the information. *What else?* She hadn't added the disk in the hoop house and its connection with the Patriotic Militia, so that went in, too.

She couldn't think of anything else to add. She ran her script. The graphic display now had a connection between the Patriotic Militia and her hoop house. But if the connection had a relationship to the killer, the screen wasn't saying. She leaned back in the chair with her hands behind her head, trying to remember what Lucinda had said. An important person in the area was also undocumented, and maybe Mike had been blackmailing him or threatening to go public with the information. Cam didn't know who it could be, though. She hadn't been around long enough to know the important people in town. And would an important person go so far as to kill Mike to keep him quiet? According to Lucinda and Ruth, that wouldn't work, since there were plenty of others in the group who also knew.

Cam saved the files and shut down the computer. No way of solving this tonight, that was certain. She was surprised Pappas hadn't returned her call. Maybe the guy actually had a life. Too bad it didn't include actually solving murders.

CHAPTER 14

Cam worked hard all Monday morning to make up for taking the afternoon off the day before. It was sticky again today. She found herself stopping frequently to wipe her forehead with the sleeve of her T-shirt. The leaves on the trees were still. No breeze buffered the brunt of the sun.

The season was picking up. The farm had had regular rains mixed in with lots of sun and long days. Plants loved this weather, even today's heat and humidity, and it showed. All plants loved it. Cam grunted as she hauled a garden cart full of weeds to the compost pile. Weeds sprouted and grew even faster than the crops.

She took a shade break at the desk in the back of the barn, where she kept her planting and harvesting record book. It was Albert's system, but it was a good one, albeit being on paper and not in digital form. She planned to enter everything into her farming software next winter, when she had time. For now, there was nothing wrong with a good old ledger book. She checked her planting schedule and hoped those beans she'd ordered would come in the day's mail. It wouldn't do to get behind schedule on an item as popular as skinny green beans.

As Cam went back outside, she thought about Stuart Wilson and how oddly he'd acted last week. Getting all in a huff on Volunteer Day, when Cam had gotten upset with him about destroying the beans, even though her reaction might have been a bit too strong. Getting drunk at the festival and harassing Alexandra about her sister. And even acting strange when Cam had asked him about Lucinda on Saturday. She shook her head. It really wasn't her problem. If he showed up on Wednesday again, she'd make sure she kept an eye on him.

When Cam popped into the house for a late lunch break, she checked her voice mail. A message from one of her subscribers dismayed her.

"We've decided to cancel our subscription because of the recent difficulties," the woman's voice stated with an apologetic tinge. "We'd appreciate having our share price returned, but understand that we're past the reimbursement period. We just don't feel safe having an association with your farm any longer."

Cam slammed her fist on the desk. Down to twenty-eight subscriptions. She couldn't afford to reimburse these people — she'd already spent the money. The murder was taking its toll on her business.

Ellie arrived right on time for her locavore badge session. All day Cam had found herself looking forward to working with the girl again. Cam, just coming out of the barn with a basket, waved at the SUV as David turned and drove down the driveway.

"How's it going, kiddo?" Cam said without thinking and then realized saying "kiddo" made her sound like an old lady, or worse, like her father.

"Meh."

"Meh? What's going on?" Ellie was not the sunny self Cam had seen in their previous encounters. "Why don't you tell me while we head out back?"

"I don't know. This kid at school? Jason? He's always talking about, like, illegal aliens and stuff. Like immigrants are from other planets." Ellie kicked a stick in the path.

So anti-immigration prejudice had filtered down to the eighth grade. No surprise, really. Cam waited.

"So I go, 'Immigrants are people, too.' And he's all, like, 'Dirty Polack.' " Ellie looked up at Cam, frowning. "What's up with that, right? It's, like, unless he's Native American himself, his relatives who came here were immigrants, too."

"Correct. What do your teachers say?"

"Oh, this is lunchroom stuff. He wouldn't dare say it in history class. Mr. Fitz would have his . . . I mean, he'd, you know, get in trouble."

"Is your family Polish?"

"Yeah. My dad's first generation. He came over to work with his uncle in construction and then, like, just stayed. My mom's family's Polish, too, but they've been here for a while. Her name is Dabrowski. Mom and Dad used to live in Chicago. You know, before me."

Cam remembered being fourteen. It had seemed like time before she had existed was time before reality. "How about we tie up tomatoes today? You can almost see them grow, they're going up so fast. I'll show you how to prune them to two leaders."

"What's a tomato leader?" Ellie looked puzzled, but at least she didn't look down in the dumps anymore.

"This kind of tomato, called an indeterminate, keeps growing and bears fruit as long as it can. Here in northern Massachusetts, that means until the frost in the fall. We get more fruit —"

"Don't you mean tomatoes?"

Cam laughed. "Well, sure. We just refer to them as bearing fruit. And, actually, a tomato *is* a fruit, botanically, because it has seeds. I think the definition is 'a flowering ovary.' I know people commonly think of fruit as sweet and vegetables as not sweet, but botany is different. Ask your science teacher sometime."

"I will. So peppers and eggplants and cucumbers, they're all fruit?"

Cam nodded. "And squash and beans, too."

"Solid."

"Anyway, if we prune the tomato plants to just two stalks — that's what a leader is — we get a bigger yield than if we let every growing tip take off. It's neater and easier to harvest, too, rather than having them sprawl all over the ground."

"Wow. Wait'll I tell Ashley."

"Friend of yours?"

Ellie nodded. "She wants to be a food scientist. She's in Scouts, too. Can I bring her with me next week?"

"If she'll work, I'll take her."

Cam showed Ellie what to do, handing her a pair of scissors and the string. They worked side by side in silence, snipping off tips that weren't the leaders, tying the unruly tops to their stakes.

"I'm glad you stood up to that boy," Cam said. "What was his name? James?"

"Jason." Ellie sat back on her heels. "He even said he'd heard my dad was illegal. I told him no possible way that was true. But he said his dad was in a, like, militia, and they knew who around here was illegal. He said Daddy was going to be in trouble, that they were going to make him go back."

Another militia member. "What did your dad say?"

Ellie frowned. "I didn't tell him. He's been kind of funny lately. Sort of, you know, like he's thinking about something important. Jason's lying. Why should I bother Dad about that?"

David Kosloski was a well-established businessman in town, with his own construction firm. He was married to an American. He couldn't be here illegally. Could he?

Cam checked the timer. Two more minutes for the pie. She checked her list. The baby mixed greens sat ready in the three-wood

Costa Rican salad bowl her parents had given her, violets scattered over the top. The salmon fillet was marinating in her special soy-ginger-lime mix. The strawberry-rhubarb pie was almost done. She'd boil water for pasta at the last moment, while she grilled the salmon. She planned to toss the gemelli with pesto frozen from last summer and top it with freshly grated Parmesan. A simple and delicious dinner. No way could she compete with Jake's expertise, so why try?

When the timer dinged, Cam pulled the pie out of the oven and let it rest, glad she'd thought to buy rhubarb from Green Spring Farm on her way home the day before. She stirred sugar into sour cream and spooned it carefully on top. She tried to steady her hand when she noticed it shaking. Sure, she was a little nervous. Not only was tonight a date with a man she liked, but it was a dinner for a chef.

"That's why I'm producing only dishes I know I can do well, right, Preston?" Cam slid the pie back in the oven and set the timer for seven minutes as Preston rubbed his head against her knee. She glanced at the table. A simple white cloth, the bucket of carnations, Marie's rose china, pink cloth napkins under the silver, a bottle of Mill

River Winery Naked Chardonnay in a chilled wine cooler. *Oops.* Candles. Cam rummaged in the hutch until she found two glass candlesticks and two red candles. Oh, well, they matched the color scheme close enough. She set them up and checked the time. Six o'clock. Jake should be here any minute.

Striding into the living room, Cam smoothed down a stray lock of hair as she checked her appearance once more in the tall oval mirror. She'd picked a gauzy pale blue Indian blouse that set off her eyes and white capri pants. The tiny bells on her silver Indian earrings jingled when she moved her head. Of course, she'd rolled the sleeves of the blouse up for cooking, and a drop of strawberry juice had landed on the pants, near her knee, which kind of spoiled the look. Cam knew she wasn't a style setter. If Jake was going to be involved with her, he'd have to learn that this was what he was going to get.

When the timer rang again, Cam dashed back to the kitchen and carefully extracted the pie, setting it on a wire rack to cool.

She looked down at Preston. "Don't you get any ideas about licking the sour cream off the top of that, sir." He only occasionally made his way onto the countertop, and this would be a particularly inopportune time to do it. Cam rummaged in the lower cupboards until she found an extra-large colander. She turned it over and covered the pie. A proper farmhouse would have had a pie keep. If Marie had had one of the cupboards with doors made of perforated metal, it was long gone now.

Cam made her way outdoors to wait in a lawn chair under the tree. A breeze that had sprung up brought the tang of fresh-cut grass. A mosquito keened near her ear and earned a slap. It was still a couple of hours until sunset. This one must have been extra hungry. She closed her eyes, trying to still her mind. A motorcycle sped by on the road. The leaves rustled in the tree above her, and a branch rubbed against another.

She got up and wandered over to the flower garden, which was in its purple phase. The Japanese irises. The pointy stalks of lupines. The delicate columbines. Cam bent over and pulled a few weeds. While she was at it, she deadheaded several of the narcissus that had gone by, a task Marie had taught her on one of Cam's first visits to the farm, twisting off the little bulging bulb where the flower had been. "The energy has to go back into the bulb in the ground and nourish it, so it will flower next year, too," Marie had said.

Cam looked back at the yard, glad she'd taken twenty minutes to mow it earlier. It made everything look tidier, nicer, even the peeling paint on the back of the house. But where was Jake? It had to be almost six-thirty. Maybe he'd had an accident. Maybe he forgot. Or maybe he thought fashionably late was cool. She realized she didn't really know if he was habitually late or not. She didn't know much about him at all, for that matter. Cam dusted her hands on her pants, as was her habit.

"Oh, rats," she said as she looked down. She didn't usually wear white for precisely this reason. A dusting of dirt now decorated the outer seam of both pant legs.

Just then a Cooper Mini with the top down pulled into the drive. There he was. Just in time to see her ruined outfit. Cam watched Jake unfold himself out of the tiny convertible. He wore ivory linen slacks with black sandals and a loose silk shirt in a bold print with blocks of black, red, and ivory tumbling every which way. To Cam's eyes, he looked relaxed and stylish. And sexy.

"Sorry I'm late," he called, waving a floral wrap full of flowers. He leaned into the backseat and emerged with the other arm tucked around a bottle of wine and a paper bag. A CD was clamped under his chin, preventing him from straightening all the way. "Help?"

Cam laughed. She relieved him of the CD, and then of the flowers when he extended them to her. "Thanks." She peered into the wrap and said, "Awww, Jake." It was dozens of pink and white carnations. "How did you know?"

"Know what?" He had the audacity to wink at her. "That you like carnations? Maybe I'm just a good judge of character."

"I guess. Anyway, thanks."

Jake assumed a stern look. "They're not local, you know."

Cam shook her head, gesturing around her with the CD. "I live, breathe, and eat local. Mostly. I don't need flowers from my dinner guest to be local, too. They're beautiful, by the way. And they happen to look great for at least a couple of weeks. It's funny. A big bunch of carnations was left here a couple of days ago. Would that have been from you, too?"

Jake's face darkened. "No, it wouldn't have happened to have been me. The competition again? What's his name?"

"Don't be silly. It was probably one of my customers." But if not Jake, she had no idea who could have left them. "So what's in the bag?"

Jake held out the paper bag. "I brought just one little contribution. An appetizer, only."

Cam wrinkled her nose. "Oh, right." *Appetizers.* She glanced up at Jake. His dark expression turned to hurt. "I mean, thank you! I totally forgot about appetizers. And I really appreciate it."

Jake's face relaxed. "I just made simple pastries stuffed with crab and truffles."

Yeah, simple, thought Cam. "What a treat," she said. "Come on in." She led the way into the house, her body aware of his following her.

Cam laid the flowers next to the sink, then drew two slender wineglasses out of the fridge. "Chardonnay okay to start? We'll have what you brought with dinner."

"Lovely."

Cam poured the wine and handed Jake his glass. "Here's to summer. Less than two weeks to the solstice."

"To summer." Jake clinked his glass with hers and sipped. "Delicious. It'll be perfect with the pastries. Give me a cookie sheet and an oven, and I'll just crisp them up."

After directing Jake to what he needed, Cam leaned her elbows back on the counter and watched him work. His ample body and energy filled the room. He glanced over once and smiled.

After he closed the oven door, Jake examined the timer on the stove and, apparently being a quick study, set it for ten minutes. He washed his hands. "Now, a wine opener. I want to let the red breathe."

The man was all business. Cam handed him the corkscrew. While he opened the red wine, she clipped the ends of the flowers and arranged them in a heavy glass vase then placed it on the table, shifting the bucket of flowers to the table near the door. She remembered to roll down her sleeves and smooth them out.

Jake set the bottle on the counter and turned to her. "There," he said. He gazed at Cam, taking in her face, her outfit, her feet — thank goodness for the red nail polish she'd unearthed in her cabinet — like he was hungry for more than dinner.

The blush tiptoed its way up her neck.

"You look fabulous, Cam. The perfect summer hostess."

Cam snorted. "Yeah, perfect." She shook her head, then gestured to her now less than white pants.

"Well, a hostess who can not only cook but can also grow the dinner, no? That's a good thing, that little bit of dirt." Jake picked up his glass and, with a seductive look in his eyes, sidled over next to Cam, leaning one elbow on the counter so he faced her. "What's on the menu, Madame Chef?"

His heat. His delicious scent. His ice-blue eyes boring into hers. She felt a little dizzy and a little damp.

The timer went off.

"Ah, saved by the bell!" Jake said as he left her side and busied himself finding a plate and a spatula, sliding the pastry cups — now tipped with a light toast color — onto the plate, offering it to Cam with a flourish.

Saved by the bell was right.

A couple of hours later Cameron took the last bite of her pie.

"That was splendid, Cameron. I must have the recipe." Jake pushed back from the table a little and patted his stomach. "What a meal."

Cam nodded, taking a sip of coffee. The pasta and salmon had been a success, and Jake had exclaimed repeatedly about the freshness of the salad. Cam had promised him as many greens as she could cut as soon as they were ready in quantity, and had made a note to herself to feed the lettuce seedlings the next morning so they stayed healthy.

"Thanks for bringing the crab thingies. They were divine."

Jake laughed with gusto. "Thingies? A technical term among farmers?" He reached across the table and squeezed her hand.

Cam sputtered as she blushed. "Hey, you're the chef. What do you call them, anyway?"

"Crab-truffle thingies." He wiped the smile off his face but not out of his eyes. "I put them on the menu every other week. They even got a thumbs-up from the reviewer last month. 'The crab thingies were divine' was in the second paragraph of the review." Jake broke down and let the laughter out until he cried.

Cam tsk-tsked, protesting, "I'll bet you wouldn't have the slightest idea what the beneficial parasite that colonizes tomato hornworms is called, so there."

Jake wiped his eyes with his napkin, the hilarity apparently subsiding. "No, my dear, I wouldn't. But you know what else I brought besides thingies?"

"A CD."

"Righto. I'm going to clear here, and then I want to put on a particular CD for you.

No, don't get up," he said as Cam started to rise. "Let me do it. You worked hard all day. I had the day off, remember?"

Cam didn't remember the last time someone cleared the table for her, but decided to sit back and enjoy being waited on. Jake's big hands made short work of it. He wandered into the living room.

"Need help with the stereo?" Cam called.

"Nah, I was an AV geek back in the old country," Jake called. He had told Cam during dinner that he'd come to the States from Sweden with his family when he was sixteen. His parents and younger brother had gone back after two years, but Jake had stayed.

The house was suddenly filled with music that sounded both Caribbean and African. The beat was catchy and regular. Jake reemerged from the living room. Bowing to Cam, he took her hand.

"May I have this dance, miss?" He pulled her to her feet.

"Wait a minute. I told you I don't dance." Cam pulled her hand back, but he didn't let go.

"Ah, but you agreed to dance in private. I don't see anyone else here, do you?"

"You win. But don't complain if I step on your toe." Cam shook her head in mock frustration. "Wait one second." She blew out the candles. "Never leave a room with a lit candle in it" was one of her mantras.

Cam let Jake lead her into the living room. He'd pushed aside the coffee table and the easy chair so they had an open space. A small lamp was the only light. It washed the room in a warm glow that didn't quite reach into the dark corners.

Jake put Cam's left hand on his shoulder, placed his right hand deliciously on her waist, and took her right hand lightly in his left. Before she could blink, they were dancing. Somehow he managed to steer her around, so it even seemed like she was following his lead, a skill she'd never been particularly good at.

The song changed, but it was the same upbeat kind of music, and Cam made it through another dance without kicking Jake in the shin or otherwise harming him. It was a magical feeling for a tall woman like Cam to feel light on her feet and in perfect sync with an even taller man, one she'd never experienced before.

The next song was much slower. Jake pulled her in close. His feet slowed. It was even easier to follow him now. The smooth silk of his shirt cooled Cam's now burning cheek. His own cheek pressed lightly on her head. They swayed and turned. Cam's body came alive and was exquisitely sensitive from the top of her head all the way down to her gaudily painted toes. But especially in the middle.

When the song ended, Jake pulled apart just enough to see her face. "See? You can dance." His voice was husky.

Cam reached her left hand around the back of his neck and pulled his face close to hers. "I guess I've never danced with a man who knew what he was doing." She was angling up to kiss him when the phone's shrill ring broke their bubble.

"Ignore it," he whispered, his lips an inch from hers. His heart beat fast next to hers.

The phone kept ringing. It was the house phone, not her cell. Few people knew the number. Cam looked into Jake's eyes. She let go of his neck and slid out of his embrace.

"I'm sorry," Cam said over her shoulder on her way into the kitchen. "Almost nobody knows my number. It's got to be important."

"Yeah. Or a Monday night telemarketer," Jake muttered.

Cam picked up the phone and said hello. She listened. Her eyes shifted to Jake. "Arrested? That's crazy!"

Jake's eyes widened. He walked over to

Cam and put his hand on her shoulder.

"Sure, I'll find a lawyer for you. I'll be over soon. Hang in there. We'll get you out. They can't hold you if you didn't do it." Cam listened. "Okay. Don't worry." She slammed the phone on the counter.

Jake gave Cam's shoulder a gentle squeeze. "Who's been arrested? What can I do to help?"

Cam faced Jake. "It's Lucinda. They arrested her for Mike's murder!"

CHAPTER 15

Jake froze. His face paled.

"I have to find her a lawyer," Cam said, frowning. "Poor Lucinda. This is just what she was afraid of. She's not exactly here legally, and she thinks if she even talks to the police, she'll be deported." Cam had a quick moment of remorse, wondering if she should be sharing Lucinda's status and fears with Jake.

"She probably will be." Jake's voice was low, ominous.

"That's ridiculous. She hasn't done anything wrong. This is all a big mistake." Cam turned back to the phone. "I'll call Uncle Albert. He'll know a lawyer." She pressed his number. "Poor Lucinda," Cam repeated as she waited. "Come on, Albert. Pick up." Cam paced into the kitchen and back.

"Uncle Albert. Hi. Do you know of a good lawyer?"

Albert asked her if she was in trouble.

"No, not for me. My friend, my customer Lucinda, she's been arrested for Mike Montgomery's murder."

"Well, isn't that something. Wait a minute while I find my address book."

When he came back on the line, Cam wrote down the number and thanked him, then hung up. She looked around. Where was Jake?

He emerged from the living room, closing the case on his CD. "I have to go, Cam."

Cam frowned. "You do? Just like that?"

"I need to. Tomorrow I have to . . ." Jake spread his hands open. "You've got a lot to do. I don't want you to have to worry about me, too." His expression was stern, but his eyes shifted around the room like a trapped animal's. "Call me later to tell me how it went."

Cam sighed. "Okay." She shrugged. The entire universe had changed course. They'd been a millimeter and a millisecond away from becoming intimate, and now he was running off. So be it.

"Thanks for dinner." Jake leaned in and kissed her on the cheek as if she was his sister. "I'll call you soon. Good luck with Lucinda."

And then he was gone.

Cam shook her head to clear it. She

pictured Lucinda in a jail cell and shuddered. She dialed the lawyer, a Susan Lee. This woman had better be a magician.

Cam knocked on the glass door of the Westbury Public Safety Complex fifteen minutes later. She tried the handle again. It was still locked. She swore. Stepping back a few paces, she scanned the front of the building with its two matching gabled roofs that mimicked the neighboring antique colonial homes along Main Street. Why a little town like Westbury thought it needed an edifice with an exalted name like the Public Safety Complex was beyond her. People used to just call them police stations and fire stations. And the public wasn't very safe when a citizen couldn't even gain access at nine o'clock on a Monday night.

She approached the door again and pressed her nose against the glass. All she could see was a long hall illuminated only by ceiling-mounted red exit signs every few yards.

"Please come around to the back door," a tinny, disembodied voice said.

Cam yelped and jumped back. Where had it come from? Then she noticed a speaker set into the stone facade. Under it was a small unlit brass sign. Cam peered at it.

AFTER 8:00 PM VISITORS ARE REQUIRED TO ENTER BY THE BACK DOOR.

Nice. She'd missed it completely.

Cam waved at the hidden camera, wherever it was, and trudged around the left side of the building. The right side housed the fire engine bays. Just in case an alarm sounded, she did not intend to be run down as they sped to their firefighting duties.

She rounded the second corner of the complex. Now she was getting somewhere. The back of the building featured a spotlight and a window set into the wall next to a door. Half a dozen navy blue Westbury squad cars were lined up in a neat row. Cam peered in the window. A space of several feet separated her from an inner window that led to a lit office. Another disembodied voice spoke, but this one seemed to correspond to the seated person behind the second window.

"Can I help you?"

Cam didn't see any particular place where she should direct her voice, so she just stood in place and spoke. "I'm Cameron Flaherty of Attic Hill Road. My friend has been arrested. Lucinda DaSilva. It's all a mistake. I'd like to see her, please. Her lawyer is on her way."

There was no answer. Cam saw the person

who had spoken to her turn and consult with another officer in the room.

A car peeled into the driveway and screeched to a stop. Cam turned to look. Out of a white Jaguar unfolded a woman as tall as Cam, in a gray suit jacket and a tight pencil skirt. Her hair was platinum and flouncy. A red leather case swung from her shoulder as she strode toward Cam on red three-inch heels that would have looked right at home on a glamorous 1930s movie star.

If this was Susan Lee, Cam was glad she didn't have to oppose her.

"Cameron Flaherty?" the woman said in a deep, throaty voice as she approached.

Cam nodded.

"Susan Lee, attorney. I got here as soon as I could." She extended her hand toward Cam.

Cam shook it. "Thanks so much for coming. I know it's just a mistake. Lucinda would never hurt anyone." She gazed at Susan, who was taller than Cam with those heels, and realized with a shock that the lawyer had to be in her sixties. Her big hair surrounded big features, with a full mouth accentuated by lipstick matching her bag and shoes. Cam didn't see a blouse under the jacket, the top button of which just covered Susan's cleavage. Still, her skin had the quality of parchment, and deep lines around her mouth and eyes gave away her age.

"Listen. Your friend isn't in good shape, being accused of murder. But I'm going to do what I can. And any friend of Al's is a friend of mine."

"Al? My great-uncle Albert?" Cam had never known Albert to put up with anyone calling him Al. "He doesn't really know Lucinda."

"Doesn't matter. You're her friend, and you're his great-niece. That's good enough for me."

"How do you know Albert?"

Susan laughed heartily. "Our mothers were good friends. He used to babysit me. He'd sneak Marie in when they were courting, and I'd feel like I was their little daughter for the evening."

Cam had trouble imagining Susan Lee ever being little.

"Al's a good man. I'd do anything for him." She cleared her throat. "Now, they might not even let you into the station, and if they do, they probably won't let you see your friend. But let's give it a try."

With that, she rapped on the window. "Susan A. Lee, attorney at law. Here about the DaSilva arrest," she declared in a loud and clear voice.

Almost instantly the door buzzed. "Just follow me," Susan said as she pulled the door open. "Once you're in, it's harder for them to get rid of you."

Cam followed. She stood behind Susan at an inner door in a lobby, glad the lawyer knew where to go and how to get what she wanted. The door buzzed, and Cam pushed through it behind Susan.

Facing them was a four-foot-high partition with a flat countertop. Cam realized this was the inner room she'd seen from the double window. A row of benches lined the wall opposite the counter, with a man and a woman the only occupants. The woman's eyes were red-lined. Tiny shreds of the tissue she worked between her fingers floated to the linoleum floor. The man scowled, arms crossed over his chest. Cam looked closely. It was Howard Fisher, the farmer from the market.

Susan laid an elbow on the counter. "Evening, Ottie. How are you, Officer Dodge?"

Cam looked up. *Officer Dodge?* "Hi, Ruth." Cam waved. She thought it prudent to leave the nickname Ruthie for when her friend was off duty.

Ruth gave a little wave back and nodded at Susan.

The woman Susan had addressed as Ottie sat at a bank of monitors and a microphone. She nodded at Susan but kept her eyes on her screens. A well-padded woman of about Susan's age, she also wore a headset. Her uniform looked different from Ruth's, with a white blouse, black slacks, and some insignia on the breast pocket. Ruth wore the full navy blue officer outfit Cam had seen her in the night of the murder.

Ruth approached the counter. "Good evening, Counselor. What can I help you with?"

Clearly Susan was known here. Cam hoped that was good.

"I have been retained to represent Lucinda DaSilva. I believe you are holding her here. I'd like to see her as soon as possible. Her friend, Ms. Flaherty, would also like to pay her a visit."

Strain pulled at the edges of Ruth's eyes. "Ms. Lee, Ms. DaSilva is being questioned at present. I'll contact Detective Pappas and let him know you are here." She turned to Cam. "I'm sorry. I can't let you see Lucinda now, Cam."

It looked to Cam like Ruth was torn between her duty to her job and her wish to

272

help out an old friend. Cam knew which would win out but thought she'd push just a little. "If I wait, can I see her when all this is done?"

Just then an inner door opened. Chief Frost walked through it with his arm around the shoulders of a thin young man, a boy, really. Cam did a double take. It was Vince, the kid who had delivered the manure a few days earlier. He looked both miserable and sullen. Cam hadn't realized he was Howard Fisher's son when he delivered the manure from Howard's Green Spring Farm.

"Here he is. I had to ticket him, and it's going to have an impact on his insurance. You can pick up the car at the tow lot tomorrow. They only take cash, mind you."

Howard stood and stuck his face in his son's. "What do you think you were doing, speeding in that wreck of yours?" His voice boomed in the enclosed space.

"The fact that the vehicle was unregistered is very serious, too," Chief Frost added.

"I'm going to . . . ," Howard sputtered.

The woman stood and grabbed her husband's arm. "Howard, this is no time for that. Vince, sweetie, we're very disappointed. But we're all going home now, and we'll decide as a family what to do." She ushered out the men in her family, one on each side, obviously experienced at keeping them apart.

Susan turned to Cam. "Why don't you go home? I'm expecting to have Lucinda out of here within an hour or two, but if I don't, it could be a long wait. I'll call you to come and get her then, shall I?"

Cam nodded. "Tell her I was here. And that I'll come get her no matter what time it is."

Susan agreed, then greeted Chief Frost. After Ruth updated him, Susan followed Ruth into the interior of the station.

"So, looks like we finally caught the farm killer, Ms. Flaherty." Chief Frost leaned on the counter. "Doesn't that make you feel safer?"

"Lucinda didn't kill anyone, Chief. You totally have the wrong person in there."

"Evidence suggests the contrary, ma'am."

"What evidence?"

"Sorry. I'm not at liberty to say."

"But it's my farm!" Cam laid both hands on her side of the counter.

"Can't help you there. It will all come out in due time."

She sighed and turned to leave.

"Oh, by the way, Detective Pappas is going to want to ask you more questions. But it's getting late tonight. You go on home.

He'll call you in the morning."

Cam reversed her steps slowly, giving the Fisher family plenty of time to leave. She was suddenly drained, and not just because she'd been up and working since five thirty in the morning. The vision of Lucinda being grilled by Pappas, or alone in a jail cell, filled Cam with trepidation. She pictured the INS speeding here to start Lucinda's deportation, her friend's worst fear. Could Susan really get Lucinda out? Chief Frost had sounded so certain about the evidence. If only Cam could find out what it was, she might have a chance to save her friend.

Out in the cool night air, she took a deep breath. It wasn't going to help Lucinda for her to be feeling sad and helpless. She strode to her truck. Climbing in, she slammed the door with a satisfying thunk. *Take that, you real killer, wherever you are.* Cam was going to find him, or her, if it was the last thing she did. Not only Lucinda's honor, but also that of the farm, was at stake. She'd already lost two shareholders' business and likely the confidence of more.

An insistent mockingbird woke Cam with its calls through the open window. She was in the middle of a dream having something to do with a Thai opera and a scrumptious buffet luncheon presided over by Johnny Depp. She had just helped herself to a plate of pad thai and delectable-looking spring rolls, and Johnny Depp had invited her to sit next to him. She desperately wanted to stay asleep and in the dream.

The bird kept on singing all the tunes in its repertoire. "Show-off." Cam groaned, dragging the extra pillow over her head. The dream had escaped her.

Cam threw off the pillow, cursing the bird. It was barely light out. She sat up. The clock read 5:10. Then it hit her. Lucinda was still in jail. Susan hadn't called her.

Cam bent over her knees, her forehead in her hands. Life was not being fair. She groaned. And it was market day.

Moving slowly, she showered, dressed in a clean T-shirt and cutoffs, and plodded downstairs. She checked both her cell and the landline phone. No messages. Cam stuck the cell phone in her back pocket. Just in case.

She ground beans and set the coffee to brew, then fed Preston and petted him while he ate. The sink held the rinsed and neatly stacked rose china plates. The wineglasses from last night sat abandoned on the drain board, a ring of red wine in the bottom a reminder of her aborted date with Jake.

After Cam poured her coffee, she added a splash of milk and turned toward the door. At the sight of the table — its white cloth bearing a smudge of soy from the fish, a pink smear from the pie, the vase of hopeful carnations from Jake — Cam sank into a chair. She didn't know if she had the energy, not to mention the emotional strength, to go out there, pick with no help, and then be all social and salespersoney at the market for the entire afternoon. She could skip this one week.

She spied her business cards sitting next to the red carnations on the table near the door. Darn it all, she had a brand-new business to maintain. Whatever happened to Lucinda, Cam was still going to be a farmer. She wouldn't be doing anybody any good if she failed to show up at market when she was just starting to build her customer base there. As Alexandra might say, Cam was building her brand, and you had to keep up momentum. Maybe she'd be able to get more information at the market about the murderer.

Cam took a deep breath and headed for the porch. If Susan needed to reach her, Cam's cell was in her pocket. She donned her work boots, finished her coffee, and strode for the fields.

■ ■ ■ ■

An hour into the market, Cam finally had a chance to catch her breath. By a stroke of luck, she'd managed to snag a shady spot. She could almost hear her bags of freshly cut greens calling out in tiny voices, "Thank you, Cam!" She'd also managed, even without help, to harvest enough to make the table look full and inviting to customers. The strawberries were coming in fast and furious, and the asparagus, while on its way out, was still producing enough for a couple of dozen bundles to be standing, points up, in a tray of water.

The weather was still warm and humid, what Marie would have called "close." Cam didn't really mind it, as long as she made sure to drink enough water. She knew the crops loved the warmth. As long as they also had enough water, that is, and the season so far had provided regular rains. If it dried out and Cam had to start irrigating, it would be a different ball game. She didn't have long enough hoses or a hefty enough bank account to bring water to the back field, where she'd planted the produce that needed more room, crops like corn, potatoes, and squash.

Her reverie was interrupted by the sight of Detective Pappas making his way down the line of vendors. Cam hadn't heard from Susan Lee or Pappas. She'd left a message on Susan's voice mail, asking what Lucinda's status was, how she was handling being in a jail cell. Cam had wanted to call Ruth, but she knew Ruth would be violating her professional boundaries if she told Cam anything, so Cam didn't even try. Maybe she'd get answers from Pappas now.

The detective stopped to speak with Bev. It was too far away for Cam to hear, but she watched them even as she made change for a box of strawberries and a bunch of irises. Bev looked over at Cam for a moment. Cam thought of looking away but waved instead. It couldn't hurt to be a little extra friendly. Bev did not wave back.

Pappas left Bev's stall and arrived at Cam's a moment later. "Good afternoon, Cam." He pretended to browse the produce while a couple finished paying for greens, spring garlic, and asparagus. After they left, he said, "You know we have Ms. DaSilva in custody."

"She didn't kill Mike." Cam folded her arms.

"We have an eyewitness who saw her in the greenhouse that afternoon. We know

Mike was threatening to expose her immigration status. And we have evidence linking her to the crime."

Cam couldn't believe it. "What kind of evidence? Who saw her in the greenhouse? She was a volunteer on my farm. She was welcome anytime, even when I wasn't home, to come by and water or —"

"We searched her apartment and found evidence that is possibly an important connection to the victim."

"What was it? Maybe somebody planted something."

Pappas held up his hand in a forestalling gesture. "I've told you too much as it is, but I felt an obligation to let you know the status."

"Susan Lee wasn't able to get Lucinda out, I gather."

"No, but there will be a bail hearing in front of a judge this afternoon. I wouldn't get your hopes up, though. It is a charge of murder."

"What about her immigration status? Is this going to get her deported?"

Pappas looked around. No customers stood nearby. He looked back at Cam and leaned over the table a little. "As far as I am concerned, the INS does not need to be involved at this stage. She is actually here legally, sort of. She has a valid tourist visa, and she has applied for her green card. Now, if she were convicted, that would certainly result in deportation. But we're a long way from that at this point."

Cam widened her eyes. Lucinda had kept saying she was here illegally. The stories didn't match. But Pappas had to know the real situation. Maybe Lucinda had been confused about it.

"Thank you, Detective, for letting me know," Cam said.

"My father was an immigrant. I have to admit I have a soft spot for hardworking people like Lucinda. She maintains her innocence. Who knows? Perhaps another suspect will turn up. But for now, it doesn't look good for her."

"Great. So it's easier to prosecute Lucinda than to find the real killer." She was about to say she would find the actual murderer for him when two Haitian women with a little boy strolled up and greeted her.

As Cam handed the boy a strawberry, Pappas gave her a little salute and walked off. She watched him go and realized she was better off not having told him of her resolve. He'd only have told her to leave police work to the police.

At three-thirty, Cam surveyed her nearly

empty table with satisfaction. She'd passed her new business cards out to most of her customers and answered several questions about organic growing methods. Her envelope for the SNAP tokens was half full, meaning a crop of low-income folks was going to be eating fresh, healthy produce for the next week. Her cell phone vibrated in her back pocket. She extracted it and checked the ID. S. A. Lee.

Cam punched the button to answer it. "Hello? Susan?"

"I'm afraid we have bad news, Cam." Susan's tone was brisk. "The judge refused to set bail for Lucinda, saying she was a flight risk. The good news is they're going to continue to hold her in Westbury. The county doesn't have a women's jail, so women are normally sent to MCI–Framingham."

"What's that?" Cam wiped the humidity off her free hand on her pants and shifted the phone to that hand.

"It's the state prison for women. You don't want Lucinda there under any circumstances. She'll be a lot better off right here in town. It's clean, and there won't be any other prisoners to harass her."

"Can I see her?"

"I think so, but only if I am along, too. I'll

try to set it up and call you back."

Cam started to thank her, but the lawyer had already disconnected. No bail. So much for Lucinda's plan for a locavore year. She wasn't likely to get locally produced meals in jail. Cam shook her head, scolding herself. What a stupid thought, when Lucinda's whole future was at stake.

"So, they finally caught my baby's murderer."

Cam jerked her head up. Bev Montgomery stood in front of her, a self-satisfied sneer on her face.

"And it was that illegal alien. Just like I thought. They ought to all go back where they belong."

"Lucinda had no reason to kill Mike."

"Like hell she didn't. He told her he was going to turn her in."

"Look, they don't have the right person. Somebody else killed Mike, and I'm going to find out who." She realized with a start that if Lucinda was in the country legally, Mike and the militia wouldn't have had a hold on her. Unless she was protecting someone else.

Bev snorted. "You? A city girl playing at farming? With all your fancy organic business? You show up in town, rob me of customers, and now you're going all private

283

detective on us? Not likely. Pappas has the right person. He's a good man, even though he is a Greek."

Cam closed her mouth. Why was she arguing with this woman? She stuck her hands, along with her phone, in her shorts pockets. The phone began to vibrate again. Cam drew it out. It was Susan again.

"Excuse me." Cam turned her back on Bev, but she sensed her eyes burning into her for a moment longer. Cam listened to Susan tell her she'd set up a visit for the following afternoon. Cam thanked her and disconnected. When she turned back to the table, Bev was gone. Cam wished she could wave a magic wand and make her gone permanently, but that wasn't going to happen. For that matter, if she had a magic wand — abracadabra! — Lucinda would be out of jail with a green card and the real killer would be put away for life.

Cam gazed at the still water of Mill Pond two hours later. She perched on a wooden bench sitting at the water's edge. Swallows swooped for insects above the water, and a kingfisher rattled hoarsely from a dead branch. The water smelled of tadpoles and early summer. Albert wouldn't mind if she was a few minutes late for dinner.

The sharp tip of Bev's comment — "You? A city girl playing at farming?" — poked at Cam, threatening to pierce her confidence. She wasn't playing. She was working as hard as she could to change careers. She was trying to make a go of hard physical work, fresh air, and supplying people with what they wanted to eat.

Maybe it was a crazy idea, though. In fact, her gifts were as a computer scientist. Even if she spent the winter using her brain, polishing and productizing her farming software, next year's season would start up again soon enough. To diversify the farm, she wanted to add chickens and fruit trees. She planned to plant a stand of blueberry bushes and several long rows of raspberries, maybe even build a pen and get a couple of pigs. It was a lot of work for a single person, and she wasn't sure she could pull it off with only the help of volunteers. She might not even have Lucinda around next year.

Cam shook that thought off. She sighed and checked her watch. Time to get over to Moran Manor. A car door slammed, and the sound of dogs barking interrupted the quiet of the tree-rimmed pond. Cam made her way toward the path that led to the parking area. From around the bend twenty yards away bounded a large black dog. It ran straight at her.

CHAPTER 16

Cam froze. The dog stopped three feet in front of her. It planted splayed feet and panted. Drool dripped from the corner of its mouth. Its eyes were trained on her and did not look friendly.

"Nice doggy," Cam said, her heart thumping in her throat. She tried to take a deep breath. She tried to muster thoughts of a curly cocker spaniel, a tactic she'd once read that could trick a dog into thinking you weren't afraid. "Nice little doggy."

"Billy! You come here." A man appeared on the path. He held back another dog on a leash, this one even bigger. "Get over here." He slapped his thigh.

Billy looked at the man and back at Cam. He turned and loped away from Cam.

"Sorry about that, ma'am," the man called.

She walked slowly toward them as he rubbed the black dog's head.

"He wouldn't hurt you."

Every dog owner's favorite words. She kept moving, her heart returning to normal, the smile on her face a lie.

"He's a good boy, aren't you, Billy?" The man wore a trim gray beard and a Red Sox hat. His business shirt, rolled up at the cuffs, and pressed dark slacks looked out of place at the pond, although his sneakers were at least appropriate footwear.

Cam passed them, giving a little wave. "Have a good walk." After she was sure the man and his dogs had proceeded down the path, she turned and watched, eyes wide. The man's forearm displayed the same tattoo as Frank Jackson's. The Patriotic Militia tattoo.

Albert pointed a crutch toward a table in the corner of the dining hall at Moran Manor that evening. "Let's eat our dinner there. We'll have a little more quiet."

Cam followed him toward the table in a tasteful room fragrant with the aromas of roasting meat and fresh bread. Aging eyes tracked them from all sides. She nodded and smiled to the senior citizens as she passed. It appeared that having a young visitor in the place was an exciting event.

Albert stopped at a table of three women

and a man. "This is my great-niece, Cameron Flaherty. Cam, Jimmy Rousseau,
Claire Rousseau, Virginia Skinner, and
Edna Rogers. We play bridge together. Well,
except for Edna."

Cam greeted them. Edna didn't look up
from the roll she was working hard to butter, but the others smiled and waved a hello.

"Nice to meet you, dear," Virginia said.
"Good to see young blood around here.
Come back soon, you hear?"

Cam said she would, then pulled out a
chair for Albert at the last table in the row.

He drew a bottle of wine out of a quilted
bag and set it on the table. "They'll come
and open it for us. Thanks for joining me,
honey. And for getting out of your farm
togs. They do like their dress code for dinner." He rolled his eyes. Albert's concession
to the dress code was the sports coat he'd
pulled on over his plaid shirt.

"You know I like hanging out with you,
Uncle Albert. And after everything that has
happened, well, I could use a nice meal and
intelligent conversation." Cam had washed
up after market and had donned a summery
dress before driving to the assisted living
facility.

They spent a few minutes perusing the
menu after giving the wine to a nervous

high-school waiter who looked like he'd tucked a shirt into pants for the first time ever. When he brought the open bottle, they gave their orders and then sipped the wine.

"It's a dry Riesling from down the road in Rowley. Perfect for a summer night, don't you think?"

Cam tasted it and agreed. "From Mill River?"

Albert nodded.

Cam took a bite of a roll, a delicious warm sourdough, then set it down. "Susan Lee is a force of nature. And she appears to adore you."

Albert laughed. "I've known her forever. She's no spring chicken, but she's done very well by herself in the law. You know, she didn't go to law school until she was in her forties. She raised three children all by herself after her scoundrel husband left them. And the minute the last kid was off to college, why, she was, too."

"I wish she could have gotten Lucinda out on bail, but the judge denied it." Cam frowned.

"Whoa, back up a little, Cameron. I want to know everything about this Lucinda. And why they think she killed young Montgomery."

Cam laid out the events of the past few

days, since she'd dropped Albert off after the Locavore Festival. "There's still something I don't get about Friday night. Lucinda left in a hurry. The next day she was late to help harvest, and she didn't look too well. Then two other subscribers, Wes and Felicity —"

"The Slavin girl?"

Cam nodded. "She's not exactly a girl, Uncle Albert. I'd say she's almost Susan's age."

"She's a girl to me." Albert waved a hand. "But go on."

"Anyway, Wes and Felicity told me Pappas had asked them about Lucinda and Friday night, as if he knew what had happened. I don't know what it was, though. And then Lucinda and I never got a chance to talk about it."

"Can you visit her in jail?"

"I'm going with Susan tomorrow afternoon."

The boy brought their meals. Cam and Albert ate in silence for a moment.

"This is good," Cam said.

"You sound surprised."

"Yeah. I didn't expect institutional chicken to be so tasty. It's a really nice mushroom sauce with what? Wine and capers?"

"We have a real chef here, and she does

wonders. It's all pretty much healthy, too."

"I should talk to her about using the farm produce in these meals."

"Now you're thinking like a business owner." Albert raised bushy eyebrows. "Make sure you charge her a good price."

"I will, I will. Getting back to the case," Cam said. "What about Bev Montgomery? She's been almost one hundred percent unpleasant to me and downright awful about Lucinda. She seems to think every immigrant in this country ought to go back where they came from."

"Yes, she does hold those views."

"Well, as far as I know, Montgomery isn't exactly a Native American last name. How does she think her family got here?" Cam heard her voice rise and saw Jimmy at the next table glance over. She went on in a low tone. "Sorry about that. It just really bothers me."

Albert nodded but didn't offer an opinion.

"And then today she also accused me of stealing her customers and playing at farming." Cam shook her head. She downed a healthy swallow of wine.

Albert reached across and patted her hand with a palm callused from decades of working with the earth. "Bev has had a hard life. Do you know her husband was killed in a tractor accident? Bev blamed it on their Jamaican farmhand, but it was Jeb Montgomery's own damn fault. What kind of farmer gets drunk and then climbs on a tractor?" Albert's mouth pulled down. "At any rate, her older sons and her daughter aren't interested in being farmers. She'd held out hope for Mike, but he didn't quite rise to the responsibility she gave him. Then he said he'd rather work for me. And now she doesn't even have him." He shook his head.

Cam rued being so irritated with Bev. Sort of. "What was it you owed her a favor for, Albert? You wouldn't tell me the other day."

"When Marie was dying, why, Bev Montgomery was over every day. She'd either be wiping Marie's brow, cleaning up the kitchen, or doing farmwork so I could be with Marie. She really came through for us. She's gruff, but she has a big heart."

Now Cam did feel bad.

"Don't let her bark worry you. I think you're doing a super job with the farm, Cameron. And I want a tour one of these days."

Cam mentally slapped her forehead for not thinking of it herself. "Of course. And thank you. I'm working hard, and I'm trying to keep the spirit of your farm going, just with an update to organic. That's what the customer base seems to want."

"The customer base. You have all these fancy ways of referring to things." Albert smiled. "And that's good."

"Would you believe we have a Web site now, too? Alexandra, one of the younger locavores, designed it and set it up for me. I just didn't have time. I'll have to show you. They must have a computer here somewhere we can use."

"I didn't tell you? I'm online now. Right in my room."

Cam's mouth dropped open. "You are?"

"Why, yes. I ordered a laptop with the Senior Geeks group they got going here, and I took the class. Just finished yesterday, as a matter of fact. I have an e-mail address and everything, don't you know. Web design is our next class, and I'm thinking of blogging about my memoirs."

"Now you're the geek, and I'm the farmer." A moment of happiness washed over her, extra rosy for the lack of it lately. "How about we start a farm blog and you can write about your farming memories? You could give growing and harvesting tips. I could publish some of Marie's recipes. They're still in her recipe box in the kitchen cupboard."

"We could do that." Albert glanced toward the door of the dining room. "Well, what do you know?"

Cam followed his gaze. Stuart stood in the doorway with a woman in a blazer that sported a name tag. On Stuart's arm was an older woman, who looked around her like she had stumbled into a new and unfamiliar universe.

"There's Betty Wilson. Hello, Betty!" Albert called to her. He turned to Cam. "Are we all done?"

Cam looked at her plate. Somewhere during their conversation she'd polished off her entire meal. She nodded. Albert was already on his feet and crutching toward Stuart and the woman, who was clearly his mother, so Cam followed.

"Betty, I haven't seen you in years," Albert said, beaming at her.

"Why, yes, Albert. How's my dear Marie?" Betty smiled sweetly, but her eyes seemed unsure. "Please tell her hello for me."

"I'll do that, Betty. Hello, Stuart. I'm Albert St. Pierre." He balanced on the crutches and extended his hand. "I don't believe we've met, although I saw you at the local food thingamabob last week."

Stuart shook his hand. "Nice to meet you,

sir. Hi, Cam." Stuart didn't smile, and a tic jumped at the top of his lip. "We're checking this place out for Mother. Aren't we, Mother?" His tone softened when he addressed her, as did his eyes.

"I'm sure you'll find a lovely apartment for yourself here, dear. Can I go home now?" She turned her face up to Stuart's.

"In just a minute, Mother." Stuart patted her hand with a wistful smile and pained eyes. He excused them and moved along on their tour with the Manor representative. Cam strolled with Albert back to his room.

"Why didn't you tell Mrs. Wilson that Great-Aunt Marie died two years ago?" Cam asked, holding open the door to his room.

"Cameron, it would just upset her. Couldn't you see she doesn't have so much going on upstairs anymore?"

"When I get old, I don't want people to lie to me."

"When you get old, you might not be able to tell the difference. Now, let me show you my new toy." Albert gestured to a chair in the corner as he lowered himself into a swivel chair at the desk. "Pull that up."

Cam sat next to Albert and watched as he showed off what he knew.

"Now, show me the farm Web site," he said.

She scooted closer and, taking over the keyboard, brought up the page. "There's an events area, a page for the CSA, and we have a customer comment area, too. See?" She clicked through the tabs. She turned to see how Albert was reacting to her baby. He looked like he'd eaten a spoiled tomato.

"What's the matter? You don't like it?"

He pointed. "Cameron, read that. It's disgusting."

Cam focused on the screen. The topmost comment was a paragraph of obscenities and slurs against her, against immigrants, against organic farming. It accused her of murder and worse.

"What! Who put that there?" She leaned in. "There's no name on it. They must have chosen the anonymous identity. But I'm taking it down right now." Her fingers flew on the keys as she logged in as administrator.

"Wait." Albert laid his hand on her arm. "Maybe you should save it. Show it to the police. They could track who sent it."

"Good idea." Cam copied the content out to a file, saving it to the desktop. She deleted the message from the page. "E-mail me this file later, will you? I'm going to have to moderate this page, I can tell."

"What's that mean?"

"I'll have to approve every comment before it goes public. Who would have thought I'd need to do that for a simple organic farm Web site?"

"There are many unfortunate souls out there, Cameron, who have never heard of moderation." Albert shook his head slowly. "Many unfortunate souls."

CHAPTER 17

Cam had just finished watering in the hoop house at eight thirty the next morning when she heard the ding of a bicycle bell. She stepped outside to see Alexandra leaning her bike against the barn.

"Hi, Alexandra. You're early for Volunteer Day."

"Yeah. Hey, funny weather, isn't it?" She gestured to the gray, overcast sky. "It's even sort of cool. For summer." She wore a red long-sleeved T-shirt and faded jeans cut off right below the knee. "So, I have to drive my sister to the bus station in a couple of hours. I thought I'd get a head start here since I can't stay until the end of the volunteer time."

"Where's your sister headed?"

"Katie thinks she's going to break into the acting scene in New York." Alexandra cocked her head. "I'd say it's unlikely she'll even break into a waitress job."

"She's not getting back together with Stuart?"

"No way. He's way too old for her, anyway."

Stuart certainly didn't think he was too old for Katie. Cam wondered how he would react to the news of Katie being gone.

"Uh, Cam? Are you going to give me a task to do? I'd like to get started."

Cam started. "Sorry. Of course. But first, can you add a moderation facility sometime to the comments page on the Web site? A disgusting message showed up on the page last night."

"Yuck. Really?"

"Yes. It was basically a rant against me and the world, including immigrants and organics. Actually accused me of killing Mike. And not in very nice language."

"You deleted it, I assume?"

"Yes, after I saved the file. I was with Albert at the time, so I had him e-mail it to me. I sent it off to Pappas this morning."

"Good. I'll set up moderation as soon as I get home. What's on the job list for farmwork today?"

"Do you mind turning compost again?"

"Not at all. I like doing that kind of work. Bring it on."

Cam grabbed a pitchfork from the barn

and handed it to Alexandra. As they walked out back, Cam patted her pocket. No cell phone.

"I'm going to run to the house and get my phone. Last week I layered fresh manure into the new bin, you know, the one on the far left. You can turn the middle bin into the one on the right, and then turn the fresh stuff into the middle bin. That all right?"

"Got it, boss."

Cam trotted to the house and retrieved her phone from the kitchen counter. She strode back to the barn, feeling like her brain was about to explode. That flaming comment on the Web site. Pappas saying they had evidence and a witness tying Lucinda to the murder. Jake's odd departure Monday night and no word from him since. Lucinda sitting in a jail cell. And Cam with a farm to run. The overcast sky and strangely cool air added to her sense of uneasiness with the world.

At noon the volunteers finished up and straggled toward the barn and their cars. It was a smaller group this week. Stuart hadn't showed. And, of course, Lucinda wasn't there. Alexandra had flown off on her bicycle an hour earlier.

Felicity approached Cam as she wiped a

weeding tool with a rag to get the dirt off before she hung it on the barn wall.

"Cam, is it all right with you if we have our first shareholders' potluck here?" Felicity tossed her braid back over her shoulder. She stood with clasped hands and a cheerful, expectant look on her face.

"That'd be fine. I don't think I have enough chairs, though."

"We'll take care of all that. Everybody can bring their own chairs. I thought we could use the share table, and then we'll bring a couple more collapsible tables."

"Sounds good, Felicity. When did you want to hold the first one?"

"This Friday. Is six o'clock okay?"

"*This* Friday?" Cam swallowed. "Don't you think that's kind of . . ." She stopped. Felicity's cheer had turned to dismay. Cam put up a hand. "No, it's fine. This Friday it is." She sighed inwardly. One more item to add to the list of things she had to worry about.

"Good." Felicity's balance was restored. "I'll send out an e-mail to the list." She looked around and lowered her voice. "Except to Lucinda, that is. Is it true she's in jail? For the murder of that disturbed young man, the one you had to fire?"

"It's true. I'm going to see her this afternoon with her lawyer. Believe me, they have the wrong person."

"She's such a nice woman. But you know what they say. The killers are often those quiet, normal-looking neighbors."

"Felicity." Cam frowned at her customer. "Lucinda is not a killer. Please don't think she is. And do me a favor?"

"What?"

"Don't talk about her as if she's a murderer. Will you do that for me?"

Felicity nodded. "I suppose." She brightened. "See you Friday! We'll have everyone bring their own plate and utensils, too, and I'll have tablecloths and such. We don't want to make any extra work for you while we build community."

Cam thanked Felicity, glad to see her leave. She'd had just about all the community she could stand for a while. She planned to commune with nothing more than solitude for the next couple of hours.

Cam waited in her truck at the only stoplight in Westbury at a little before three o'clock. She looked down and checked her outfit, khaki slacks and a navy blue blouse. She brushed a bit of lint off one sleeve. An official visit to a jail seemed to warrant a somber outfit. She wondered if she should have brought Lucinda anything. Maybe she needed a change of clothes or a toothbrush. She could probably use a decent meal, but Cam guessed the jail wouldn't allow that. She'd ask during the visit what Lucinda needed and what the police would let her bring.

A discreet beep from behind made her look up. The light had turned green. Cam gave a little wave in her rearview mirror and drove the last couple of blocks to the station. She pulled in and parked next to Susan's Jaguar. What a car. Cam peered in at pristine white leather seats and a red dashboard. She thought fondly for a moment of the sporty Audi she'd owned as a single software engineer, heated seats and all. She'd been single with a hearty salary. Now all her money was in the farm, and she still thought it had been a good move. Most of the time.

Cam squared her shoulders and strode into the station. Susan stood at the reception counter, tapping her enameled fingernails on the top. Today she wore a navy pinstriped pantsuit, again with the red heels and red leather case.

"There you are," Susan said to Cam in a brisk tone. "We're ready now." Susan directed this at a young officer Cam hadn't seen before who stood behind the desk.

Cam's heart rate doubled. She'd never been inside a jail before. She was glad the officer held the heavy door for her. Her palms were so sweaty, she wasn't sure she'd be able to grasp it herself. And she hadn't even done anything wrong.

The officer led them into a small conference room. The walls were painted an institutional beige and needed a touch-up coat. Susan turned full circle, looking at every wall, then up at the corners and ceiling. She glanced sharply at the officer.

"We will not be recorded, correct?"

"No, ma'am."

"Thank you. We'll see Ms. DaSilva now." She turned her back on him. "Sit down, Cameron." Susan gestured at the table and chairs in the middle of the otherwise bare room. After the officer left the room, Susan sat across from Cam.

"They'll probably record us, anyway, even though it's illegal. At least they don't have a two-way mirror in here, although they might have a camera." She drummed her fingers on the tabletop. "What can you do?"

Cam tried to still her nervous hands by clasping them in her lap. That felt silly, so she moved them to the top of the table.

The door opened. The officer ushered Lucinda in ahead of him and pointed to a chair. Dark patches caved in under her eyes, and her skin was pale. Her glorious mane of curls was twisted back in a messy knot. She wore what looked like scrubs, except Cam had never seen them in any hospital in that shade of orange.

As Lucinda sat, Cam reached her hand out to touch Lucinda's, but at the glare she got from the officer, she pulled it back.

"Hey, *fazendeira.*" Lucinda mustered a weak smile.

Susan shot a pointed look at the officer. "Leave us now, please."

"You have twenty minutes," the officer said, then turned and left.

When the door clanged shut, Cam was as imprisoned as Lucinda.

"Thanks for bringing Cam, Susan," Lucinda said.

"I'm so sorry you're in here, Lucinda. We all know you're the wrong person to be accused of Mike's murder, but what do we do now?" Cam opened her palms.

"Let's start by going over everything we know." Susan proceeded to list Lucinda's activities in the days before the murder, as well as where she'd been that day and what her dealings with Mike had been.

"Wait," Cam said. "Do we know what this

evidence is they say they have?"

Susan shook her head. "I haven't gotten that information yet."

"Or who the witness is?"

Susan shook her head again.

"Lucinda, did you come back to the farm at the end of the day that Saturday?"

"No! But I was just home, by myself. Nobody could have seen me at the farm, but nobody saw me at my apartment, either. What about the Patriotic Militia? They said I killed Mike because he was going to turn me in. What if Mike was threatening another undocumented person? He could have been the one, you know, who killed him." Her face pleaded first with Cam and then Susan.

Susan didn't look up but tapped out notes on a tablet device she'd pulled out of her red case.

Cam rubbed her forehead. She looked at Lucinda. "Didn't you say something about a big cheese?"

Lucinda nodded.

"I saw David Kosloski act very strangely at the festival," Cam went on. "Ellie told me he's first-generation Polish, which means he's an immigrant. He has an accent when he speaks. And he's a well-established businessman in town. I'd call that a big cheese."

Now Susan looked up. "I'll check out his immigration status."

Cam had another thought. Jake had an accent, too. He was sort of a big cheese, too, with an entire restaurant at stake. Was that why he left so abruptly when he heard of Lucinda's arrest? Cam decided to keep this thought to herself for the time being.

"And speaking of immigration status, Lucinda," Susan went on, "you know your visa is still valid."

Lucinda's eyes widened. She shook her head. "I thought it expired."

"No. So you're in no imminent danger of being deported. If you are convicted of a crime, it's a different story. You're all right for now on that front."

"I must have gotten the dates wrong. The INS isn't exactly the easiest office to deal with, and their paperwork is really confusing." Lucinda's look of relief was a small spot of joy in the meeting.

"Listen, Alexandra talked with me about Stuart this morning," Cam said. "Well, not really about him, but about him and his former girlfriend, Alexandra's sister, Katie."

"Stuart," Lucinda groaned.

"What?" Cam leaned toward her.

"Oh, you know, he and I were sort of flirting at the festival. He, um, came home with me. But then I got really sick to my stomach. Before anything, you know, romantic happened. He was kinda nice to me, and then he left. Just hearing his name makes me feel sick again."

Cam frowned. "I was really sick Friday night, too. Do you think we both ate the same bad thing?"

"I don't think so. Everybody at the festival would have been sick, then, right?"

"I guess so." Cam didn't believe that for a minute. She and Lucinda must have tasted something spoiled. Except the only food Cam sampled was Jake's. *Oh, crud.*

Susan glanced at the big schoolroom clock on the wall. "We have seven minutes left. How are they treating you?"

Lucinda's smile was a pale reflection of her usual beam. "Okay, I guess. Can I get a decent hairbrush? They gave me a little kit, you know, toothbrush and soap, but the hairbrush is no good with this mess." She smoothed back a few escaped curls. "And underwear would be nice."

Cam rued not bringing anything. "I'll get that stuff for you, Lucinda. Anything else?"

"How about getting me out of here?" Her eyes filled.

"I'm working on it," Susan said. "But until they find a different suspect, it'll be difficult.

And now that they have you, my bet is they aren't looking too hard for anyone else."

Lucinda slumped in her seat. She sank her head onto her arms on the table.

"Couldn't she at least have house arrest, or whatever they call it?" Cam asked. "You know, one of those bracelets."

Susan said she was working on it.

"How's the farm doing, Cam?" Lucinda asked.

"I'm getting along. It's tough without my best volunteer, though." She smiled at Lucinda. "We're going to get you out of here. I promise." This time she reached for Lucinda's hand and squeezed it.

The door banged open. Chief Frost stood in the doorway. "Good afternoon, ladies. I'm afraid your time is up." He moved to Lucinda's side and took her elbow as she stood.

"Thanks for coming, you guys," she said with a wistful look.

"I'll see you soon." Cam tried to put on a hopeful, positive face.

"We'll let ourselves out, Chief." Susan stowed her device and stood.

He nodded and led Lucinda away.

Cam followed Susan as her heels clicked down the hall. Cam glanced over her shoulder. Lucinda's orange scrubs disappeared around the far corner.

Cam sat in her truck in the police station parking lot. She rested her head on the steering wheel. If she didn't find the murderer, Lucinda was never going to get her freedom back, and she'd be sent back to Brazil, too. Cam didn't know why Lucinda had needed to leave her own country, but she did have faith in Lucinda's integrity and honesty. *Not from long experience knowing her,* Cam acknowledged to herself. She just had a feeling.

She laughed to herself. *A feeling?* She'd always been too much of a brainiac to let feelings creep very far into the equation of her life. It must be the physical work of farming that was letting her nonmental side emerge.

She straightened and shook her head. Back to the business at hand. It was only three thirty. She did a search on her phone and started up the truck. While she was all cleaned up and presentable, she might as well try her hand at detective work.

Ten minutes later she stood at the reception desk of K-One Construction, David Kosloski's company. No one occupied the orange and blue chairs in the sunny waiting room. No one sat behind the desk. But the door of the office, housed in a small Cape on the main road, had been unlocked. Cam assumed it was open for business. She cleared her throat in lieu of pressing the button on the old-fashioned half-sphere bell on the desk. She looked around the waiting room. The walls held a dozen black-and-white photographs of tasteful houses, a condominium complex along the Merrimack River, a group of smiling men wearing work clothes and hard hats.

She peered more closely at one photo, of a perky little girl seated at a small desk, looking at a blueprint. It had to be Ellie at a younger age.

"Can I help you?"

The slightly accented voice from behind her startled Cam, who turned in its direction. A petite woman with pale skin and dark hair pulled back in a ponytail stood behind the desk. She wore a black T-shirt and black jeans and looked a few years younger than Cam. Several small silver hoop earrings traveled up the outside edge of both ears, and a dozen silver bangles decorated each wrist.

"I was looking for David Kosloski. He's a customer of mine."

"It's Wednesday," the woman said in a "Don't you know anything?" kind of voice.

"That's right. May I speak with him, please?" Cam gestured around the room. "It doesn't look like I'd be interrupting anyone's appointment."

"He's not here. He's never here on Wednesday afternoon." The tone continued.

"I see. Do you think I could find him at home?"

The woman rolled her eyes. "Only if he lived at the Polish Club in Lawrence. He sponsors the free health clinic there every week."

"I didn't know that. That's very generous of him."

"Would you like to make an appointment?" The woman cocked her head, as if that was unlikely.

"No, I . . ." Cam took a closer look. "Hey, are you related to him? You look a lot like Ellie." She didn't know why she hadn't noticed earlier. Ellie cocked her head the same way. And they had the same coloring and petite build. The accent, now that she thought of it, sounded like David's.

"Yes. Eleanor's my niece. I'm David's sister. My name is Aniela." She folded her arms on her chest. "What do you sell, anyway?"

"I'm Cam Flaherty. I run the farm they're members of." She decided not to extend her hand, given Aniela's body language.

Aniela nodded. "Ellie talked about you." She looked down at the desk and straightened some papers.

"Well, thanks. Nice to meet you." Cam turned to go. "I'll stop in tomorrow. I just have a quick question for him." She glanced back, but Aniela had disappeared. Cam let herself out. David's sister hadn't been exactly forthcoming. That had to be bad for business.

So much for sleuthing. Cam stood on the small porch and thought. A car destined to be ticketed in the speed trap just ahead whizzed by. The speed trap was a big revenue source for the local police, Ruth had told her. And it sat just before the Food Mart. Cam nodded. Maybe there was more investigating she could do today, after all.

She picked up a plastic basket at the door of the Food Mart. She needed a few groceries, anyway, and this way it wouldn't look as if she'd come here only to query Stuart, if he was even at work. She tossed in a *Boston Globe,* then selected a half gallon of one-percent milk, a pound of butter, a sourdough baguette, and some extra-rich chocolate ice cream. At the checkout counter lately she often got strange looks from customers with carts full of fruit and vegetables, along the lines of "You poor ignorant thing with your basket full of unhealthy food." This amused Cam. They didn't know she had a farm full of produce at home, at least at this time of year.

As she rounded the end of the cookie aisle on her way to the meat counter, Cam stopped. Stuart was speaking in a raised voice to someone. The other voice sounded a little like Bev Montgomery's.

"I told you why!" Stuart said, almost yelling.

Cam eased around the corner. Stuart stood behind the meat counter with an older woman, her fists set on ample hips. Not Bev, after all. Cam thought she must be the store's manager or owner. Her steel-gray hair was cropped, and her clothes were a sensible pair of dark slacks and a dark blouse under the blue jacket all Food Mart employees wore.

The woman glanced at Cam. "We'll deal with this later, Stuart. You still have four more hours on this shift. You can take lunch when you've finished those ribs." She gestured at the cutting board behind Stuart, then exited the meat area and headed for the front of the store.

Cam looked at Stuart. His narrowed eyes

followed the woman until she disappeared into the next aisle.

Cam cleared her throat. "Hi, Stuart. A little trouble with the management?"

Stuart whipped his head at Cam. "What do you want?" He glared at her with a flushed face.

"Hey." Cam held up her hand, palm out. "We're friends, right? I was looking for a steak and thought I'd say hi," she lied. "What's wrong with that?"

"Nothing." The anger drained from his face. "Nothing. How are you, Cam?"

"Good. Missed you this morning at the farm."

Stuart stopped what he was doing, then turned back to Cam with a tray of steaks that looked freshly cut, their red meat glistening.

"These are excellent if you like rib eye."

Okay, don't answer me. Cam nodded. "Sure. Wrap me up a couple."

"They're expensive," Stuart warned.

"It's all right. I don't eat meat much. I'll splurge." She smiled at him. "So you heard Lucinda was arrested for Mike's murder?"

"I heard." Stuart busied himself with wrapping the meat in white paper. "Guess that makes you feel better, that the killer isn't walking around out there anymore."

"Oh, she's not a killer. No, they have the wrong person. Totally the wrong person."

Stuart looked up. "Oh?"

"Absolutely."

"Is that what the police say?"

"No. They're the ones who arrested her." Cam snorted. "But they're wrong. You'll see. Lucinda said she got really sick after the festival." Cam waited. Would he acknowledge going home with Lucinda?

"That's too bad." He weighed the meat and wrote the price on the white paper with a black marker.

"It was nice of you to help her out. While she was sick." Setting her basket on the floor, Cam examined a package of chicken while keeping Stuart in her field of vision.

He, in turn, busied himself tidying up a pile of sausages. "Yeah, I got her a glass of ginger ale afterward."

"Did you get sick, too? Because I was really sick after I got home. I wondered if it was food we all ate there."

"No, I was fine."

A woman and a little boy came around the far end of the aisle.

"Can I get you anything else?" Stuart asked.

"I'll just take this chicken. Nice chatting with you." She picked up her basket and added the chicken. She started to leave and then turned back. "Say, did Felicity contact you? She's organizing a potluck at the farm Friday night."

Stuart nodded. The woman leaned over and started to ask him a question. Cam waved and walked away. She hadn't learned a thing except that he was in trouble with his boss.

Cam checked the connection to the gas bottle under her small grill on the brick patio. She cocked the switch on the lighter but didn't press the button to start the flame. She felt the connection again, making sure it was tight. She held her breath, turned on the gas and, pointing the lighter at the grill from as far away as she could, released the spark. The flames flared in a nice controlled fashion. She breathed again.

She drew her sweater around her as she waited for the rack to heat. She sat with a glass of merlot in hand and the newspaper on her lap. The day's cool temperature had settled into an inland fog. The light was dim, even though sunset was still an hour away. The moist air crept in through her pores until she shivered. Still, it was better than sitting in a jail cell.

She went into the house to call Pappas,

but he didn't pick up, so she decided to leave a message. She was meandering through what Lucinda had said about Friday night when the voice mail apparently reached its limit. Cam sighed and punched the off button with bit more vehemence than necessary. She'd have to explain when he called back.

Returning to the patio, Cam waited for the grill to heat. She'd rubbed the steak with kosher salt, freshly ground pepper, and a clove of garlic. The baguette warmed on low in the oven. She planned to finish her indulgent dinner with a bowl of ice cream, read a little, and call it a night.

When she flipped to the Metro section of the *Globe,* a headline caught Cam's eye. She gripped the paper in both hands.

BURNING HOUSE NEARLY TAKES
GIRL'S LIFE; SITTER CHARGED.

A chill crept through Cam, one unrelated to the weather. She again saw the flames licking at the bottom of the door. Felt the heat pressing in. Heard her voice calling out for her mother. Wondered where Zachary, her teen babysitter, had gone. Experienced a young girl's paralysis at knowing no one could hear her.

Her cell phone buzzed in her pocket. Cam shook her head to clear it. She looked at the display. She didn't recognize the number. Maybe Pappas was calling her back from a different phone. She'd better answer it.

"Hello."

"Cammie, is that you?"

"Mom! Where are you?"

"We just got into San Francisco from Bangkok. What's this we hear about a murder on the farm?"

Cam closed her eyes and counted to ten, banishing the memory the news article had drawn up from the depths of wherever she'd banished it to for all these years.

Mom. It was just her current-day, still-absent mother. And what ever happened to, "We've missed you, dear," or "How are you, honey?"

"Have you been talking to Albert?" Cam asked.

"No, we saw it on the Internet once we got back in range and wanted to check out the local news. You must be so much more at ease now that they've caught the murderer."

Cam sighed, but she didn't have time to count to ten again. "Is this your own cell, Mom?"

Her mother said it was.

"I'm in the middle of cooking dinner, and I don't want it to burn. Can I call you back?"

They arranged to talk later, and Cam disconnected. What she really didn't want to burn was her own feelings, shielded from conflagration for so long by her immersion in the satisfying and logical work of coding. If farming was gradually lowering her emotional defenses, what would happen when her parents breezed through town again? When they showed up and failed to try to find out how she was, as they had been doing for so many years. She knew, or at least Marie had told her, that her mother and father meant well. They just didn't have people skills, either. Cam had apparently come by that honestly.

She set the steak on the hot grill and put history, both ancient and recent, out of her mind. Twelve minutes later she brought the plate in and sat at the table. She savored her first mouthful of juicy steak and rolled the flavors of the seasonings and the meat on her tongue. Perfection.

Perfect food bought her thoughts a direct ticket to Jake. She hadn't heard from him since he left Monday night. She tore off a piece of crusty bread and sopped up a bit of the juices with it. She chased the bread with a swallow of wine. Jake was still there in her brain. Cam was the one who had left their embrace to answer the telephone. Maybe Jake was waiting for her to call him and fix things up. But he was the one who had split, hadn't offered to help her, had looked alarmed. Shouldn't he call her?

Preston sidled over and laid his paws on her leg, asking with his tiny voice for a morsel of rare beef. Cam cut off a bite and laid it on the floor for him.

"Preston, what do you think?"

He ignored her as he ate.

"Shouldn't he call me? And why do I feel like I'm suddenly sixteen again and angsting about a boy?" Which was exactly how Cam felt.

From outside came a noise like a big object being knocked over. Cam froze. What was that? And who? Had she locked the door after her dinner was ready?

She crept to the door, trying to stay out of sight of the windows. She locked the door and the dead bolt. With the day's cool weather, all the windows were already shut and secured. Cam turned off the lights. She listened. Another noise, and then the outdoor floodlight lit up.

Cam peered out onto the patio but couldn't see anyone in the pool of light. Still keeping it dark inside, she found the remote to her seldom-used television and switched it on. Careful to stay out of the light from the screen, she found a news talk show and turned the volume up as she had done before. At least it might sound like there was a conversation going on inside.

She returned to the table. The outside light from over the top of the café curtains cast enough illumination on the table so she could see her food. It was at least equivalent to candlelight. Cam cursed the noisemaker, whoever it was, but she wasn't going to let some sound ruin her dinner. She had good locks, a cell phone in her pocket, and an excellent steak.

As she picked up her knife and fork, Cam spied one window in the room whose curtains were not fully drawn. She got up and reached for the cloth to draw it shut. She took one more glance at the patio and then laughed out loud. At the edge near the back door, a raccoon had tipped over the trash barrel and was devouring the fat Cam had cut off the edges of the steak. Almost no food made its way into Cam's trash, but animal meat and fat were an exception, since they weren't appropriate for the compost. Other bits of trash were scattered over the bricks.

Well, let the little guy have it. She could clean up the patio tomorrow. Cam switched the light back on and turned off the TV. She was going to get her dinner, after all.

After she finished savoring her meal and reading the rest of the day's newspaper, she pushed back her chair but remained seated. For the moment, her search for a murderer was at bay, as were her worries about Lucinda. She relaxed with a warm glow.

Cam looked at her cell phone on the table. In a rush, so she didn't change her mind, she pressed Jake's cell number. When he didn't answer, she left a simple message that she hoped to speak with him and that he could call her back anytime. She looked at the phone for a moment and then pressed The Market's number. Might as well go all out.

"The Market," a perky female voice said. The clatter of dishes and voices behind her made it sound like the restaurant was fully booked on a Wednesday night.

"I'd like the kitchen, please." Cam knew the kitchen had its own extension.

"Okay, but they're pretty busy in there."

"I'm a personal friend of Jake's." Cam winced, wondering if this was a big mistake.

"Hold on. I'll transfer you."

"Kitchen." Jake almost spat out the word.

"Who's this?" The background was even noisier, if that was possible, although these were sounds of water boiling, fat spattering, vegetables being chopped with a vengeance, line cooks calling out orders.

"Hi, Jake. I just wanted to —"

"I can't talk, Cam. I'll call you tomorrow. Or the next day."

Her ear hurt as he slammed down the receiver. Her heart hurt, too, even though she'd been a fool to expect him to talk during the dinner rush. Living in a shell was so much more comfortable.

CHAPTER 18

Cam spent the morning tilling, hoeing, and thinking. She wished she could go talk with David Kosloski, but farming chores called out for attention like a crying baby. Things would only get worse if she didn't tend to them.

This time Rust Bucket started up like a charm. Cam pushed it between the rows in the back field, the tiller's rotating blades turning over the soil in the paths and at the edges of the rows, uprooting the crop of freshly sprouted weeds. Corn didn't take well to competing with weeds for nutrients and moisture, and neither did young potato starts. When the edges of the corn were cleared, Cam pulled a CobraHead cultivator at the end of a pole gently between the corn plants, its single curved hook neatly slicing through weeds and aerating the soil. After she tilled next to the potatoes, Cam spent another hour hoeing the freshly turned soil up around the plants in a long mound along the rows until only the very top potato leaves showed. In a couple of months that range of miniature foothills of dirt would be filled with potatoes.

By midmorning the fog had burned off and the sun shone dry and hot again. Cam shed her long-sleeved shirt for the tank top she wore under it and rolled her pants up to the knees.

She finished the morning cutting greens and picking strawberries. It was Thursday, one of the days she had committed to delivering produce to Jake. After last night's call, though, she wondered if he still wanted it. And then wondered again at the wisdom of getting involved with someone she already had a professional relationship with. The embarrassment of thinking Jake could talk during his busiest time of night continued to sting, as did that of him hanging up on her.

She strolled into her kitchen at eleven thirty. As she drank down a tall glass of water, her cell phone rang. She checked the display, which read THE MARKET. She groaned. "Let this be an easy call," she whispered to whichever spirit watched over relationships.

After Cam answered, Jake said, "Cam, I'd

like to fix you lunch. In my apartment."

"Today?" Cam asked.

"Yes, as soon as you can get here."

Cam looked down at her muddy legs and dirty clothes. "I'd love it, but I'll have to clean up. Say, twelve thirty?"

"Deal. Do you happen to have my greens and berries?"

"Freshly picked. But wait. Where do you live?"

Jake laughed. "It's just upstairs from the restaurant."

Cam said she'd see him in an hour and disconnected. That laugh had sounded like the normal Jake. Maybe he wanted to make up, to get their budding relationship back on track. Still, she had no idea of his mood or what had been going on during the past few days. She wondered if it was safe going to his apartment. He was a Swede. What if he was the undocumented immigrant who put a pitchfork through Mike's neck? She did not have the same kind of instinct about Jake's innocence that she did about Lucinda's, even though she had trusted Jake enough to kiss him and be kissed.

She shook her head. Those were crazy thoughts. He had owned the restaurant for years and was well known in the community. She marched upstairs for a quick shower, then pulled on clean capris and a blouse. Surely restaurant employees would be right downstairs from Jake's apartment. And she'd have her phone with her, after all.

"So, what do you think?" Jake gestured around the room with a broad sweep of his hand. He again wore black-checked pants with a black T-shirt. Very large bare feet poked out from under the pants.

"It's lovely, Jake." Cam wasn't just being nice. The plain lines of the off-white walls and gleaming hardwood floor in the large room were brightened by a simple red couch, accents of blue and yellow, and a three-foot-tall houseplant in front of the bow window. An abstract painting in the same colors hung over the couch. A glass coffee table was home to several chefs' magazines and the day's paper. A small glass table and two blue upholstered chairs at the end opposite the window separated the rest of the room from a small kitchen. The table was laid with yellow place mats, red cloth napkins, and silverware.

A box fan in the window blew the air around. Jake gestured to a still ceiling fan. "Sorry it's a little warm. If I turn it on, I'm afraid I'll get a haircut I didn't plan on."

"Good choice. You're pretty close to the ceiling as it is."

"The house was originally built two hundred years ago, right after the big fire in this section of the city. People must have been shorter then."

Cam stood a few feet away from Jake, her purse over one shoulder. She suddenly couldn't think of a single thing to say to continue the conversation. She glanced out the window, at the painting, anywhere but at Jake's eyes.

Jake cleared his throat. "Come and sit down, Cam. Lunch is all ready." He gestured to the table and then walked behind it to the kitchen area. "I made simple sandwiches. I'll finish them in the broiler. But first, a glass of wine with lunch? I have a nice light Côtes du Rhône breathing. Or would you rather have seltzer?"

Cam sat and took a deep breath. "I'd love a glass of wine." She seemed always to want a glass of wine lately.

Jake delivered her wine and held out his own. "Thanks for coming." They clinked glasses. His expression remained serious.

Cam said nothing but took a sip.

"Now, it'll just be a second." Jake turned to the counter, slipping a pan into the oven. He left the oven door open a crack and stood watching it.

"How long have you been in this building?" Cam's voice quavered a little. She didn't know if she was nervous because of their previously budding romance or worried because there was a chance Jake was a murderer.

"More than a decade. I bought the building, renovated downstairs for the restaurant, and then gradually fixed up the apartment." He drew the pan out. "You can't beat the commute."

Cam watched as he slid two portions onto waiting plates, added several other things, and turned toward the table.

"Voilà. Grilled portobello and goat Gouda melt on sourdough." He set a plate at each place, fetched his wineglass off the counter, and sat.

Cam studied the plate. The toasted top slice of bread, spread with what looked like pesto, lay open on a bed of watercress. Brown dots on the white cheese, which was sprinkled with flecks of rosemary, still bubbled slightly from the broiler. The cheese oozed over a blackened mushroom as big as a small steak. The crust of the bottom bread slice peeked out at the edges. She leaned over and sniffed, then straightened.

"This looks and smells heavenly. But it doesn't look so simple to me."

"It is, believe me." Jake scooped watercress onto the top of his sandwich, added the top slice, and then cut it in two. "Dig in." He took a large bite and then set the sandwich half down.

Cam followed suit. They ate in silence for a moment, if the sound of chewing and swallowing a delicious meal can be called silent. But even as Cam ate, she wondered when they were going to actually start talking. Or if.

She took a sip of wine and then opened her mouth to speak.

Jake spoke at the same time. "Cam, I must apologize for leaving so quickly Monday night." His eyes darted around the room before settling back on hers. "I don't know if I can explain it."

"I thought I should apologize for answering the phone. It was really nice dancing with you." Cam set her elbow on the table and her chin on her hand.

Jake sipped his wine. He studied the half of his sandwich remaining on the plate. "All right. I'll tell you. When my parents went back to Sweden with my little brother and I stayed, I became an illegal alien. My father had come here on a work visa that permitted him to bring his family. I had become an American kid in those two years. I wanted this life, and I refused to go back. In Sweden it's either very dark or very light. The government takes care of people, but they also regiment them. I liked this freedom you have."

"And you couldn't just apply to stay?"

"I was young and stupid. I started getting restaurant jobs and found I loved cooking. I was paid cash, under the table. Nobody seemed to care or ask for my papers. Now, since nine-eleven, the INS is much more vigilant. Homeland security and all that. But by then I had already bought this place."

So Cam's idea about Jake had been correct. "But what made you split when I said Lucinda was in jail for the murder?"

"Listen, we're both immigrants. Mike and that group of his had threatened to expose me. I could lose everything, Cam." He stood. "Everything!" He was nearly shouting. He paced toward the window.

Cam kept her eyes on Jake as she put a hand down the side of her chair and into her purse, which she'd hung there, and grabbed her phone. She slipped it into her pants pocket just as Jake turned back toward her.

"I left because I didn't want you to see how glad I was that they had arrested Lucinda."

"She didn't kill Mike, Jake."

"How do you know?" His eyes narrowed. "Did they let her go?" Jake approached the table until he loomed over her.

"No, the police think she killed him, but I know she didn't."

"If she didn't kill him, who did?"

The question hung in the air between them like a bubble of explosives. Cam wasn't sure if she should try to pop it or wait for it to waft away.

"Did you?" she asked. Now she'd done it. Her heart started racing. Her throat tightened. She gripped the phone in her pocket but wondered if it would be better to just race for the door.

He regarded her with those pale eyes. He threw his head back and laughed, then sank into his chair. "You think I killed Mike Montgomery? It was Jake Ericsson in the greenhouse with the pitchfork." He laughed again, more quietly this time. "For the record, I didn't."

"You acted so oddly. You're an immigrant. I just wondered . . ." Cam realized she no longer wondered. She believed Jake.

Jake frowned. "I guess I had just cause.

Isn't that what they say in court? And I'm still worried about that damn group. I know there are plenty more where Mike came from."

Cam agreed. "I went online. They're scary, what they write, how they talk."

"Didn't you think it was a little scary to come here, to my apartment, to be alone with me, and accuse me of murder?" Jake reached out a hand and covered Cam's.

"Hey, I'm a big girl. Plus, I had my trusty phone." She drew it out of her pocket. Just then the descending out-of-battery-power tones played. "Oops. Anyway, how do you know I don't have a black belt in kung fu?"

"Do you?" Jake raised one eyebrow.

"No." She smiled. "I'm going to finish my lunch now that we've gotten that out of the way. I'm sure you have work to do this afternoon, and so do I."

As they ate, they talked about how the crops were coming along, Jake's plans for a monthly wine-pairing dinner, anything but murder.

When they were finished, Cam rose and thanked Jake.

He walked her to the door. "You're still not completely sure I didn't kill Mike. I hope you'll believe me when they find the actual murderer."

"They?" Cam shook her head. "*They* think they have it all buttoned up with Lucinda behind bars. They're not really looking anymore. The last thing Pappas said to me was, 'Perhaps another suspect will turn up.' Those aren't the words of an active investigator. No, if anybody is going to find the killer, it's going to be me."

"Shouldn't you leave it to the police? You could get hurt, Cam. If I had been the criminal, you might never have gotten out of here alive." He leered at her. "I have a very large walk-in freezer downstairs."

As he put his arm around her, Cam shivered. She didn't know if it was from attraction or fear. Maybe she was still wondering about him. "I'd better get going. That was a great lunch. I appreciate it. And thanks for not using your cleaver on me." She mustered as big a smile as she could.

Walking down the stairs, Cam glanced back up and called, "I'll see you Sunday."

Jake stood backlit at the door to his apartment. His expression had returned to somber, and he loomed as large as an ogre.

Cam checked her watch after she climbed into the truck. Might as well take advantage of the clean clothes again for a visit to David Kosloski. She debated calling first but then remembered her dead phone. It wasn't until she pulled up in the K-One Construction parking lot that she wondered what she was going to say, and then wondered why she hadn't wondered that yesterday. If David was here illegally, and if the militia, with Mike as the messenger, had said they were going to expose him, David had a lot to lose. His successful company, his reputation in the community as a generous donor to charities, his ability to support an ill wife and a daughter. Would he have killed Mike, though? Cam had no idea if any of it was true. Her head hurt from all the ifs. But there was one more. If any of it was true, would David even talk with her about it?

He certainly wouldn't talk if she stayed sitting in her truck. Cam climbed out, took a deep breath, and opened the door to the office. The scene was different today. A man bent over blueprints on the reception counter, and a couple sat in chairs, the woman clutching a folder.

The door to the back opened. David Kosloski, a folder in his hand, ushered an older woman out.

David's eyes fell on Cam where she stood just inside the door. "Cam, what can I help you with?" He walked across the room to her. His mouth smiled, but his eyes did not participate.

"I wondered if I could talk with you for a few minutes."

"Is it about Eleanor? She's been behaving herself, hasn't she?" His brow sprouted new lines.

"She's great. No, it's not about her." Cam lowered her voice. "I just wanted to ask you . . ." She looked around the busy room. What had she been thinking?

"Aniela said you were in yesterday, too. Asking questions." David matched Cam's low tone. His kindly expression changed. His eyes flew wide open, and his nostrils flared. "What's this about, Cam?" he hissed through a clenched jaw.

"I've been hearing things about a militia group harassing immigrants," Cam said, almost whispering. "I wondered if . . ."

"Not here. Not now." His eyes darted around the room and then back at Cam. "Why don't you just go back to your farm and mind your own business?"

"This obviously isn't a good time. I'm sorry to bother you." She turned to go, then paused. She asked in a normal voice, "Will we see you at the shareholders' potluck tomorrow?"

Kosloski nodded, his face once again that of the busy entrepreneur, but his eyes daggers into hers.

Cam spent the rest of the afternoon hand weeding in the heat, trying to still her mind in the company of earthworms and crows uncurious about murder. As the sun made its way toward the horizon, a breeze finally came to visit. It cooled her brow and rustled the tops of the trees. She wished it brought answers, too.

She stretched, surveying the back field. At least part of her world was in order. The potato shoots were already pushing up through their hills. The three hundred garlic plants, their white bases thick and healthy, their green leaves bowing gracefully to the sides, were getting ready to throw up their pointy, alien-looking scapes. The soil in the rows of corn was dark and largely weed free.

She layered her hands on the top of the hoe handle and leaned her chin onto them, staring out at where the last field bordered the woods. The question of who killed Mike Montgomery was not right with the world. David Kosloski and Jake had both acted oddly, almost threateningly, when Cam tried to talk with them about their immigration status and the militia. She was new to town, of course. It was illogical to assume that everyone she asked questions of would be forthcoming.

And then there was Stuart. It seemed like she was missing information about him. As the lazy red disk of sun slid behind the trees, she checked her watch and made a plan. First, she'd call Tina and see if she knew the circumstances of Stuart's leaving the company. After that, she had an idea of one more source to check.

Peering at mailboxes along a dark country road, Cam drove slowly, thinking of what Tina had said. She hadn't known anything specific but had said she thought Stuart was laid off partly because of his temper.

Cam stopped, checked the address on her phone, and resumed. The narrow road was in serious need of repaving and wasn't doing her truck's shock absorbers any favors. Then the way appeared to end. When she reached that point, she saw instead that it took a sharp turn to the right. The number on the mailbox at the turn had faded from black to barely readable gray, but Cam thought it looked like a seventy-nine. She turned into a winding graveled drive with even more ruts and potholes than the road.

The house, when she arrived, was a small two-story farmhouse. The moon hadn't yet risen, and the sky was inky.

"Mrs. Wilson?" Cam raised her hand in a wave as she shut the truck door behind her. A diminutive person, backlit from the room behind her, sat in a rocking chair in the dark of a wide covered porch. "Hello?" Cam called.

No response. Cam, carrying a bag, picked her way along a gravel path toward the house. Stuart's car wasn't in the drive, and Cam didn't see a garage. At the bottom of the steps, Cam paused. "Mrs. Wilson? I'm Cameron Flaherty. I met you the other night. My uncle is —"

"Albert St. Pierre. And your great-aunt was Marie, God rest her soul. Come on up, dear." The woman, now in silhouette, beckoned to Cam and then patted the wicker chair next to her.

Cam climbed the stairs and sat, wondering if she was doing the right thing. But Stuart's mother might be able to speak to her son's innocence. It was worth a try. She might have a few moments of clarity here in her home territory. At least she now seemed to know that Marie had left this world. The older woman leaned toward Cam, half a weathered face now in the light. Cam took the hand she was offered, the skin a cool wrinkled leather glove over knobby knuckles. She set the bag on the floor.

"So you've chosen the farming life, I hear. Tell me, how is my old boyfriend, Albert?" Mrs. Wilson smiled at a long-ago secret.

"He's doing well, Mrs. Wilson. He seems to like Moran Manor. We saw you there just the other night, remember?"

"I can't say that I do."

"Well, Albert's making friends there." That she didn't remember didn't surprise Cam at all, having witnessed the older woman's bewildered expression in the dining room. "I know he misses Great-Aunt Marie, but he's thriving."

"He was quite the looker in his day." She winked at Cam. "A bit older than I, of course, but not too much. Then Marie, why, she just snatched him away from me. But we grew to be friends by and by. Such a shame she passed over ahead of her time. Now, were you looking for my boy?"

Cam was startled at the change of subject. "Yes, I guess I was." She stalled. "He must still be at work, though." Cam had planned on him being there until the Food Mart closed at ten.

"Or maybe out with one of his girlfriends. Although I hear that Katie girl left town. They all leave town sooner or later." Mrs. Wilson's sweet tone turned suddenly sour. "Good riddance, after she dropped my Stuart for that poor boy."

"Poor boy? Who was that?"

"Oh, girlie, let me tell you." Mrs. Wilson lowered her voice to a harsh whisper. She leaned toward Cam.

Cam reciprocated the lean. Was this going to be the piece of information she needed? Her heart was drinking at a nightclub with a really loud band. Its pounding drowned out the chorus of crickets and the periodic buzzing of cicadas in the background.

"The way they move me around every night, I don't know who sees whom, or even who I'm seeing," Mrs. Wilson said. "They move all my stuff, they put it back in exactly the same place, but when I wake up, I'm in a different room. Every damn morning."

Disappointed, Cam smiled politely. She hoped. "Who are 'they'?"

Mrs. Wilson looked left and right, and then back at Cam. "You know. They're trying to confuse me." She tapped her forehead. "But I know what's up. I can tell."

"I'm sure you do. Getting back to Stuart, was he upset Katie started going out with someone else?" Cam silently urged the lucid part of Mrs. Wilson's brain to wrest power from the confused part.

Mrs. Wilson leaned back in her chair. She nodded. "Yes. Poor Stuart has always had a little problem with his temper. He comes by it honestly. Got it from his father, rest his soul."

"Oh?"

"Why, yes. Could be that's why young Katie left him for the Montgomery boy. Didn't make things any better, though."

"The Montgomery boy. You mean Mike?" Cam's thoughts raced. Could that be who Katie left Stuart for?

"My old friend Beverly is in great pain now." Mrs. Wilson nodded again.

Cam narrowed her eyes. Which part of the old woman's brain held sway now? Of course. Small town. Everybody was friends or at least knew everyone else. "Mrs. Wilson, did Stuart confront Mike, Bev's son?"

The older woman did not respond. She began to rock with a steady rhythm. The claws of her hands gripped the chair's arms like she was about to take off in flight. An unevenness in the porch floor made the rockers give a *ba dump, ba dump, ba dump.*

Cam glanced at her watch. That was apparently all she was going to get out of Stuart's mother. "Well, I have to run now. It was nice talking with you."

Stuart's mother met Cam's eyes for a moment, then resumed staring at a memory beyond Cam's reach.

Cam had just stepped off the last stair when a car tore around the corner and blasted up the drive. Stuart.

He threw open his car door and was shouting at Cam before he even got out. "What are you doing here? Are you harassing my mother? Can't you see she's got dementia?" He strode toward Cam.

She could almost see the smoke pouring out his ears. He must have gotten off work early. She kept her eyes on him as she moved toward her truck and thought fast. "Hi, Stuart. I brought you the rest of your share." She pointed to the bag on the porch. "Remember you left it Saturday? And I wanted to tell you about the farm potluck tomorrow night." She smiled the smile of a confident farmer and hoped it came through. "Your mother and I just had a nice chat about her and her old boyfriend, my great-uncle."

"I'll bet that's not all you talked about." Stuart now stood face-to-face with Cam, except that his red face and boiling eyes were a couple of inches below hers. "And don't you remember? You told me about the potluck yesterday." He folded his arms and glared. "I didn't realize dementia was catching."

"Oh, that's right." Cam lightly smacked

her forehead. "It's such a busy time of year, I forgot about that. Well, I'll be going. See you tomorrow." Cam slid to the side. She took one step before Stuart's hand shot out and grabbed her right arm. The cool evening air turned suddenly cold despite the heat of his meaty hand on her bare bicep.

"What else did you talk with my mother about?" Without taking his eyes off Cam's, he raised his voice. "Mother? What did you tell Cam?"

The bumping of the rocker was the only response. The cicadas' buzz zoomed to a crescendo and then fell silent again.

"Excuse me, Stuart. Let go of my arm." Cam kept her voice calm as she returned his gaze. "I'll see you tomorrow."

He squeezed her arm in a vise grip before releasing it, then dusted his hand on his pants as if he'd touched fresh manure. "Get out of here," he spat. He turned and stalked toward the house.

Cam drove away as fast as was safe, bumping along the country lane until she reached the main road. He was right, of course. She had taken advantage of a senile old lady. She took one arm off the wheel and tried to rub the impending bruise from where Stuart had gripped her. Her heart didn't relax until she was almost home.

Chapter 19

The reds and blues on the screen mocked Cam. She'd thought displaying all the facts in the spreadsheet graphically would help her brain get a handle on who did what and why. But that was stupid. She shook her head. She didn't process things graphically. Hers was a brain that hungered for numbers and algorithms, not pictures.

She pushed back in her chair and took a sip of the scotch she'd poured. The time display in the corner of the screen read nine thirty. She ought to climb those stairs and go to bed. Dawn was going to show up early. But the image of Stuart's angry face in front of hers nagged at her. Was he just protective of his elderly mother, or had he been afraid his mother had let Cam in on a secret? Trouble was Cam hadn't learned what the secret was.

She replayed the conversation with Mrs. Wilson. She'd said all the girlfriends left eventually. And that Stuart had a temper. That didn't seem so earthshaking. The question Cam had really wanted an answer to — whether Stuart had confronted Mike about stealing Katie from him — had gotten only rocking from Stuart's mother.

The house phone rang into the silence. Cam jumped in her chair. Who was calling a farmer this late in the evening? A quick jolt of panic buzzed through her. She pictured a person out in the darkness, peering over the top of the café curtains, watching her answer.

She reached for the phone. As it continued to ring, she checked the caller ID, but it read only PRIVATE NAME, PRIVATE NUMBER. Might as well get it over with.

She pressed the TALK button. "Hello?"

"Cameron? Pappas here, returning your call."

Cam blew out the breath she didn't know she'd been holding. "Hello, Detective. Any news?"

"I thought you had information for me." His voice was terse. "Your message was cut off while you were in the middle of a story about Lucinda becoming ill. I don't understand how it relates to the case."

"Well, the thing is, I was sick after the festival, too. It just seemed odd. Plus, Stu-

348

art had gone home with —"

"I know that." Pappas cut her off. "I'm sure you both just ate a bad dish from one of the vendors. There was apparently no food permit pulled for the event, by the way."

"I didn't organize it." Cam didn't enjoy being scolded.

"So what other critically important facts have you uncovered?" Pappas didn't sound like he believed Cam could have come up with anything even remotely useful.

"I found out Alexandra's sister, Katie, was dating Mike Montgomery. Did you know that?"

"Alexandra Magnusson, your subscriber?"

"Right. Her sister had been seeing Stuart Wilson but apparently dropped him for Mike. Stuart has a bit of a temper, and I thought you might want to check it out."

"Why would that be? We have a suspect in custody, as you are well aware."

"Maybe Stuart went to see Mike. Or maybe he has information about the real murderer. Lucinda did not kill Mike. I am sure of that. Also, what if Mike told Katie something? What if she heard about a person who was after Mike or had been threatening him?"

"Does Katie live at home with her sister?"

"She did, but she left town yesterday." Cam leaned back in her chair and put her feet up on her desk.

Pappas's groan came through loud and clear. "Where did she go? And why didn't you tell me earlier about this Katie?"

"I just found out tonight that she was dating Mike. Anyway, Alexandra said Katie went to New York."

"State or city?"

"City. Maybe Alexandra knows where Katie is staying." *Or maybe not,* Cam thought.

"I'll check it out. Anything else?"

"No, I don't think so." Cam's eyes fell on the infrared light where it sat on the counter. Should she tell him about it? She should have turned it over earlier. She wasn't in the mood for more reprimands. "No, that's it."

"Thank you. I'll be in touch." Pappas disconnected.

Cam splashed just a little more scotch into her glass. She sipped it as she paced from one end of the house to the other and then back. Pappas certainly hadn't given a moment's credibility to her idea that maybe she and Lucinda getting sick the same night might be related. She didn't know how if it wasn't from food poisoning. She stopped still. Poisoning. Maybe it had been deliberate. But by whose hand? She had no idea who would want to get both her and Lucinda out of the way at the same time.

She resumed her pacing and her thinking. As usual, Pappas hadn't answered any of her questions. Although he at least had the grace to act surprised about Katie going to New York City.

She thought of Katie, a young person exploring a big city. She almost envied her, with no responsibilities to customers, no murders to solve, no jailed friend to free.

A ray of light jabbed Cam in the eye as the mockingbird ran through its repertoire on a branch outside her bedroom window. She groaned and closed her eyes again. It had to be near six if the sun was already aiming at her pillow. A late start for a farmer. That last scotch had been one too many. Still, work called.

She sat on the back porch with her coffee. The cool of the evening had continued into the morning, but yesterday's breeze was gone. Thin clouds high in the sky promised another still, warm day, and the lingering rosy color in the east was a guarantee of rain later, if the old adage "Red sky in the morning, sailors take warning" had any validity.

Cam cocked her head at a sound. It was early for Tully to be driving up his gravel driveway. *Wait. Driving up?* Where had her neighbor been? He was old and not in the habit of either staying out all night or going for early morning coffee runs. She stood and peered over the lilacs at the border of the yard. Tully's drive paralleled Cam's but extended much farther back. When the trees were in leaf, like now, she could barely see the neighbor's house, which was set so far back, it was on a level with Cam's back field.

A vehicle crept slowly away from the road. Not Tully's ancient Cadillac. On the contrary. If Cam was not mistaken, the ratty red pickup was the farm truck Bev Montgomery drove. And Cam was pretty sure Bev didn't have a breakfast date with Tully. Albert had once mentioned a long-standing feud between the two. This morning was getting interesting.

Cam darted into the house, grabbed her cell phone, and made her way to the barn, following the far edge of the property. She peered out the back door of the barn. The truck had pulled off the drive under a line of trees that extended to Cam's property line and joined the woods rimming the back of her fields. Sure enough, Bev Montgomery climbed out and started in the direction of the potato and garlic field. A black bag of some kind was slung over her shoulder.

Cam's anger rose. What was Bev doing skulking around her property? And what was in the bag? Cam was about to find out. She headed for the field but kept to the far side, weaving behind the hoop house, circling behind the compost area, ducking under cover of a long row of five-foot-high grapevines. Cam pushed aside a cluster of wide, flat grape leaves and peered through.

Bev stood in the middle of the potato rows. The bag was on the ground. She had a bundle in her hands. It looked like she was trying to open a package. Cam slid her phone out of her pocket, held it out in front of her, and snapped a couple of pictures. She strode around the edge of the vine.

"Hey!" Cam set the camera in the phone on zoom and clicked two more photos, capturing both Bev's startled look and the package. "What are you doing?"

Bev glanced back at the package and fumbled with it for another moment. Which left Cam with enough time to stash the phone in her pocket and rev her long legs into running stride. Bev looked up and swore loud enough for Cam to hear. As

Cam arrived at her side, Bev dropped the package on the ground. She snatched up her bag with one hand and reached into it with the other, her eyes wide and wild.

"Stop right there," Cam demanded. She grabbed both the bag and the arm in the bag. A loud noise exploded. The dirt sprayed up from the ground a few inches from Cam's foot. A hole smoldered at the bottom of the bag, and smoke escaped from the half-open top. "What the heck? You have a gun in there?"

Bev cursed. She slammed her hip into Cam's.

Cam kept her grip on both Bev and the bag. Her ears rang from the noise with a din that almost blocked out Bev's voice. She squeezed Bev's wrist as tightly as she could. "Drop the bag, Bev." Cam tugged at the bag, careful not to pull it toward her.

Bev didn't drop it. She tried to twist away from Cam, but Cam had the advantage of height and youth. And the disadvantage of both hands already occupied.

"You and your organics. You're taking all my business away," Bev snarled. "I can't believe Albert let you do this to me."

"Bev, drop the bag. Then we'll talk." Cam's voice shook.

Bev still struggled. Cam had no choice.

She wasn't about to be the recipient of a wild bullet from an out-of-control woman. She lifted her knee and brought her farm boot down hard on the insole of Bev's worn sneaker and then drew her foot back and aimed for Bev's kneecap.

Bev screamed as Cam connected. She released the bag and fell on her side, clutching her knee.

Cam walked the black bag several yards away and placed it on the ground with care. She rejoined Bev, kneeling at her side.

"I'm sorry to hurt you, Bev. But you come onto my land, and then you try to shoot me? And what's this package?"

Cam reached for it. She examined it, turning it over. It was the size of a small radio or a book. She peered at the label. *Leptinotarsa decemlineata.* Cam's eye's widened. She glared at Bev.

"You were going to introduce Colorado potato beetles? Onto my potato crop?" Cam's voice rose. "Really? You think I don't have enough troubles?"

"That's exactly what I wanted to do. Add to your troubles until you decided farming was too much for you." The vehemence in Bev's voice was gone, replaced with a plaintive tone. "Go back to your city job, and keep your hands clean."

Cogs clicked in Cam's brain as she sank to her haunches. "You were responsible for the other sabotage, weren't you? The rhubarb? The arugula?"

Bev nodded. "I wanted to stop you."

"Did you put Mike up to using chemicals on my crops, too?"

"I might have." Tears filled her eyes. "But he didn't get a chance, did he? For all I know, you killed him."

Cam sat in silence. So that was one mystery solved. But not the mystery of the murder. Bev did not kill her own son.

CHAPTER 20

Cam stared at Bev. What was she going to do with her? She stood and extended her hand to Bev. "Can you stand up?"

Bev gazed at Cam's hand for a moment, took it, and Cam pulled her up. Bev dropped Cam's hand as she tested out the leg Cam had attacked.

"It hurts, but I don't think you broke anything." Bev hobbled in a slow circle.

Cam kept an eye on the bag, glad Bev hadn't gone near it. She didn't want to have to disable the older farmer a second time.

"Good. I really am sorry I hurt you. But I thought you were going to shoot me." Cam folded her arms. "Were you?"

Bev didn't meet her eyes. "No." Her eyes flared. "But you have to be prepared. In certain states, you come at me like that, I can shoot. Perfectly legal."

"But not in Massachusetts!" Cam had heard about those so-called self-defense laws and the kind of violence they encouraged.

"No, not here. I have a license to carry, though."

"And, anyway, you were the one trespassing on my land. You were the one trying to ruin my business. If I come running at you, I'm the one protecting my property, aren't I?"

Bev nodded, slowly. "I'll be going." She headed for her bag at the end of the row of potatoes.

Cam stuck her arm out and blocked Bev. "Uh-uh." She shook her head.

"I'm taking my bag with me."

"No way." Cam shook her head again. "It's mine now, or at least until I figure out what to do with the gun."

"Give me my keys, then. They're in the outside pocket."

Cam gingerly retrieved the keys and tossed them to Bev.

Bev glared as she caught them. She turned and limped away. When she reached the neighbor's field, she paused. She looked back at Cam and opened her mouth.

"Good-bye, Bev." Cam waved.

Bev shut her mouth and kept walking.

Cam heaved a deep breath. She leaned over the black bag and held it open. The only thing in it was a stubby gun with a black handle. Its cylinder looked like the ones Cam remembered from old cowboy movies. The rest of the business end of the gun was of a smaller diameter and had the word *bodyguard* printed on its side. Cam shuddered. She could easily have had her foot blown off or worse. She had been on a shooting range with Great-Uncle Albert as a teenager but hadn't touched a gun since.

Cam added the package of beetles to the bag and lifted it with care. She held it out in front of her so her knees wouldn't jostle it and walked toward the barn and the house. At the sound of tires crunching on gravel, she glanced toward the neighbor's field. *Good.* Bev was headed for the road.

But where was she going to stash the weapon? She didn't want to leave it in the truck. She'd have to call Ruth to find out what to do with it. There was no good place to lock it up in the house. Cam wandered into the barn and looked around. *Ah, just the ticket.*

On the back wall of the barn, in her tools area, hung a wall cabinet. Albert had locked up pesticides in it, but it was empty and scrubbed clean now. Cam gingerly drew the gun out of the bag and deposited it on the bottom shelf of the cabinet. She wondered if she should try to unload the weapon but decided not to mess with it any more than necessary. It would be safe here. Cam turned the key in the lock and pocketed it.

Now she had to figure out what to do with the potato beetles. That was easier. She wrapped them tightly in a plastic bag and then in another. She shoved them firmly to the bottom of the trash barrel and made sure the lid was clamped on tight afterward. The world did not need more *Leptinotarsa decemlineata.*

What a morning it had already been. One that called for more coffee and a call to Ruth, in that order.

"What do you think I should do?" Cam asked Ruth, who had sounded sleepy but had insisted she was up before listening to the story of Cam's early morning drama. "Do I take the bag to the police station? I'd hate to get Bev in trouble, but I'd also hate to get shot at again, either accidentally or on purpose, which is why I kept it."

"Gee, Cam. I wish you hadn't called me."

Cam's heart sank. She hadn't really thought through the consequences. Now that Ruth knew what had happened, of course, she'd be obliged to do whatever police procedure required. Cam waited.

Sounds of Nettie and Natalie squabbling quieted after Ruth admonished them to finish their cereal and get their shoes on.

"Bev was trespassing, correct?" Ruth spoke in a low voice.

"Right." Cam wondered if Frank was in the room and Ruth didn't want him to hear.

"Do you want to press charges on it?"

"Not really. But what do I do about the gun?"

"You should take it into the station. I'm off today, but they'll check to make sure she holds a legal license. You can let them return it to her. That will keep it out of her hands for a few days, anyway. I'll put in a call and ask them to move slowly on it."

"Thanks, Ruthie. I appreciate it."

"Hey, it's Friday. I'm sure they're too busy to deal with it today." Ruth cleared her throat. "In fact, I highly suspect nobody will have time to call for her to come and pick it up until at least Monday. If she even owns it legally. That'll give Bev time to cool off."

"Is she going to get arrested for firing it, though?"

"Since you say the gun discharged accidentally and it happened on private property, no, I don't think so. Nettie, leave her alone!"

Cam laughed. "Tough morning?"

"Every morning is a bit tough. Especially when I'm on duty until six in the morning. I just got home a little while ago."

"Ouch."

"Yeah. Well, they'll be off to school by eight, and then I'll sleep. Bye, Frank."

Cam heard a door slam.

"We're the proverbial ships passing in the night sometimes. Listen, I gotta run, Cammie. Be careful with that gun. It's probably still loaded."

"I will. Oh, I just remembered. The subscribers are having a potluck in the barn tonight. Bring the girls, if you want. Should be fun. Six o'clock."

After Ruth said she'd try to make it, Cam said good-bye and hung up. She'd take the gun over to the station later. It was safe in the barn for now.

Cam spent the rest of the morning working. In an effort to preserve her mental health, she tried not to accompany the working with thinking, at least not about murder. But when she turned on the hose at nearly midday and strolled into the hoop house to water the seedlings, the image of Mike lying dead on the ground drew a shudder through her from the crown of her head to the tips of her toes. Cam drew a hand through her hair, surprised it wasn't standing straight up from the memory.

Hair. Cam swore. She had promised Lucinda a decent hairbrush and a pack of new underwear. Two days ago. What kind of a friend was she? Cam turned off the water and strode to the house. She grabbed her purse and keys and strode right back out to her truck. She made it to the Newburyport shopping center in record time while staying a hair under five miles over the speed limit.

After purchasing several packs of cotton bikinis in jailbreak-wild colors and in a size two down from her own, Cam went to the drugstore next door. She threw a good sturdy brush into her basket, then added her own favorite deodorant, a pack of wipes, a lipstick in a color she thought Lucinda would love, a box of pads, and a pack of disposable razors. Then she put the razors back. The police might not even allow the lipstick and wipes. Cam had read stories about weapon-grade material, like needles and files, being smuggled in to prisoners in seemingly innocuous items like lipstick.

She moved to the candy aisle and added a pack of dark chocolate miniatures. Everybody needed chocolate, didn't they? And if the station wouldn't let Lucinda have it, maybe Cam could use it as a gentle persuasive offering to let her have a short visit with Lucinda. Not a bribe, certainly not a bribe.

In her truck, Cam drew a notepad out of the glove compartment and scribbled a note to Lucinda. She hoped she'd be able to see her, but had an idea she wouldn't be allowed. She wrote that she hoped life wasn't too tough, and that she was sure Lucinda would be exonerated soon. She stuffed it in the bag of purchases and drove off.

She stood at the Westbury PD's reception counter fifteen minutes later. A stony-faced woman was on duty. Cam's heart sank.

"Hi. I have a few things for Lucinda DaSilva." Cam held up the semiopaque plastic bag.

"Name please?" The officer glanced at Cam, pursed her lips, and returned her eyes to her monitor and keyboard.

"Sorry. Cameron Flaherty. Eight Attic Hill Road here in Westbury." Cam looked down at her clothes. She would have pursed her lips, too. Dirt smudged her yellow T-shirt, and her khaki work shorts showed smears of green and flecks of brown compost.

The officer tapped on the keyboard. Without looking up, she said, "Things?"

"Yes, she asked for a hairbrush and some underwear." Cam peered at her name tag.

"I also picked up a couple of other toiletries, Officer Kingsley."

"List them."

"Deodorant, lipstick, wipes, pads. And chocolate."

"Put them there." The officer pointed to a lower spot in the counter, then grabbed a form from a printer and slid it under the clip of a clipboard. "Sign this."

Cam laid the bag in the assigned location. She took the clipboard and signed her name under the list of items. "Could I go back and say hi to her? Just for a minute?"

The woman's glare was enough of an answer. Cam didn't think chocolates would sway her even a millimeter. She thanked the officer and turned to go. She paused at the outer door. Voices grew nearer from the hallway leading to the interrogation rooms and the jail cells. One sounded like Susan Lee. Was the other Detective Pappas?

Susan emerged from the doorway, followed, indeed, by Detective Pappas. When Susan caught sight of Cam, she closed her mouth, mid-sentence, apparently. She nudged Pappas, who fell silent, as well.

"Cam, what brings you here?" Susan said. She walked toward Cam, heels clicking.

"Hi, Susan." Cam nodded at Pappas. "Detective. What's going on?"

"The detective had a few more questions for Lucinda, so I sat in on the session."

Cam raised her eyebrows. She waited for more. And waited.

Susan smiled politely. "As I said, what brings you here?"

"I told Lucinda I would bring her a few, uh, personal items." Cam didn't need to elaborate about the bikini underwear, deodorant, and sanitary supplies in front of Pappas. Not to mention the chocolates. She tilted her head toward the bag, which was still on the counter.

"Good," Susan said.

"I asked if I could see her, but Officer Kingsley here wouldn't facilitate that. How is Lucinda? Any chance she'll be getting out soon?"

Pappas excused himself without meeting Cam's eyes and went back through the inner door.

Cam was about to ask Susan if she could get her in to see Lucinda when Susan's phone played a bit of Bach. Susan pressed a button on the phone and sailed out the door, already talking, already moving on to the next client, the next case.

Cam sighed and exited, too, as Susan's Jaguar slid out of the parking lot onto the road. She stood and watched it drive off.

366

She was still without answers. What had Susan and Pappas been doing there? Maybe the case had turned. Perhaps Pappas had finally uncovered information that made him doubt Lucinda's involvement in the murder. That would be a big break. She hated to think of Lucinda getting used to living in a jail cell. Cam wished Pappas or Susan had let her in on the secret, though.

As she drove slowly toward home, she rued her decision to let the shareholders have their potluck on the farm tonight. Socializing was the last thing she wanted to do. She'd have to cook. She'd have to clean up the barn. She'd need to set up the couple of tables she had and then clean herself up. Investigating, thinking, trying to use her intellect to solve the mystery of who killed Mike Montgomery were what drew her. Instead she'd have to spend the evening smiling and talking with customers over dinner in the barn.

The barn. Cam smacked herself on the forehead. She was supposed to have brought the gun to the police station. She had completely forgotten about it in her guilt about not having gotten Lucinda her supplies the day before. Well, it was locked up. Nobody at the potluck would even know about it. She hoped.

■ ■ ■ ■

Cam gazed at her spreadsheet. She knew she should be either in the kitchen, cooking, or out in the barn, preparing for the potluck, but the lure of the computer overrode the tasks that would lead to an evening of chatting and smiling. The logic of columns and rows and their underlying bits and bytes calmed her in a way her fellow humans didn't, in a way she'd never really been able to explain.

Jake. She felt pretty sure that she didn't need to keep him in the suspect column. She highlighted his row and dragged it down to the others section, which she'd added at the bottom, and then considered the rest of the other names and everything that had happened in the past two weeks. She thought about David Kosloski, his strange behavior, his sister at the office. She mused on her conversation with Stuart's mother and her allusions to his temper. She recalled her encounters with Frank Jackson and with Bev. Something was still missing, though. Running the graphics script didn't help. The solution nagged at the back of her brain but stayed stubbornly there, instead of coming to the forefront.

Cam pictured Lucinda sitting in jail until frustration shrouded her mood like a heavy, itchy cloak. She shoved her chair back with a bang.

CHAPTER 21

An hour later Cam sprinkled a handful of violets and chive flowers on top of the mixed greens in her wide salad bowl. The lettuces were really taking off, as were the arugula and mizuna, so she had cut a full basket for her contribution to the potluck, and the cutting had soothed her raw feelings in a way the computer had failed to. She checked her watch — four o'clock — then covered the salad with a clean, damp dishcloth and placed it in the refrigerator. She would whip up a vinaigrette at the last minute. Cam smiled to herself as she strolled out to the barn. Vinaigrette had caught on in the last decade, but she'd heard waitstaff in restaurants call it "vinegarette." She was willing to bet they didn't realize they had Americanized it without meaning to. Jake's waitstaff knew better, but not those in less fancy establishments.

Cam looked around the barn and sighed.

Cleaning for dinner guests had just taken on a whole new meaning. She grabbed the push broom and set to work clearing the old wooden floor. When she'd emptied a couple of dustpans into a bucket and dumped that in the compost area, she dragged the farm table to the back of the space. She spread the colorful market cloth over it. People could put their offerings there. She set up her collapsible market table in the middle. She arrayed three cheap plastic chairs and unfolded her four lawn chairs, then added an old metal folding chair that had been Albert and Marie's. Felicity had said she'd also bring tables, hadn't she?

She sneezed as she surveyed the space. It looked kind of bleak. Cam snapped her fingers. That was what it needed. Striding to the house, she thought of picking a few bouquets of flowers, too. She rummaged in a kitchen drawer until she found a half dozen strings of tiny white lights, plus the two strings of hot-pepper lights she liked to put up at Christmas. Cam loaded an orange extension cord into her arms, as well. The clock on the stove read four thirty, so she was still good for time. Felicity had said she would come early, at five thirty or so.

Cam took the lights back to the barn. As

she walked, she heard a noise like a distant train and looked up. A sudden wind had set every deciduous leaf to vibrate and every evergreen needle to purr. The treetops swayed. A massive cloud as dark as charcoal approached from the west. *Uh-oh. Could be a stormy potluck.*

Cam began stringing the lights around the walls. The old plank walls provided plenty of nails and other protrusions to hang the wires from. A bang sounded, and the rear of the barn darkened. Cam looked up with a start. The back door of the barn had swung shut with force from the wind.

She connected the extension cord to the last end, plugged it into the wall, and stepped back to survey the effect, hands on hips. The tiny white points lit the dark shadows, and the reds and oranges of the pepper lights warmed the room into festivity. The light seemed to illuminate that back part of Cam's brain, too. All the bits of information she'd been accumulating now fell into place. Her eyes widened. She had to call Pappas.

She patted her pockets and cursed. No cell phone. She'd have to call from the house.

"Looks pretty."

Cam whirled, her heart racing. "Stuart!

You startled me."

Stuart stood ten yards behind her near the wide door, one hand in his pocket, the other hanging on to a knapsack slung over one shoulder. Wind blew in through the doorway, making his thin hair poke out in odd directions. He gazed at her through narrowed eyes, his head slightly cocked. The edges of his mouth pulled down.

Cam faced Mike's killer.

CHAPTER 22

"You're early for the potluck." *What is he doing here?* She had to keep calm. Stuart couldn't know she knew he was the murderer.

"I know." Stuart reached back and slid the door shut. He dropped the heavy latch into its slot.

"We should leave that open." Cam started for the door, her heart pounding.

"Too windy. Gets on my nerves." Stuart walked slowly toward Cam.

Cam tried to move around him. "People are going to start arriving any minute now." Felicity wasn't due for another hour, but Stuart didn't know that.

"Not a problem." He grabbed her arm. "I put a sign on the driveway saying the potluck was canceled."

"Why'd you do that, Stuart?" Cam tried to twist away. She could smell her own fear.

"Let's sit down and have a chat." He let

go of her arm as he gestured to the nearest chairs, then sank into one of them.

"Thanks, but I have way too much to do," Cam said with what she hoped was a calm smile. She edged toward the back door, keeping an eye on Stuart. "Gotta cut flowers, and the dish I'm cooking for the potluck is in the oven," she lied. "You're welcome to sit and wait, though."

"It's not going to work."

Cam twisted the knob on the door. The door wouldn't open. She rattled it and pushed it with her shoulder. It didn't budge.

"Told you it wouldn't work."

Cam faced Stuart, her stomach a stone.

"I padlocked it from the outside. Now, come and sit down." With a cold smile, he patted the chair next to his.

"You padlocked my door?"

"I was afraid you wouldn't want to be alone with me in here. Guess I was right."

Cam's fear morphed into anger. She marched toward the wide door he had slid shut. She had no intention of spending another minute alone with him. Out of the corner of her eye she saw him lean down and do something with his pack.

Stuart rose and grabbed Cam in a sudden move. He twisted her right arm behind her. His other hand waved a long knife with a curving blade. The knife he'd brandished at the butcher counter. The knife she'd last seen dripping with blood.

He held the blade against her neck and forced her down into one of the molded plastic chairs. "I asked you to sit. I asked nice. Now see what you've made me do."

Cam struggled, but her arm burned where he held it twisted. "Let go of me."

Stuart's pressed the knife to the side of her neck. The blade stung her skin.

"Okay, I'll talk to you!"

Stuart released the pressure on her throat. "And you'll sit there like a good girl?"

Cam cringed inwardly but nodded. Stuart let go of her arm. He pulled up a chair, directly facing her.

"Now then." Stuart's voice had an edge to it. He placed his hands on his knees and leaned forward. "You've been poking around in my business. I heard you've been asking questions about Katie. *My* Katie. And then, last night, you harassed my poor old mother."

"I . . ." Cam began, shaking her head.

Stuart pointed the knife at her. "I know what you've been up to. And it's going to stop."

Cam's thoughts sped. How was she going to get out of here? "I heard Katie left you for Mike."

Stuart leapt out of his seat. He kicked at the leg of her chair, jangling her nerves.

Bad move. Now she'd made him mad. Cam couldn't help cowering.

He paced toward the door and back. "She didn't leave me. He *stole* her. She was so innocent. So beautiful. That rat took her from me."

"Not according to her sister, he didn't."

Stuart walked away.

"Alexandra says she was tired of your temper." Cam realized she was yakking out of fear. She was only making him madder. *Better get that under control before he goes over the edge.* Without the overhead light or the illumination from outdoors, the barn was dim despite the strings of lights. Shadows threatened from corners.

"Listen, there's nothing wrong with getting mad when the situation calls for it." Stuart's flushed face glistened with sweat. Shadows of red and green streaked his cheek closest to the pepper lights. "I've been in a lot of angry-making situations lately." He ended up in front of Cam. He glowered down at her. He tapped the knife blade against his palm. The blade still bore traces of blood.

"Why don't you sit down?" Cam kept her

voice way more level than she felt. "You look hot."

He stayed on his feet. "Your snooping around is one of those situations. You couldn't just leave well enough alone, could you? I heard you telling that statie about my temper last night, about me and Mike."

"You heard me?" Cam thought back. She had spoken to Pappas the night before. "Were you listening at my window?"

"I'll bet you thought your secret admirer left you those carnations."

Cam peered at him. "You left those?"

"That little ladybug on the bucket? It's a real bug."

She felt like an idiot.

"I've been listening to you for a week now. You talk to yourself a lot, you know."

Cam shuddered. What had he heard her talking about? "You have a lot of nerve."

Stuart nodded with a smug smile. "And they have your little friend Lucinda in jail. They think she did it."

"But she didn't!"

"Well, maybe not." He giggled.

At the sound, Cam's anger turned back to fear. This guy was off his rocker.

"I'm the one who tipped them off about that." Pride tinted his voice.

"About what?"

"Oh, that she'd been seen in the green-house that afternoon. And when they searched her place? They found Mike's cigarette case, the one the stupid militia gives all its members. It conveniently had Lucinda's fingerprints on it. How did they get there?" Stuart said in a singsong voice, smiling an awful parody of innocence.

A chill drew through Cam as if it were January and not June.

"You poisoned Lucinda's drink, didn't you? What did you put in it?" As Cam waited for his answer, she tried to figure out how she was going to take this lunatic down. She was taller than him by a couple of inches, but he weighed more and likely had the adrenaline-fueled strength of a madman on his side. And then there was the knife.

Stuart turned his head toward the sliding door. Cam heard it, too — a persistent knocking.

"Cam? Are you in there? I came early to help set up," a high-pitched voice called. "Cam?"

Ellie. Cam had to convince the girl to go away. "Ellie, go back home. I'm busy right now," she called out.

"I can't. My dad already left."

As Cam rose, Stuart smacked her hard across the face and snarled in a low voice,

"Sit down and shut up."

"Ellie, run! Get help!" Cam yelled through the pain.

Stuart strode to the door and opened it, knife in hand.

Ellie saw him and turned to run.

Stuart grabbed her by the arm. "Come on in, young lady," he growled and yanked her in. He pointed the knife at her. He let go of her for a moment to drop the door latch in place, then placed his hand on the back of her neck.

Cam realized he must have lied. He didn't put a sign up, or David wouldn't have dropped Ellie off. Cam's sense of helplessness almost overcame her.

Ellie looked around, bewildered. "What's going on, Cam? Why's it so dark in here?" She tried to slip out of Stuart's hold without success. "You're hurting me."

Stuart marched Ellie over to the chair next to Cam's and pushed her down. He waved the knife in her face.

"You're the butcher from the Food Mart." Her face paled.

Cam couldn't let him hurt Ellie. No more helplessness.

Stuart kept his hand on Ellie's shoulder. He said, "Don't even think about getting up, Flaherty." He took aim and delivered a hard kick to Cam's knee.

Cam moaned as she bent over her knee, massaging it with her hands.

Ellie turned to Cam, eyes wide. "This dude is nuts."

Cam nodded, her eyes stinging with tears of pain.

Stuart let go of Ellie and set the knife down behind him. He drew a roll of duct tape out of his knapsack. He grabbed Cam's hands. When she realized what he was doing, she turned her wrists so her palms faced inward when he taped her wrists to the chair arms. He wound the tape around Cam's left wrist and the chair three times. He glared at the diminishing roll. "Damn chintzy tape."

Cam saw Ellie's eyes on the knife. The girl rose, but Stuart blocked her way. He shoved her back into her chair.

"Sit down, kid." Flecks of saliva flew into her face.

The girl turned her face away and toward Cam with a look of determination fit for a fighter.

Stuart tore off another piece of tape and wrapped it once around Ellie's wrist and the arm of her chair, then taped her other wrist and Cam's.

"Sorry, girls. Can't have you running out

to call Westbury's finest."

Cam surreptitiously tried to move her wrists and realized she could, just a little.

Ellie fixed her eyes on Cam. Cam gazed back, trying to convey more hope than she felt.

Stuart slammed back into his chair and pulled it so close his knees almost touched Cam's. One of his legs vibrated up and down. His eyes sparkled, and he blinked fast. "Now, what were we talking about when this little twerp so rudely interrupted us?"

Ellie opened her mouth, but at a little shake of Cam's head, she shut it again.

"Oh, yes. It was how I made sure Lucinda was tabbed for the murder. But Cameron here seems to want to undo all my hard work."

"They're going to find out the truth," Cam said.

"How?" He leaned down so his eyes were inches away from Cam's. "There is no evidence linking me to Mike's killing. I made sure of that."

Cam didn't have an answer. "What did you put in Lucinda's drink at the festival?"

"Same thing I put in yours," Stuart said. "I had a little extra. Waste not, want not. Isn't that what they say?"

His grin chilled Cam.

"Why did you kill Mike? Lots of people get their feelings hurt in love, but they don't murder the competition." Cam stole a glance at Ellie, whose wide eyes pulled at her.

Stuart rose. He breathed fast, nearly panting. "He stole my girl. Nobody steals from Stuart Wilson. I told him to meet me at the farm after I saw you leave that day." He waved the knife in the air.

He'd been watching her. She felt an irrational urge to scrub herself under hot water for a very long time. "So you planned to kill Mike?"

"Well, maybe, maybe not. But he wouldn't even apologize. He flaunted the fact that Katie had been with him the night before. That they had screwed that morning." Stuart looked at Ellie. "Sorry, kid. That's the way the world is." He peered at a dark corner of the barn. "So I knocked him down and used your pitchfork. Good riddance."

So that was why Mike had died. "But why did you do it on the farm?"

Stuart shot her a look that said, "Why not?" He began whistling a tune.

"That's, like, a Doors song," Ellie said. " 'Light My Fire,' right?"

"You're a smart chick. How'd you know

that?" He leaned in, leering at her.

Ellie turned her head away with a look like she'd smelled fresh manure. "My dad likes to listen to that group."

Stuart turned to Cam and winked. "Come on, baby, light my fire," he sang in a creepy imitation of the original, stretching *fire* out into two syllables. He stuck his hands in his pockets and surveyed the barn. His eyes lit on a bale of salt-marsh hay in the corner. He stashed the knife in his knapsack. He strode to the bale and dragged it toward the large door.

He strolled, still whistling, to the corner of the barn where Cam kept the rototiller, the lawn mower, and gas cans. He hefted one of the cans.

"Great. It's full," Stuart said in a cheery voice, glancing over at Cam. He resumed his whistle as he wandered around the barn.

Cam stared at Stuart. Her palms sweated. Gasoline. He couldn't. He wouldn't. Cam watched through narrowed eyes.

"Sorry, girls. It's going to get a little hot in here." He turned and strolled back to the gas cans, whistling again. He opened the pour spout and the air breather hole on the largest can. He carried it to the bale and poured until the can was empty, shaking the last drops onto the hay.

"Stuart, stop!" Cam yelled. "You could claim self-defense for Mike's murder. But three people dead? You'll never get away with it. They'll find you."

"Maybe. Maybe not. You know. Another tragic farm accident. 'Newbie farmer stores gas near dry hay, loses life, barn.' " Stuart strode back to the machine area and grabbed a manual for one of the devices. He sauntered back to the bale. He tore out pages and crumpled them until he'd covered the top of the bale with paper.

"Cam, he's setting a fire." Blue veins stood out on Ellie's pale forehead as she whispered.

"I know. We'll get out, though." Cam swallowed. How would they escape this? She feared for the lovely old barn. She dreaded death by burning far more.

"Enjoy your sauna, girls." He picked up his knapsack and strolled away with another horrible giggle. Stuart unlatched the wide door. Backlit, he reached into his knapsack and drew out a long object. He held it down, pointing it at the bale, and clicked.

CHAPTER 23

Cam held her breath.

Stuart clicked another time. He clicked several more times. He threw it hard against the wall.

"Damn lighter." He strode to Cam's side. His face and neck had turned ruddy again, and the crazy, calm whistler had been replaced by a raging maniac. "Matches. Where do you keep matches?" His voice rose until he was almost screaming.

Cam looked over at Ellie. "I don't keep matches in the barn," she lied. "Too dangerous. Anyway, this is crazy. Cut us loose and let's talk."

Stuart answered her with a heavy slap across the cheek. Tears filled Cam's eyes, but she kept her mouth shut. He slapped her even harder in the other direction. Then he glared at Ellie.

"You know where the matches are, kid?"

Ellie shook her head, fast.

Stuart looked wildly around the barn. Suddenly the calm demeanor ruled again. He strode to the far corner, which Cam had been keeping her eyes firmly away from. The corner where she kept her charcoal grill. The corner with the shelf holding a collection of matchbooks.

"I'm sorry, Ellie," Cam murmured.

Stuart lit a match. He held it to the corner of the matchbook until the thin cardboard began to burn, then threw both the match and the lit matchbook on the soaked hay.

The flames whooshed.

CHAPTER 24

Stuart lingered until flames licked at the wall. He waved at Cam and Ellie. He slammed the door closed behind him.

The thud of the thick plank of the outer lock falling into place was the worst sound Cam had ever heard. Smoke wafted up toward the high window above the wide door, the cracked window Cam had never gotten around to fixing.

She froze. She was back in the burning house again. Six years old. Alone. Terrified. Flames crawling closer. Smoke thickening. She coughed.

"Cam!" Ellie scooted her chair close to Cam with her feet. "Hey, what's going on with you? We have to get out of here."

Cam shook herself and took a deep breath. *Right.* She'd gotten herself out then; she'd get them out now.

"I have my Girl Scout knife in my pocket. Can you get it?" Ellie angled her chair so her left hip was as close to Cam's right hand as possible.

"You rock, girlfriend." Cam wiggled her hand under the tape. She had hoped by keeping her wrists vertical when Stuart taped them that the tape would be looser. He seemed to have brought extra-sticky duct tape, though. She couldn't get her hand free.

The fire crept up the wall. She had to get her hand loose, and quick. An image of a trapped animal arose in her mind. The kind of animal that gnaws its paw off to escape the jaws of a trap.

Cam bent over her right wrist. She chewed on the tape. The chemical taste of the plastic was acrid on her tongue, but not as bitter as the prospect of burning alive. Cam bit and tore at the binding, coughing from the smoke beginning to fill the barn.

"Brilliant," Ellie said.

Out of the corner of her eye, Cam saw Ellie bend over her own wrist and bite at the tape, too. The fire crackled as it fed on the timbers that had been drying for centuries. Cam bent over her wrist again. They were almost out of time. Chew, spit, gnaw, pull. She was down to one fiber. She twisted her forearm and pulled her hand free.

Ellie pointed her chin at her pocket. Cam

slid her hand in and closed it over a pocket-knife. She drew it out. She held it near her other hand but couldn't get her fingernail under the slot in the blade to flip it out. She switched the knife to her taped hand and pried.

The knife opened. Cam cut her other hand loose. She freed both of Ellie's. Cam pulled the girl to her feet.

The thick smoke almost obscured the flames on the far wall.

"Cam, we're locked in." Ellie's voice quavered.

"I'll get us out." Cam took Ellie's hand and pointed to the right of the back door. "Lie on the floor over there until I get the door open. You stay there, okay? Girl Scout's honor?" Cam squeezed the girl's small hand and tried to beam confidence into Ellie's frightened eyes.

Ellie nodded. She held up the middle three fingers of her right hand and set her mouth in a determined line. She ran for the area and lay prostrate on the floor.

A bang sounded from the rototiller. Cam didn't look. She didn't need to see gas tanks exploding.

Cam ran for the cabinet on the wall near the back door, where she'd stashed Bev Montgomery's gun. She scrounged in her pocket for the key, desperately glad she hadn't yet changed out of her work clothes for the potluck. She inserted the key in the lock and tried to turn it. It balked. Cam swore and coughed. She drew it out, turned it over, and tried again. It wouldn't turn. She threw it down. So much for trying to shoot the lock off the back door.

A crash sounded behind her. Cam whirled. The old hayloft on the far wall, above the wide door, collapsed. Cam turned her back on it. Cam's heart raced. She couldn't give up. She had to save Ellie. And Cam had to get herself out of this hell of fire.

She glanced up. The clerestory window above the door. They might get out, after all.

"Ellie, turn away and cover your face." Cam grabbed a shovel from the wall. She took aim and hurled the shovel javelin-style at the window. The thin old glass shattered as the shovel fell back into the barn. Cam pulled her T-shirt over her head and off.

"Here's the plan," Cam said to Ellie in a short, fast burst. "You wrap my shirt around your hand. I boost you up. You knock the glass out to the outside."

Ellie nodded with wide eyes.

"Lay the shirt on the bottom of the window. That'll protect you from the sharp edges of the broken glass. Then jump out. Try to steer away from the granite step, and roll when you land."

"How are you going to get out?" Ellie said in a rush.

"I'll be right behind you." *I hope.* "Work quickly. It'll be a furnace up there."

"Got it." Ellie wrapped the shirt around her right hand. "I'll stand on your shoulders."

Cam laced her hands into a step. In a flash, Ellie was up, her weight light on Cam's shoulders. Cam glanced up. Ellie shoving glass out with her improvised mitt. Ellie folding the cloth into a cushion. *Hurry.*

"See you out there," Ellie said. A second later she was off Cam's shoulders and out.

Cam heard a cry as she upended a bucket under the window. She looked up. Shards still stuck out, and it was going to be a lot tighter fit for her than for petite Ellie. An explosion blasted a corner of the barn a few yards away. Cam took a deep breath. She stepped onto the bucket and set her hands on the hot cloth at the base of the window. She worked her legs up and through.

She landed with a thud and a sharp pain in her shoulder. She winced, squeezing her eyes shut. When she opened them, flames licked out the window she'd just fallen from. She rolled away from the building, then pushed herself to standing. Ellie lay curled up nearby.

"Ellie!"

The girl remained still, not responding. Cam scooped her into her arms. Ellie's eyes remained closed. Cam staggered toward the house as the burning barn crashed down behind them with a sound like a thousand memories dying.

CHAPTER 25

Cam tripped on a root of the ancient maple in the yard. It sent her sprawling on the grass, but she managed to protect Ellie's head from the fall. She pulled herself to sitting, Ellie still unconscious in her arms. Felicity and Wes appeared from somewhere, Felicity running to Cam and Ellie with her arms full of tablecloths. And a Westbury fire truck roared up the drive, all lights and sirens, with two Westbury police cars right behind.

Cam blinked. Smoke tainted the air. A coat of ash filmed the leaves of the tree. She took a deep breath and then coughed.

"Cam! What happened? Is Ellie all right?" Felicity dumped the tablecloths and knelt next to Cam. She stroked Ellie's cheek.

Ellie opened her eyes. "I'm fine. I think." She looked up at Cam, then wriggled out of her arms and sat cross-legged, rubbing her eyes. "Gross. What stinks?" She wrinkled her nose.

Cam, suddenly weak, sniffed. "It's the smoke, Ellie." She suddenly wanted to restore human contact. She put her arm around the girl's shoulders.

"Oh, yeah." Ellie turned wide eyes to the flaming wreck that had been the barn.

"You have cuts all over you." Felicity pointed to Cam's arms and legs, which were indeed riddled with scratches and cuts from the broken glass.

Cam looked down, startled to realize she was clad from the waist up only in her sports bra. Even her stomach was cut.

Felicity handed her a blue-and-white tablecloth, which Cam gratefully wrapped around her shoulders.

Firefighters poured off the engine. Two hurried toward Cam and Ellie. One carried a kit with a red cross on it. He knelt in front of Ellie and asked how she was.

The other firefighter shouted at Cam over the noise of the fire, "Ma'am, anybody in there?"

"No," Cam called back.

The firefighter turned toward the barn. "Surround and drown," she called out and then began barking orders.

Firefighters in bulky suits pulled flat hoses out of the back of the vehicle, its emergency lights still flashing. They dragged the hoses closer to the barn. Another couple of fire-fighters connected the hoses to the side of the engine. They began spraying the closest side of the inferno. It hissed and steamed like an angry dragon. The hose writhed on the ground, three firefighters struggling to tame it. A spray of water fanned out from a connection, creating a strobing blue-and-red light show. Another engine pulled in behind the first.

A police officer appeared from the road, followed by Chief Frost, who made a beeline for Cam as he spoke into a phone and then pocketed it.

"Are you all right, Ms. Flaherty?"

"I think I am. But my barn isn't." She raised her voice above the din of engines running, flames crackling, more sirens speeding toward the farm, an air horn blar-ing, commands being shouted.

"What happened? Careless with the barbe-cue?" He folded his arms and looked down at her with raised eyebrows.

Cam opened her mouth to object, but El-lie spoke first.

"No! A guy tried to, like, burn us alive in there." Ellie frowned at the chief. "He lit it on fire and then locked the door on his way out. Cam rescued us."

"Is that true, Cam?" the chief asked.

"Yes."

Ellie snapped her head toward the back of the property. "Hey, there he is."

Jake strode around the corner of the hoop house with a yelling Stuart fighting to get loose. Jake clamped Stuart's neck firmly in the crook of his elbow and held one of Stuart's arms twisted up behind his back, making him walk in front as they skirted the engines and hoses.

"Anybody want this guy?" Jake brought Stuart to a spot a few yards away from Chief Frost.

Stuart glared daggers at the chief. "I didn't do anything," he snarled.

Frost looked from Stuart to Cam and Ellie. "Stuart Wilson locked you in the barn and set it on fire?"

"Yep." Cam shuddered. "Not just locked us in but taped us to chairs. But Ellie had her Girl Scout pocketknife, and we not only got free, but got out. And just in time."

"It's your word against mine," Stuart spat.

"Well, here's another word for you," Cam said. "Stuart told us he killed Mike Montgomery."

"He did?"

Cam looked up at the new voice. Pappas had materialized.

397

"Yes, he did."

"I never said that." Stuart's strident tone was defiant.

"You did so. I'm a witness," Ellie said. "I'm glad this dude caught you." She glanced up at Jake.

Pappas nodded at Chief Frost. He and the other officer took over for Jake, cuffing Stuart's hands behind his back.

"Stuart Wilson, you are under arrest for the murder of Mike Montgomery and very likely arson and attempted murder, as well." Pappas read Stuart his rights. "Let's go." He and the police officer steered a cursing, struggling Stuart toward a cruiser.

Cam extended a hand to Jake, who helped her to her feet. "Thanks. But how . . . I mean, why are you here? How did you . . ."

He blushed, looking around at the listening group before returning his eyes to Cam. "I wanted to see you again. I called your cell and your house, but you didn't answer, so I came out here, anyway. When I drove up, Stuart was just standing in your driveway, staring at the barn. Something didn't seem right."

"Boy, were things ever not right." She leaned down and rubbed the aching knee Stuart had kicked.

"When I called to Stuart, he started running away, toward the back. I smelled smoke and saw some coming from the top window of the barn. I called nine-one-one. Then I chased him out to the fields." Jake smiled. "He didn't have a chance against these long legs." He laid an arm over Cam's shoulders and gave a squeeze.

Cam winced at the pressure.

Jake drew his arm back with a quick move. "Sorry. Did I hurt you?" His heavy eyebrows pulled together.

"I banged it when I landed. It'll heal." She nudged him with her shoulder, leaning into him, until he replaced his arm.

"I'm just glad you're all right. You too, Ellie." He patted Ellie on the back with his free hand.

"Cam?" Ruth, wearing red capri pants and a white T-shirt, loped toward them. One twin in each hand ran to keep up with her. "What happened? I heard on the scanner as we were heading out here for the potluck that your barn was on fire."

"It's a long story, Ruth. We're fine. He's not, and that's good." She nodded her head toward Stuart, who was being carefully folded into the backseat of the cruiser.

"Mommy, why's the building burning?" Nettie pulled on Ruth's hand.

"I'm not quite sure, honey. Let's make

sure we stay out of the firefighters' way, all right?" She glanced at Frost. "Hey, Chief. Everything under control?"

Chief Frost greeted her and the girls. "We got it covered."

Cam shook her head to clear it. "Chief Frost, Lucinda is free now, isn't she?"

"I would say so. It looks like we were wrong about that arrest."

Cam nodded. She leaned into Jake's solid form. The relief at it all being over — Lucinda free of suspicion, Cam free from trying to track a killer — washed through her, her legs suddenly as unsteady as hollow cornstalks.

"Cam?" Felicity tapped Cam on the shoulder. "I hate to say this, but what should we do about the potluck?"

The potluck. Several dozen subscribers were about to descend on the farm. No barn to eat in, no tables to eat off of.

"There will be no potluck here tonight," Frost said. "Ellie has to get checked out at the hospital, and you do, too, Cam. You both could have had a concussion and smoke inhalation damage."

"But . . ."

"No buts." Chief Frost crossed his arms.

"Let's just postpone the potluck until tomorrow night." Felicity bounced a little on the balls of her feet.

"I need to get statements from you to-night, too," Frost added.

A bicycle bell dinged a few yards away. Alexandra dismounted. "You sure know how to light a bonfire. But did I just see that scumbag Stuart in the back of a police car?" She shed a full backpack and stuck her hands in the back pockets of overalls printed with smiling vegetables.

Cam nodded. "You can thank him for the bonfire."

"Well, good riddance. Are you all right?"

As Cam nodded, she began to shiver. "Maybe."

Frost looked at her and motioned to the firefighter who sat with Ellie. "Might have shock setting in here." The firefighter wrapped a blanket around Cam's shoulders.

"You're going to need help picking in the morning," Alexandra said, raising her eyebrows.

Cam slapped her forehead. "Tomorrow's share day." She looked around at the group and then gazed at the ruins of the barn. "I don't have tools. I don't have baskets. I'm not sure I'll even be able to walk tomorrow." She rubbed her stiffening knee again, and the bruise on her shoulder twinged.

Alexandra spread her arms wide. "We'll

all help. It'll be a pick-your-own share day. How about that? Right, people?"

Felicity nodded. "Of course. We'll each bring tools, scissors, baskets. Whatever we have."

Wes spoke up. "I'll contact everyone tonight."

"I'll help. We can split up the list," Alexandra offered.

"Wow. Okay. You guys are the best." Cam wondered if her inner glow showed through to the outside.

Darkness crept in around the edges of a perfect June Saturday evening. The core group of subscribers, plus Ruth, her twins, Albert, Cam, and Jake, sprawled on Cam's lawn. The remains of the barn lay dark and forlorn like some giant's abandoned campfire. One charred post still jutted bravely toward the sky.

The potluck had been a success. Wes had fetched Great-Uncle Albert and had brought a comfortable chair out from the house for him to sit in. David Kosloski had been keeping Ellie close by his side all evening. Even the ever-tasteful Irene Burr had shown up, bringing an elegant platter of tiny herb quiches in puff pastry, which, she said when complimented on them, her cook had prepared. Everyone had clapped and cheered when Lucinda arrived. Cam was the first to give her a big hug, surprising herself with the pleasure of giving her friend an embrace. Up to now, hugging had never been one of Cam's favorite activities.

"Sorry I couldn't help out this morning. To be out of jail and in my own bed was just too delicious." Lucinda looked like she could still barely believe her fortune had changed.

Cam then took a moment to explain to everybody how Stuart had framed Lucinda and what had transpired in the barn, earning another round of applause for Ellie and her.

"We got out because Ellie here is resourceful. We made a good team." Cam cocked her hand at Ellie in a gun imitation. The girl returned it with a smile.

"Stuart's one sick dude," Jake said. "When I got here, he was just standing there, watching the barn burn. That's bad enough, but knowing you and Ellie were trapped inside?" Jake shook his head and whistled. "I hope he never gets out of prison."

"I also found out that the night of the festival, when I was so ill, that was Stuart's doing, too," Cam continued. "Whatever he put in your drink, Lucinda, he slipped into mine, as well."

Lucinda rolled her eyes, and Jake, sitting next to Cam, squeezed her hand.

The subscribers dined on the collection of dishes. They sipped beer or wine, chatted, and watched the girls run around the yard, trying to catch Preston. Jake had contributed sautéed scallops with braised spinach, Cam's favorite. Each of the rest of the dishes featured at least one ingredient from the morning's shares, even Alexandra's cheesecake with strawberries and mint spread over the top.

Cam spied little Natalie looking wistfully at Preston, stretched out on the porch steps. Cam walked to her side and knelt.

"Do you want to pet him?"

Natalie nodded.

Cam rose and took her hand. At Preston's side, she guided the girl's fingers over his luxurious fur and watched a smile invade Natalie's face.

"He'll let you stroke him. Just stay away from his tail, okay?"

Natalie nodded as Preston's purr grew louder under her touch.

Cam felt a hand on her shoulder and turned.

Ruth squeezed. "Thanks, Flaherty." She lowered her voice. "This one never gets as much attention as her fearless sister. Hey, sorry about the fire." She gestured to the blackened ruins of the barn. "You did good getting yourself and Ellie out of there."

Shuddering, Cam stared at the charred mess. She'd tried all day not to dwell on the nightmare of the day before, to stay too busy with the harvest to think about it. "It was my worst fear," she whispered.

"What do you mean?"

Cam nudged her away from Natalie and the rest of the group. They stood together on the driveway.

"Our house almost burned down when I was six. I was in it."

Ruth's eyes widened.

"My parents were out, and they left me with a teenage babysitter, a boy named Zachary. I guess he was smoking and was careless. A curtain caught fire while he was outside, talking to some friends who had dropped by. When he tried to get back in, the door was locked because he'd let it latch on the way out. I'd been playing in my room with the door closed. I was trapped, Ruthie." Cam's voice shook.

"That's terrible." Ruth's eyes sought out first one daughter, then the other. "What happened?"

"I was so scared. I kept screaming for my

mother, even though I knew she wasn't there. The heat." Cam's throat thickened. "I felt it through the floor, burning my bare feet. The smoke started as little puffs under the door. Then it poured in. It choked me, stinging my eyes. I could barely breathe. I hid in the closet, but then I remembered a fireman who visited my preschool had said to get out, not to hide. I managed to crawl along the floor to the window. I knocked the screen out and jumped. Luckily, I landed on the porch roof under my window, but when I jumped off that, I broke my wrist." She extended her left arm, which still bore a faint white scar, and let out a breath.

Ruth stretched her arm around Cam's shoulders and hugged her.

"I've been careful with fire ever since," Cam said. "And then this happened. Now Ellie will have to live with the same memories as she grows up."

"I don't think so. She wasn't abandoned. You worked together and rescued yourselves. Just like you did back then, Cam."

"I've never told anyone the story. At the time, I didn't know how the house caught on fire. My father filled me in on the details later. You can bet that babysitter was out of a job." Cam smiled, surprised at how light she suddenly felt. "Time to move forward."

Ruth nodded. Natalie ran up and caught her hand.

"Mommy, Preston let me pet him!"

As Cam watched them return to the steps, David Kosloski approached her. He asked if he could speak to Cam for a moment.

"In private," he added.

"Sure," Cam said. They moved farther down the driveway, toward the road.

David cleared his throat. "I need to apologize for being rude to you on Thursday, Cam. I have been very concerned lately."

"Does this have to do with the militia?"

A dark cloud passed over his face. "How did you know?"

"Just go on."

"They threatened me because of a mistake I made long ago. I came to this country on a tourist visa, to my relatives in Chicago. I met Myrna, my wife, there. We married, moved here, had Eleanor. I established my business, Myrna discovered she had multiple sclerosis." His eyes held years of sadness.

"I know. I'm so sorry."

"So, I was married to a citizen, nobody ever questioned me, but in fact I am here illegally."

"Ellie told me a boy at school said as much."

"She never told me! The poor girl. Her mother has a fatal wasting disease, and her father is a liar." The lines around his eyes deepened.

"David," Cam said, laying a hand on his arm. "Why don't you apply for your green card? I don't really know how it all works, but you have been married for what? Almost two decades?"

He nodded.

"It might take some time, but even if you have to leave the country for a little while, your business is well established, and your employees can cover for you. Then you'd never have to worry again. You could even apply to be a citizen, if that's what you want."

David took a deep breath and his face lightened, like a weight had fallen from his shoulders. "I'll think about it. Thank you, Cam. I haven't been able to confide in anyone. I don't even know why I told you, except, well, you saved my Eleanor's life." His voice thickened.

"Hey, she saved mine, too. We're even. And I promise you I'll watch out for her. I'm getting to like the kid."

"You'll have to come to our house for dinner soon, meet Myrna. You'll like her."

Cam agreed. They strolled back to the picnic area, David mussing Ellie's hair as he sat down next to her. Jake relaxed on the ground with his back to the old tree. Cam eased herself down on the grass in front of him, leaning back against his bent knees.

Lucinda sat up straight. She cleared her throat. "Listen, everybody." She waited until the group fell silent. "I need to thank Cam for believing in me. If she hadn't, I'd still be in that jail. She got me a good lawyer, she brought me stuff, but mostly she knew I wouldn't kill anyone. The police thought I did, and they gave up looking for the real guy."

"That's for sure." Cam shook her head, then glanced at Ruth. "Present company excepted."

Ruth winked at her.

"And it was Uncle Albert here who got you the lawyer," Cam said.

"It was my pleasure, Lucinda." Albert patted his heart.

"So thank you, *fazendeira.* I owe you one. And thank you, *Tio* Albert."

Smiling at her, Cam relaxed against Jake. This socializing thing was growing on her. She cleared her throat.

"It's my turn," Cam said. "I need to thank

409

everybody for pitching in this morning. I couldn't have done it without you. I want you to know I'm going to keep this farm going. The fields are fine, and I plan to rebuild the barn."

"I'm pretty handy with a hammer," Alexandra said. "We can have an old-fashioned barn raising."

"Sounds good to me," Cam said.

Others chimed in with offers of help.

"It's the 'plus' in Produce Plus Plus." Lucinda squeezed Cam's hand.

"I knew there was a reason I let you change the farm name." Albert pointed at Cam. "You're doing a great job so far. Don't let anything stop you."

Cam knew how close she had come to being stopped. The bulk of the season's work was ahead of her, but now she knew she wasn't alone in the effort. Being comforted by that was a new sensation. She decided she liked it.